Death as Concept

Death as Concept

E.E. "Doc" Murdock

H.O.T. Press
Publishing fine books since 1983

H.O.T. Press
Los Angeles, California
www.hotpresspublishing.com

ISBN: 0-923178-41-4
ISBN-13: 978-0-923178-41-3

Books by E.E. "Doc" Murdock

Novels

- **The Storyteller of Cottage H**
- **The Robots of Cottage H**
- **God's Messenger – God's Victim**: A *Bildungsroman* Stockholm Syndrome Novel
- **The Pain Artist:** An American Hikikomori
- **My Vietnam War**
- **A Psalm for Cock Robin**: A Harp and His (Dead) Mother Mystery
- **Crueltown**: A Drew Steele Los Angeles-Las Vegas Mystery
- **The End of the Civil War**: A Drew Steele Civil War Mystery
- **Who Owns Arizona**: A Drew Steele Civil War Mystery

Textbooks/How-To Books

- **How to Write Fiction: Tools and Techniques**
- **Self Management: A Guide to More Effective Study**
- **Computers Today**
- **Computers the Easy Way**
- **Windows the Easy Way**
- **DOS the Easy Way**
- **HyperCard the Easy Way**
- **dBASE the Easy Way**

History/Political Books

- **From Washington & Adams to Trump & Biden:** The Stories behind the Story of Every Presidential Election, With Special Focus on the *Volatile* Presidential Election of 2020
- **From Washington & Adams to Hillary & Trump:** The Stories behind the Story of Every Presidential Election, With Special Focus on the *Volatile* Presidential Election of 2016

Acknowledgments

I am indebted to the members of the Ojai Writing Workshop who provided valuable feedback as I worked through the many drafts of this book. I would also like to acknowledge the help of all my students at California State University, Long Beach who taught me so much. And of course, without Zoe, this book would not exist.

This one, especially, is for Zoe.

Prelude: Dead, Almost

"Here's one."

"Leave him. He's dead."

"Don't think so. Look. His chest is going up and down. A little."

"Well, he's not gonna make it. Just look at the state his body's in."

"Didn't . . . shoot."

"Hey, he talked."

"What? Talked? How could he?"

"I don't know, but he did."

"Okay. Throw him in the chopper. But do it fast. We gotta lift off, like now! We're gettin' low on fuel, and we're for sure gonna take fire gettin' the hell out of here."

Chapter One

In my mind, I call him my wheelchair chauffeur. Even though I'm getting so I can walk fairly well, whenever I'm supposed to be somewhere, he still comes to fetch me with his trusty wheelchair. This time, I know we're not going to physical therapy because they told me to put on my uniform. No use asking him where we're going; even after all the times he's wheeled me to physical therapy, or to all my surgeries, he never talks to me. Maybe he's seen too many sad cases like me come and go. To him, I'm just another wounded soldier with yet another sad Vietnam story he doesn't want to hear.

He wheels me all the way down a long hallway to a completely different wing of the building. I wonder where he's taking me this time.

We come to a glassed-in office. He wheels me into it, parks me in front of a desk, and leaves, still without a word.

A woman is behind the desk. A second louie. Maybe forty or so. Black hair, pulled straight back Typical for female officers. She doesn't have a speck of gray in her hair. Dyed?

She's busy writing on a form and doesn't look up at me. Should I interrupt her? She may be an officer, but I've noticed that most of the patients in this hospital, even lowly privates like me, don't bow all that much to rank. I ask her, "Are you writing about me?"

She doesn't answer, and she doesn't look up She just keeps on writing. I wonder if that's the style she likes to portray, tough, busy, in charge.

I'm not going to let that stop me from talking. In Vietnam, I got known as a loner, quiet. But after all the many, many months I've spent in hospitals since then, I've been learning how to interact more with people, so I ask her, "Am I that interesting?"

This time, she at least looks up at me. But then, she looks down at the form again, and her pen is poised above it. She asks, "What do you plan to do now?"

Aha, a real question. This is almost becoming an actual dialogue. I should keep it going. "You're asking me what I plan to do next?"

"Yes. I need to write down your plans. If you have any."

"Plans?"

"Yes, your plans when you leave here."

"Leave? Does that mean I'm leaving this hospital?"

This time she does look right at me. "Nobody told you?"

"This may be a hospital, but it's still military. Nobody tells a lowly private anything."

"Be that as it may, Mr. Murphy, we need to get through this exit interview." She looks down at her form again. "I need to write down your plans. If you have any. Do you want me to write that you have no immediate plans?"

"How could I have any immediate plans? I didn't know I was leaving."

"Well, you are leaving. Don't you want to leave?"

"Uh, I guess. In fact, yes, I do want to leave. I've been here way too long. Uh, do you have any idea how long I've been here? I don't know for sure, but it seems like a long time."

She glances at her form. "It doesn't say.'

"Well, it's been a long time. I know that at least. And before they brought me here, I was in another hospital back in Vietnam. I was in that hospital for a long time too. No wonder it doesn't say. I've been in hospitals so long they lost track of me."

Her pen is still poised above the form, but she continues to look at me. "I doubt they lost track of you. It just doesn't say how long you've been hospitalized. Not on this discharge form anyhow."

"Discharge form? Do you mean I'm being discharged out of this hospital, or discharged out of the Army?"

"You are being discharged from the military, Mr. Murphy.

I'll ask you again, do you want me to write down that you have no immediate plans?"

No kidding? Is this moment the last moment of my short-lived military career? "Right. Yes, you can go right ahead and say I have no immediate plans. In fact, you can say I have no plans at all, immediate or otherwise."

She writes something on the form, and then she looks back up at me. "Do you have any marketable skills?"

"What's that?"

"I means what are you good at."

Should I answer her honestly? Well, if this is the moment I'm being kicked out of the Army, why not? "What am I good at? Following orders, I guess. I did that well. If you mean a job, my job was killing the enemy. Sometimes. Not that often. But don't write any of that down. I'm not sure about that part. Maybe it wasn't my shooting that killed them. You can never tell for sure whose shots did it."

She frowns. "Well, obviously you can't do any of that anymore."

"You asked me what I was good at. Actually, maybe I wasn't so good at that. I'm not sure how you tell."

"All right then, just tell me what you did before you joined the service."

"Join is an inappropriate verb. I got drafted."

"An inappropriate verb? What, were you an English teacher or something?"

"An English teacher? Me? Are you making a joke?"

"Uh, let's get back to filling out this form so you can go."

She's back to looking down at the form, her pen still hanging in the air as if it can hardly wait to drop down onto the paper.

She looks back up at me again, but her pen is still ready to write. "Just tell me what you did before you were drafted."

"Like a job, you mean? I didn't do anything. I was a student."

"So you never worked?"

"Oh, sure I worked. There was a lot of work to do around the school. Fixing. Pounding in nails. Pulling nails out. Sometimes painting. Are you going to write all that down?"

She's frowning again. "Mr. Murphy, I think we'd better start over. I am your discharge officer. My job is to complete your paperwork and explain your discharge parameters."

"Parameters. That's a good word."

"Yes, well, I'm here to explain your disability severance pay, among other things."

"Severance pay? You mean I get money?"

"Yes, disability severance pay is a one-time, lump sum payment. It says here you qualify for a partial disability rating. Thirty percent."

"Thirty percent?"

"Yes, you are in that category."

"What would one hundred percent mean?"

"The percent only refers to your capacity to fulfill duties in the service."

"So thirty percent means I'm only thirty percent capable of fulfilling any duties in the Army?"

"Not you personally. It's only an evaluation number."

"What would zero percent capable of fulfilling my duties would mean? That I'm dead? I did almost die, but it probably doesn't say that on your form."

She looks back down at her form. Is she avoiding eye contact with me. Did my talking about death remind her of something? Did she know someone who got killed over there?

She taps her pen on the form, and says, "It's only an evaluation number. As I said."

"I didn't."

She looks up at me. "Didn't what?"

"Die. I didn't die."

"Well, obviously you didn't."

"I almost did. I was supposed to. Everybody else in my patrol group died."

For the first time, the expression on her face changes. "Oh, I'm sorry to hear that."

She's still looking at me, so I guess she wants me to continue. "Yes, they all died. But I got lucky. I think I was blown up so bad, the enemy thought I was dead. Or about to be dead, so they didn't bother to shoot me. They shot all the others."

"I'm very sorry to hear that, Mr. Murphy."

She quickly looks back down at her paper. Did I upset her?

"Not your fault, Ma'am. Oh, and you can call me Murph. That's what everybody called me. When they were still alive, that is."

She's still looking at the paper. Is she having some kind of emotional response? I think I did upset her. Now that I'm actually alive, I want to be a real person from now on, but I didn't want to upset her. Doesn't she hear these kinds of stories all the time? Maybe not. Maybe nobody else talks about what brought them to this hospital. Maybe I shouldn't be talking about it either.

She picks up a book and reads from it. "For a thirty percent disability, severance pay will be an amount equal to two months of basic pay for each year of service. That includes active service and inactive duty points. It says here you were in active service for two years, counting your time being hospitalized. And because you were injured in active duty, you would normally receive credit for three years of service, but because you were wounded in an active combat zone, your severance pay will be based on six years of service." She looks at me. "Do you understand?"

"I guess so. It means I get extra money."

"Yes, that's right. However, it will take a few days to generate the check. The check will be sent to whatever mailing address you give me." Her pen is poised above the paper again." Now, what is your mailing address?"

"I don't have one of those."

"You don't have a mailing address?"

"No, Ma'am."

"Well, they can also send it to your parents' address."

"I don't have any of those either."

"Any of what?"

"Parents."

"Oh, are your parents deceased?"

"No, they never were."

She looks startled. "What?"

"Well, I guess I had some, like everybody. At least a mother, I suppose. But I never knew her. I grew up in an orphanage. In Arizona. From when I was a baby. It was an orphanage for Pima Indian boys that had been abandoned. It was way out in the desert, on a Pima reservation. A Catholic priest was in charge. The priest and the other boys raised me. They told me they took turns bottle feeding me when I was real little. "

"So, you're a Native American?"

"Uh, I haven't had anybody call me that."

"Well, are you?"

"I guess so. The priest told me my mother was Pima, but he said I obviously had white blood in me too. He wouldn't ever tell me more than that."

"Well, you do have thick dark hair and dark eyes, but it doesn't say anything here about you being Native American."

"Does it matter?"

"No, not really. I guess the only question is will you go back there, and if so, do you know its mailing address?"

"Go back there? I'm not sure. I hadn't thought about it until now."

"Well, we need to know where to send your severance check."

"I don't know if the orphanage even has a mailing address. It's way out in the desert, like I said."

"Oh, never mind. You can notify us when you get a mailing address."

"Uh, do I get any walking-around money until then?"

"We have no facility for that."

"Another good word. Facility."

"Maybe tomorrow I could get you a clothing allowance. That would give you a little money."

"I can't keep wearing my uniform?"

"Certainly you can. Now, back to the mailing address issue. Wherever you end up, you should let me know your address. Or you could get a post office box."

"I guess I could do that."

"All right. Let us know when you get a mailing address. In the meantime, here are your discharge papers and a pamphlet with a list of resources available to you." She hands them to me, and says, "I've written my phone number on the back of the pamphlet. Call me as soon as you get a mailing address." She picks up her phone and punches in a number. "He's ready."

I guess that means she's done with me, and somebody is going to come get me. I use the waiting time to leaf through the pamphlet. I only see one "resource" that looks interesting. I hold it up to show her. "It says 'Educational Benefits.' What's that?"

"It means the government will pay for your tuition if you want to go to college."

"Oh. Well, yes, maybe I could take some classes."

"It's up to you. The pamphlet tells you how to get that type of benefit. But it only pays for tuition and books. Not housing or food."

"So, I'd still have to get a job or something."

"Well, you'll have your severance check. That should last you for a while."

"Oh, right."

My wheelchair chauffeur is back. He grabs the handles and spins me around so fast I barely have time to look back and wave at her. But she's already gone back to writing. What is she writing now? That Murphy doesn't have any skills at all. Doesn't even know who his parents were.

Maybe she's writing that I'll probably get myself into trouble. If that's what she thinks, she doesn't know the new me. I swore if I ever got out of that jungle alive, I'd make something of myself. I did and I will.

Chapter Two

My wheelchair chauffeur takes me out through the building's front door and says, "End of the line, buddy."

"Hey, you *can* talk!"

"I gotta go, buddy. Good luck."

I guess he wants me to hurry up and get the hell out of his limousine chair.

As soon as I stand up, he turns and hurries away. More patients to take care of I guess. Amazing how fast he can move pushing that wheelchair.

So, here I am outdoors. I haven't been outdoors since . . . I can't remember since when. Since the jungle, I guess. I look up at the sky. It's a clear day, but the air looks kind of thick. Big city air, I guess.

I shuffle down the long sidewalk toward the street. After all the surgeries and endless physical therapy, I've learned how to walk pretty well. I remember asking one of the doctors back in Vietnam if my legs would ever work right again. All he would say is, "You never know." I suspect he had his doubts, but didn't want to say that.

After I got back to the good old U S of A, and they put me in this VA hospital, I asked the physical therapy guy that same question. He said he hoped so. He sounded about as unsure about it as that doctor in Vietnam. They must have a rule: don't discourage the poor guy, no matter how bad it looks.

In the end, he did encourage me to try to walk, and when I started making progress, he made me work hard until I got better at it. Now, after all the surgeries and all those many months in the physical therapy room, I can walk in a way that looks almost normal. I hope. And because the explosion hit right behind me, with my back and my legs getting most of the damage, my face ended up without a mark on it. So, if people don't see me shuffling along, they might not even suspect I got hurt at all.

Out at the wide street, a lot of cars are going by. I watch them for a while, but I know sooner or later, I have to decide where to go. Should I go left or right? There's no real reason to go either way. What does it matter which direction I take if I was supposed to be dead anyhow?

But I shouldn't start thinking like that. I'm alive, aren't I? And people that are alive have to decide what to do every day, every minute. The true fact is, now that there's nobody to give me orders, I have to start making my own decisions.

Okay, decision one should be where to go. I know I'm in Los Angeles. I guess I could stay here for a while, but what would I do here? I don't know anybody in this city, and just seeing the number of cars whizzing past already feels a bit overwhelming. But I don't want to feel overwhelmed. I want to feel like I can do anything, so I should look around and see all the possibilities.

I look up at the afternoon sun. That direction is west. What is west of here? The ocean. I flew over that ocean going to Vietnam. I could go look at that ocean again right now. Or maybe not. For some reason, that edge of this big country seems like a dead end. Nowhere else to go from there.

What about the other direction? East. I turn that way. That direction is the whole United States. Wide open to me. Arizona is east. Do I want to go back to Arizona, to the orphanage, like that discharge lady suggested? Well, I could. If I get to be alive and have to go somewhere, I could go to a place I already know. Now that I think about it, that orphanage out in the Arizona desert is actually the *only* place I've ever been, except for Oklahoma, where I did my basic training. After that, the only other place I've been is the Vietnamese jungle. I didn't much like the hot and sticky jungle. The Arizona desert, on the other hand, is hot and dry. I did like being out in the hot and dry desert. I spent a lot of time wandering around that desert by myself near the orphanage. I liked doing that a lot, so, if I can go anywhere I want to, why not go be in that desert again?

I might not want to stay there forever, but I wouldn't mind seeing my teacher, old Father Saul, again. He knows I got drafted and went into the Army. In fact, he was the one who made me register for the draft in the first place, even though he wasn't sure exactly how old I was. He's probably been wondering if I'm still alive, or if I got killed in Vietnam.

Although it seems like I left the orphanage a long time ago, I guess it actually wasn't, so I'm sure he'll remember me. And he liked me. He said I was the smartest student he'd ever had. That was right after he told me I'd probably never amount to anything. He cared for us boys, but he could be harsh like that. His way of spurring us on.

"Do you need help?"

I turn. It's a woman in the kind of nurse's uniform they wear inside the hospital. I smile to show her I don't mind her saying that to me. "Do I look like I need help?"

Now she seems embarrassed. Maybe I said the wrong thing.

"Well, it's only that you've been standing there for quite a while. Like you can't decide which way to go."

I smile to let her know I'm not one of the crazies they have here in this VA hospital. "That's it exactly. I'm not sure which way to go. How does a person decide which way to go if you don't really have anywhere you have to be? It's a dilemma. That's a good word. Dilemma. Don't you think?"

"I guess so. Well, I do have somewhere I have to be. Inside the hospital, I mean. I'll be late for work."

"Well then, you'd better get right in there." I bow to her and use my hand to gesture toward the hospital entrance. But then I wonder why I did that. I've never bowed to anyone before in my entire life. Have I changed that much? Maybe being almost dead and then not dead changes a person.

She seems like she wants to go, but she can't quite get herself moving. She says, "All right then. I'd better get going. Nice to meet you."

"Is that what we did? Meet?"

"Well, I guess we . . . "

She seems confused. Did I say the wrong thing again?

She points toward the hospital entrance. "Actually, I'd better go. I don't want to be late." She hurries away.

I watch her go. That was odd. But kind of interesting. At least it proves I can talk to people if I want to. I said some things to her that felt different than the way I used to talk to people. For some reason, it feels like I could have said anything I want to her. I'm alive aren't I? Alive and out of the Army. That means I'm free as a bird. Where did I hear that? It's a funny idea. Are birds free? I look up to the sky, but I don't see any birds. Maybe they don't have many birds in a big city like this. There were lots of birds in the Arizona desert. Not so many in the Vietnam sky. Maybe they'd all gotten blown up there, or shot down. I actually did see a guy try to shoot a bird with his rifle. Just for fun. To me, it seemed like a weird thing to do, but the other guys thought it was funny. Luckily, he didn't hit it.

I watch some more cars go by. There are people in those cars, mostly one person per car. I bet I could talk to them too, if I wanted to.

I'm still thinking I can do anything, but I do have to decide what to do first. I can go left, or I can go right. Or I can just stay here and watch the cars go by. It's an amazing thing to be alive when you didn't expect to be. It kind of opens up all kinds of possibilities.

It feels like I'm having odd thoughts, unusual thoughts for me. I doubt if other people—the people going by in those cars, for example, or that nurse that just talked to me—are having these kinds of thoughts. So why am I? Is it because of what happened to me? Because I almost died, but then didn't?

Whatever it is, I know I can't just stand here all day. Maybe I should start by going back to Arizona. See how old Father Saul is doing. Then I can decide what to do next.

Okay, if I want to go to Arizona, how will I get there? I don't have any money.

Looking at all the cars going by, I guess I could hitchhike. I've never tried that, but some of the older boys at the orphanage told me people will pick you up if you get a piece of cardboard and make a sign telling drivers you're a student. I guess I could try that.

Decisions. Odd how much of my life I didn't have to make many decisions. At the orphanage, Father Saul took care of us and made all the rules. At basic training, there was always somebody making the rules, and all the decisions. It was the same in Vietnam. And mostly the same in the hospitals I've been in since then. Other people decide what you're going to do. But now, it's up to me.

I decide. I start walking east.

Chapter Three

If I'm going to hitchhike to Arizona, I'll need to find the highway that leads to Arizona. But first, I need to find a piece of cardboard to make myself a hitchhiking sign.

Despite the pain in my legs and my back, I'm moving pretty well, and I haven't walked too far when I come to a freeway. The sidewalk goes under it, and I can hear a lot of cars up there. I wonder if any of them are going to Arizona.

There's a raggedy old man sitting under the freeway. He has a metal cart on wheels that seems to be stuffed full of crap like plastic bags and cloth. I stop in front of him. "Hey, old man. You got a piece of cardboard you could lend me?"

"Who you calling old?"

He sounds pissed off. "Well, you are old, sir. A lot older than me anyhow. Uh, do you have a piece of cardboard?"

"How about you go to hell."

I smile to let him know I'm not mad at him. Why should I get mad at anybody, no matter what they say to me? I'm alive aren't I?

There's another man on the other side of the street. Like this old man, he also has a cart on wheels that's full of stuff, and he seems to have made himself a sort of tent out of a blue tarp that's tied to the cart. Is he living here under this freeway?

As I cross the street, the guy watches me come. He's just about as raggedly as the other guy, but he's not as old. Hard to tell how old he is, but he's dressed young, in a T-shirt and jeans. His long blondish hair is tied back with a string and he has a dirty red bandanna covering his head.

I walk right up to him. "Hello, sir. I'm looking for a piece of cardboard. I need to make a sign. For hitchhiking, you know."

"That right? Where you headin'?"

"I'm thinking I might go to Arizona."

"Why? It's just as warm here in California."

"I don't really know why. Because I grew up there, I guess. Actually, I've never been anywhere else."

"Okay, I'll help ya make a sign. Make 'em all the time." He stands up and digs into his cart. He pulls out a torn piece of cardboard that looks just about big enough to make a pretty good sign. It's like he had it ready. Is he the official sign maker for guys who live under the freeway? He digs down deeper into his cart and pulls out something even better than the black crayon I was expecting; it's a black marker. This guy really must be the local sign maker. What does it mean that I ran into this guy exactly when I needed a sign? When I get time, I need to think more about why things happen like that.

He sits back down and puts the piece of cardboard on his lap. He pulls the top off of the marker and looks at me. "Okay. Whatta ya want this here sign to say?"

"Well, I was told if you say you're a student, people will pick you up."

"Yeah, but you're obviously not a student. You got an Army uniform on."

"Oh, right. Well then, just write soldier to Arizona."

"Uh, you sure about that?"

"I guess so. Why not?"

He shrugs. "Whatever ya say, buddy."

He starts making the sign: SOLDIER TO, but then he stops. "Where you going in Arizona? Phoenix?"

"Sure. Phoenix is okay. Put that. The place I'm going to is near there."

"Yeah, saying Phoenix is better than just Arizona. Phoenix is warm. Otherwise, you might end up in Flagstaff. Too cold there with winter comin' on pretty soon."

So this guy knows Arizona. I wonder if he's hitchhiked all over the country. Maybe that's why he's been making hitching signs—for himself.

He finishes making the sign and holds it up: SOLDIER TO PHOENIX.

It's a good sign, spaced out about perfect. This guy knows what he's doing.

"Well, thanks, mister. Sorry I don't have any money to pay you."

"No problem. Now here's what you do. Go up a couple of blocks, and you'll find an on-ramp that gets cars onto this here freeway we're under. Stand there and maybe somebody'll pick ya up. Now make sure you get yourself next to the southbound on-ramp. That's the direction they'll be goin' if they're gonna be eventually headin' east toward Arizona."

"Okay. Thanks, sir."

He waves me away, and I head out in the direction he told me, hoping it isn't too far. My legs and back are starting to hurt quite a bit.

It doesn't take me long to find the on-ramp he was talking about. I find a good place to stand where somebody will have room to pull over and give me a ride. I sure hope I don't have to stand here too long. The pain in my back and legs is reminding me that despite the supposed success of all my physical therapy, I always had a bed to go back to when the pain got too intense.

Lots of cars are going by, and I show every one of them my sign. But nobody seems interested in stopping to pick me up. In fact, they all seem to be in a heck of a big hurry.

When a man in a car finally does slow down enough to read my sign, I hold it up to show him.

In return, he shows me his middle finger and speeds off.

Why did he do that? Doesn't he like soldiers?

After a lot more cars go by, another car slows way down.

It's a couple. A man and a woman. I bet they'll give me a ride.

The woman in the passenger seat rolls down her window, so I smile at her and point to what it says on my sign.

She yells, "Baby killer!" Then, they speed away.

What? Why would she think I was a baby killer? The people in this city are turning out to be very weird.

A lot more cars go by, and then another one slow down to look at my sign. It's another couple, younger this time. The woman rolls down her window, just like that last woman did, but this one doesn't yell anything, she just spits at me.

Luckily, she's not a very good spitter so her spit doesn't quite reach me. That does it. For sure, I'm not going to get a ride here. Now I know why that sign maker guy didn't think I should say on my hitching sign that I was a soldier. Obviously, they don't like soldiers here in this city. I wonder why.

I guess I'd better go back to the sign maker and get him to make me a new sign, one that doesn't say anything about me being a soldier.

When I get back to the freeway underpass, I'm in luck; the sign maker guy is still sitting there. I explain what happened, and he does the kind of little laugh that's not really a laugh. "Yeah, they think every soldier they see was in Vietnam."

"Well, I *was* in Vietnam."

"I wondered if you were. The way you limp along when you walk. Wounded over there, eh?"

"Yes. My group went out on patrol, like normal, but this time—"

"Fine. Well, give me your sign. I'll fix it."

I guess he doesn't want to hear about how I just about got killed in Vietnam. Maybe nobody wants to hear something like that.

While I sit down on the curb to rest my aching back and legs, he takes my sign and flips it over. He takes out his black marker and writes STUDENT TO PHOENIX. He holds it up to show me. "There. That better?"

"I guess."

He looks me over. "You're young enough to be a student, but they ain't gonna believe it with that Army uniform you're wearin'. But maybe I could make use of an Army shirt. We could make a trade. Let me see what I got." He digs into his cart. He has all kinds of stuff in there, plastic bags filled with cans, and other bags that seem to be filled with cloth.

Clothes? Is he the clothes supplier around here as well as being the sign maker?

He pulls out a light blue shirt and holds it up for me to see. It's a dress shirt with a button-down collar. It's really wrinkled, but it's a pretty nice shirt. "Pretty fancy," I say.

"Too fancy for ya? I thought people might be more likely to pick you up if you looked . . . I don't know, normal."

"I guess that might be good. So we can trade?"

"Yep."

I take off my Army shirt, and he hands me the blue shirt. I put it on, and it actually fits pretty good. The sleeves are a little short, but that's not a big deal.

"Well, ya better get a move on back to that on-ramp. Ya don't wanna be out here hitchin' in the dark, do ya?"

"Oh right. Okay then, thanks. For the sign, I mean. And for the shirt too."

He waves me away. I guess that means he's tired of helping me.

Now that I know the way to the on-ramp, it doesn't take me long to get there. I go to the same place I stood before and hold up my sign. Just like before, the cars speed right past me. I hold up my sign to every one of them, but nobody stops. I'm getting worried. That sign maker guy said it'll be getting dark before long, and nobody is stopping to give me a ride. But at least they're not spitting at me.

Finally, a fairly young guy in a fancy red sports car pulls over and says, "Hop in."

I get in quickly, grateful for the chance to finally sit down.

It's an exciting feeling to be in an auto for the first time in my life. I've been in military vehicles a few times, but this car is a lot more comfortable, and a lot lower to the ground. It is exciting, but a bit scary at the same time. I wonder how many new things I'm going to get to experience in this post near-death life of mine.

Once the guy has successfully merged his car into traffic, he glances at me and says, "Phoenix, eh? Why you going there?"

"It's where I grew up. I'm going back there."

"How old are you?" he asks.

"I'm not sure. About twenty, or maybe twenty-one. Why?"

"Just curious. College student?"

I wonder why he thinks that. Maybe he thinks I'm too old be a hitchhiking student. Maybe my time in Vietnam, as short as it was, aged me. But that pamphlet the Army discharge lady gave me said they'd pay for me to go to college, so I say, "Right. College."

"Sure you don't want to hang around here for a while. You could make a few bucks."

"Really? Doing what?"

"You know. You could do something for me." He reaches over and squeezes my knee. "How about it?"

From that squeeze on my knee, I'm pretty sure I'm not interested in doing whatever it is he wants. I move his hand off my knee and say, "No thanks."

"Up to you."

The freeway branches and he turns west. He's not going east? So why did he pick me up? I say, "So, you're not going to Arizona?"

He does a sort of non-laugh laugh that I think must be intended to be sarcastic. "Not hardly, kid. I'm doing you a favor taking you this far. You were on the wrong freeway. You want to be on this freeway, the ten, but you need to go the other way." He doesn't say another word as he pulls over and lets me out.

I get out, and he burns rubber roaring away.

He's left me standing on the darn freeway. I'd better get off it quick.

I hurry as fast as my aching legs will carry me to the next exit and manage to get down the offramp without getting clipped by any of the cars that are zooming past. A couple of them honk their horns at me in an irritated-sounding way.

When I finally make it down to a surface street, I see that there's an underpass a lot like the one back where I met that sign maker guy. Nobody's hanging out under this underpass though.

I go to the other side of the freeway. There's an on-ramp, and a sign that says "10 East." I guess that's the freeway the fancy sports car guy meant when he said the ten would take me east toward Arizona. I find a place to stand and hold up my sign.

This on-ramp isn't as busy as the last one, but there are still plenty of cars going past, and just like the last time, they all seem to be in a big hurry.

Finally, a guy in an old pickup truck slows down to look at me. He seems to be having trouble reading my sign, but eventually he stops and waves for me to come. I hurry to his truck as fast as my aching legs will carry me and climb in.

The driver is a white-haired old guy. I thank him for picking me up, and he says, "My name's Foucher. What's your name, kid?"

"Murphy. But everybody calls me Murph."

As he pulls back into traffic, he says, "Okay, Murph. I should tell ya I wouldn't have stopped if I thought you really were a student like your sign says. Are you?"

"I . . . uh, I'm thinking about it."

"You're wearing a nice shirt like maybe a student would wear, but them's Army pants, aren't they?"

"Oh . . . yes. I just got out. But I am thinking about going to college."

"Student or not, don't matter to me one way or the other, son. Smart thing your sign said you were a student and not a soldier. People are all het up about Vietnam right now. Don't much like what they been seein' on the TV."

"Is that right? What've they been seeing?"

He turns to look at me. "Where you been hidin', son?"

"Uh, I've been in the hospital. Actually, a couple of different hospitals. For . . . well, for a long time."

He glances at me. "So, you haven't been seein' the TV news, eh? Well, you haven't missed much. Same thing, every night. News and more news about Vietnam. Killin' and more killin.' And news about anti-war protests. Of course, the politicians are on the TV too, makin' hay over all of it. Lotta rah rah.

They keep on tellin' us we're winnin' that stupid war, but everybody knows we're not."

What he's saying is kind of shocking. Why didn't I hear anything about that kind of thing? No wonder they didn't have any TVs on my ward in that VA hospital. I don't know what to say about it, so I just say, "I never saw any news photographers over there. Not where I was anyhow."

He again turns to look at me. "So, you were in Vietnam, eh? When did you get back?"

His question makes me realize I don't even know how long I've been out of Vietnam. I say, "I guess I don't really know when I got back here to the states, sir. I was in the hospital like I said. For . . . for a long time."

"Wounded, eh?"

I suspect he probably doesn't want to hear about how I got blown up, so I just say, "Yes."

He doesn't look at me. He's keeping his eyes on the road ahead, and he isn't driving his old truck very fast. In fact, I can see in the outside mirror that cars and trucks keep on pulling in close behind us, and they dart around as soon as they get the chance. People here in California sure do want to go fast. A guy in a red car yells something as he roars past. I couldn't hear what the guy said, and Mr. Foucher doesn't respond to it.

Mr. Foucher remains quiet while he avoids some cars entering onto the highway. I look over the inside of his old truck. It's old, but it seems to be in pretty good shape. He must be a man who likes to take care of his things.

After remaining quiet for some time, Mr. Foucher says, "I was in the big war. The real war. Not that Korea one. That one never did make any sense to me. Vietnam don't either for that matter, but what the hell do I know? All I know about is the war in Europe. I was in a big battle there. Ever hear of the Battle of the Bulge?"

"Yes, sir. The school I went to in Arizona taught us a lot about wars. All the way from the Thirty Years War to World War Two and Korea and Vietnam. We learned a lot."

"Sounds like a pretty good school."

"I guess it was, sir. The Catholic priest teacher was hard on us, but he taught us a lot."

"You don't have to call me sir. You're not in the Army here."

"All right, sir. I mean, okay."

"Listen, son. I'm not goin' to Arizona. But I am goin' a ways east. To Indio. Ever heard of it?"

"No, sir."

"Name's Foucher."

"Oh, right. Uh, no, I've never heard of a place called Indio. Is it a big city?"

"Naw, real small. It's as far as I'm going, but it'll get you quite a ways out of LA. Probably easier to get rides out there."

"Okay. That'll be great."

"Now, since we're gonna be stuck together in my good old truck for a while, why don't you tell me about Vietnam."

"Well, there's not much to tell, actually. The firebase I was at was out in the jungle."

"Hot?"

"Yes. Unless it was raining. Then it was a little cooler."

"I meant hot as in combat."

"Oh, that. Some, but not too often. Not all the time, I mean. Probings mostly."

He glances at me. "Probings?"

"Mortars. And a few incursions. At night. But they never got past the wire or through the Claymores."

"Claymores. What's that?"

"A kind of exploding mine. With trip wires."

"Over there in Europe, we had to deal with mines too, but we had specialists that went ahead of us to clear 'em. But that wasn't me. I was never in the lead. But one time I did get hit with shrapnel. Some kind of artillery. Hit my leg. Like I said, in the Battle of the Bulge. They patched me up, and after that, all I had to do was load trucks. Day and night, loadin' trucks. Bout broke my back."

As the miles go by, Mr. Foucher keeps talking about his war experience. "I got to Europe late. Up until then, I was in England. They had me loadin' ships. Me, a ranch kid from Indio, California, loading big ships in England. Seems like I spent most of the war loading stuff. Got sent over to France on one of those same ships I'd been loadin' and got sent right out to the German border. A forest. Artillery shells blowin' up all over the place. All we could do was run forward a few yards, and then hit the dirt. It was foggy the day I got hit. And damn cold."

If he asks, I'm ready to tell him how I got blown up in much the same way, how I had lots of injuries from an explosion, but he barely pauses his talking to take breaths. I don't mind. I like hearing about his war experience, and I can tell he's getting into reliving it as he talks. I've been learning people don't much want to hear about war, so he's probably happy to have found somebody who'll listen. The guys in Vietnam said I was a good listener. I guess it's because I like to hear about other people's experiences.

Mr. Foucher scratches the side of his head and says, "After I got hit, it was all real confusin'. Couldn't tell which way was up. I got up, but I didn't know which way to go. Nothing around me but holes in the ground from the artillery. And shattered trees. But I'll have you know that even though I could barely walk and everything was blowin' up all around me, I still didn't run away. Kept walkin' til I found a medic. Cold. Damn cold. Bout froze to death before I got help."

As he continues to talk, I'm glad he isn't asking me any more about my experience in Vietnam.

I wouldn't have much to tell him anyhow since I spent most of my time at that small firebase, deep in the jungle. His telling me about the Battle of the Bulge makes his war sound dynamic and exciting and makes Vietnam seem small and insignificant. But as he talks, I realize it didn't feel like that to me. Even out there in the jungle, it felt like I was part of something bigger, something important. But then maybe every soldier feels like that.

Mr. Foucher obviously did, and he's enjoying telling me about it.

He's still rambling on about his war experience when we pull into the town of Indio. Like he said, it's not much of a town, but it's somehow surviving smack in the middle of a really dry-looking desert. I'm expecting him to just let me out by the side of the highway, but he pulls into a big gas station full of big trucks. He gets out, but before he closes his door, he says, "Wait here a minute, son. I know a guy here. A mechanic. I'll see if he can get you a ride to Phoenix in a semi."

I do as he says and wait. It's a fairly busy place, with lots of trucks pulling in and out. It'll be great if he can get me a ride all the way to Phoenix. It's getting to be late in the afternoon, and I'd rather not be out here in the dark trying to catch a ride.

It isn't long before Mr. Foucher is back. He hops in and hands me a candy bar and a Coke. "You're in luck," he says. "My mechanic pal introduced me to a guy that was in Korea. He's haulin' some steel to Phoenix. I told the trucker you're a wounded vet, and he said he'd take you all the way to Phoenix if you promise not to talk about Vietnam. Okay?"

"Fine with me, sir."

"Okay. Let's go. The guy's waitin'."

As Mr. Foucher leads me around behind the gas station to where a lot of big trucks are parked, he tells me he enjoyed talking to me.

I say, "I enjoyed it too, sir. It was good to meet someone who was actually in the second world war."

"Yeah, and I was glad to hear more about this country's latest war, as crazy as it is."

I nod and don't remind him that I hardly said anything about Vietnam. He was the one that did almost all of the talking. Actually, that was okay with me; it made the miles go by pretty fast, even in his slow-moving old truck.

He leads me to an idling flatbed semi-truck that's loaded with long steel poles.

Mr. Foucher shakes my hand, and seems about ready to say something, but just then the truck's passenger door swings open, so I just thank him again and climb up into the truck.

The truck driver is a big guy with a black beard, and I'm hardly inside when he puts the truck in gear and starts to slowly move forward. As we pull out, I wave goodbye to Mr. Foucher, and he waves back. I'm kind of sorry to leave him behind. He was a long-winded talker, but a really nice old guy. He even got me something to eat and drink, first I've had since lunch today at the hospital.

The trucker pulls us out onto the highway without a word. He's the silent type. I met a few like that in Vietnam, and I quickly learned not to bother them.

Although I know he wanted to make sure I wasn't a talker, I do want to be friendly, so I say, "Thanks for the ride, mister."

He nods, but he keeps his eyes on the road and still doesn't say a word as he shifts through the big truck's gears. Unlike the clean inside of Mr. Foucher's truck, the floor of this big truck is a mess, with lots of candy bar wrappers and crushed soda cans. He has a couple of small pictures of near-naked girls taped to the dashboard. The pictures seem to have been cut out of magazines.

Even though he's not a talker, I should still try to be friendly. I say, "Mr. Foucher gave me a ride from LA. He told me all about what he did in World War Two."

"Uh huh."

"He told me he got wounded at the Battle of the Bulge."

The trucker doesn't respond to that.

"He said he got hit with shrapnel, but they kept him in the war. Loading trucks."

The trucker still doesn't respond. He may not like to talk much, but maybe he'd like to talk about his war experiences, like Mr. Foucher did. "He said you were in Korea."

Finally, the trucker turns to look at me. He points up toward the ceiling of the truck. "Hear that CB radio?"

I assume he's talking about the little radio that's attached to the truck's ceiling just above the windshield. It's squawking staticky nonsense. I say, "Uh, yes. What about it?"

"I like to concentrate on my driving. How about you just listen to that radio and tell me if you hear anything about smoky bears."

"Smoky bears?"

"Yeah. Cops. They hang out on this road. They got radar."

I understand what he's telling me. He wants me to shut up so he can listen to the radio. "Got it," I say.

The evening darkness is coming on quickly as we head on through the flat desert. I keep silent and eat my candy bar and drink my Coke. But I do listen carefully to the CB radio. I'm starting to learn how to understand what they're saying, despite the static and the trucker lingo. And I'm learning that almost everything begins with, "Breaker 1-9." But as we roll on, after several hours of listening, I still haven't heard anything about any smoky bears.

As we plow on through the darkness, going amazingly fast for such a big truck, I'm trying to stay focused on the staticky CB radio, but the boredom of it is making me sleepy. A wave of exhaustion rolls over me, and it dawns on me that this is the first time I've been out of a hospital bed at night in a long time. Nevertheless, I'm determined to stay awake and listen to the CB radio.

I feel the truck slow down, and I realize I must have fallen asleep with my head leaning against the truck's door. I can see the lights of a big city ahead, so maybe we're almost there. I wonder how long I slept.

I sit up straight and do a little stretching, but my aching back is reminding me that this is the first time in a long while I've done this much sitting upright.

As we pull into the outskirts of the city, the truck driver says, "Where do you want me to drop you?"

He sounds irritated. He's probably mad at me for falling asleep instead of listening for smoky bears on his CB radio.

"Oh, anywhere is fine. Where are you going?"

"Goin' right through Phoenix. This load's goin' to Mesa. Know where that is?"

"Yes, I know exactly where Mesa is. That's close to where I'm going. I'll stay with you until we get there, if that's all right with you."

He doesn't say anything, so I guess he doesn't mind me staying with him.

As we go through Phoenix, I look at the many buildings and the many cars. Even though the orphanage I grew up in wasn't all that far from here, I've never been in Phoenix before. It's a bigger city than I guess I expected, and a lot of the buildings look new. I wonder if that means it's a growing city.

The trucker drives us out of the city, across a short stretch of desert, over a long bridge, and then down into a smaller city that has only one tall building, a white concrete structure identified as Hayden Flour Mill. Before long, we go around a sweeping corner and on our left is a collection of very new-looking buildings. I see a sign that identifies it as Arizona State University. So we must be passing through Tempe. Father Saul was always hoping some of us would "graduate" from his orphanage school and go to that university. Tempe wasn't that far away from the orphanage, but as far as I know, nobody ever did go there. Maybe with the Army education benefits, I could take some classes there. I don't have a clue what's involved in being a university student, but that discharge lady at the hospital said the Army would pay for me to go to college if I wanted to, so I should keep it in mind.

It doesn't take us long to get to another town. It must be Mesa, the closest town to the orphanage.

The driver carefully pulls his big truck into what looks like an unloading place for construction materials. As usual, he doesn't say a word as he parks his truck. I think about apologizing for falling asleep and for failing to listen for smoky bears. I could explain why I'm so tired, but the more I think about it, the more sure I am he wouldn't want to hear it.

When he pulls to a stop, I just say, "Well, thanks a lot, mister. I guess I'll get going."

Of course he still doesn't respond, so I get out without saying anything more. My legs and back are stiff from sitting so long, but after I do some of the stretching exercises they taught me in physical therapy, I feel a little better.

I walk out to the main street. It's dark, but I figure if this is Mesa, all I have to do is find a street that heads north. That'll get me to the reservation. And once I'm on reservation property, I'm sure I can find the orphanage building.

I soon find a street that heads north and start walking that way. Although I have to stop often to rest my legs and back, it isn't too long before I get to an area of fewer homes and more orange groves. It must mean I'm close to the edge of the city. I keep walking, and soon I come to a highway. I cross the highway, and I'm into the desert. My legs and back are hurting even more, but I made it—I know I'm now on reservation property! I sit in the dirt to rest and look up at the stars. How many times have I been out at night sitting in this very desert, looking up at those same stars.

But I can't stop now. I get up and start moving again. Despite the lack of a moon, I'm sure I can find my way to the orphanage. All those years of exploring this desert at night taught me how to read the lay of the land. Back then, I didn't pay much attention to where I was going, but I never got lost because the lights of the city are always to the south, and the mountains are always to the east. Also, I learned to recognize every slope and ravine and cactus patch that was anywhere near the orphanage. Tonight, I know all I have to do is stay on this slight upslope until I start to recognize the part of the desert that's near the orphanage building.

The darkness of the night and the brilliance of the stars overhead bring back the memory of the only other time I was ever in the city of Mesa. It was the one time Father Saul chose me to be the one who got to go into town to buy a few supplies.

After I bought the bag of supplies at the store, I lingered in town for a long time, amazed at all the things there were to see: people and buildings, stores with things for sale, and more cars than I thought existed in the whole world. And women. And girls. I had never seen *any* females, not once in my entire life. Of course I knew females existed: there were pictures of women in some of the books Father Saul had us read, and he even explained what he called "the birds and the bees," about male and female anatomy and how babies are made. But it was really different to actually see females walking around, in the flesh. Most of the women were wearing dresses, but some of the girls my age were wearing shorts.

When I finally started walking back to the orphanage on that long ago night, from the positions of the stars, I realized I'd gotten so caught up in looking at everything in town, I'd missed supper time. As I walked through the darkness that night, I was very hungry, and all I could think about was how Father Saul would have already rung his big iron bell to call all the boys in to take their seats at the long wooden eating table, and how wonderful it would be to be there with them, enjoying the usual joking and laughing about silly stuff as we all ate together. Father Saul made us good food, even though it was pretty much the same meal every night. We called it Father Saul's "miracle stew." We called it that because it seemed like a miracle that he could continue to somehow find enough potatoes and other vegetables to make the meal for us. That night, I was pretty sure Father Saul would be very angry at me for not coming right back with the supplies.

He always demanded that we do as we were told, and he made a big point that learning to be responsible was an important lesson we needed to learn as we progressed toward adulthood. I knew I'd made a big mistake by staying away for so long. I stopped and crawled into a shallow ravine to think about what to do. I spent a long time that night, lying out here in the darkness, listening to the calls of night birds and the occasional mournful howls of distant coyotes.

I hoped if I waited long enough, Father Saul and the boys would already be asleep by the time I got there. That way, I might be able to sneak in and find my cot in the darkness of the dorm without anybody knowing what time I had come in. As I lay there that night, looking up at the stars, it hit me that the reason Father Saul had asked me to get so few supplies on my first trip to town, was to test me. And I knew I'd failed his test.

But when I finally got back to the orphanage that night, he was still waiting up for me. He said when I didn't come back, he'd been very worried. But when I couldn't come up with a good explanation about why I'd been gone so long, he got really angry and said I would never again get to be the one selected to go to town to get supplies. He said if I wasn't going to follow his orders, maybe I shouldn't even be in his orphanage. I never again did get to go to town, but he didn't kick me out of the orphanage. He said I was too young to be out on my own.

Now, here I am, years after that incident, shuffling along that same route, going back to see Father Saul after leaving to fight in a far-away war. This time I'll be able to tell him I passed his test. I went to war and did my duty just like he wanted me to. I'll be proud to tell him I was in a combat unit, and I did whatever was required of me. Until that is, I got seriously wounded and almost died. Most importantly, I'll be able to tell him I didn't get into the booze or the drugs like most of the other solders did, and I didn't forget any of the important lessons he taught me about how to be a good person.

But all of a sudden, I'm feeling unsure of my directions. I stop. Have I passed the place where I should have turned to get to the orphanage building?

No, not yet. It's probably only that I'm not moving as fast as I did when I was a kid. And my aching back and legs are probably also slowing me down. They're hurting so much it's tempting to just stop and sleep here in the desert tonight. After all, it's a warm night.

But no, I only have to keep walking a little longer, and then I'll be able to sleep indoors on a nice cot, surrounded by the other boys. I fight off the pain and keep going.

Soon, the old navigation memories return, and I know it's time to turn. Sure enough, shortly after I've made the turn, I come to a dry wash that I remember from the many times I explored this area. I drop down into it and follow it until I know it's time to come up out of it and turn west.

And as soon as I'm out of the wash, I see the building in the distance. Despite the moonless night, I can make out the familiar shape of the orphanage building against the background stars. How well I know that ramshackled old building. It's only been a few years, so I know the school building, with its attached dorm, will be exactly the same as always. They won't have any lamps lit this late at night, of course, and all the boys will be asleep in the dorm.

I head toward the dorm building, trying not to make any noise; no use waking everybody up. When I get closer, even though it's very dark, the place seems even more ramshackled than I remember it. But it's probably just my faulty memory; the place always was a wreck. It was everything us boys could do to keep it from falling apart, especially when the winter rains came. For many years, I was the youngest and smallest boy in the orphanage, so I was the one who got nominated to climb up onto the roof in the pouring rain to slop the tar onto wherever the other boys down below would tell me the leaking holes were.

I creep into the dorm, trying to be especially quiet to make sure I don't wake up any of the boys. Odd that it's so quiet in here. Nobody is snoring, and that gives the place an almost empty feel. Maybe it means there are fewer boys in the orphanage now. I wonder why.

I guess I'll find out more about that in the morning when I talk to Father Saul.

In the darkness, my knee bumps into one of the cots. Thankfully, it's empty, and I fall right onto it.

The moment I lie down, it hits me how exhausted I am and how much my injured back and legs are aching.

No need to worry about that now. Time to get some sleep. I can already feel my eyelids getting heavy. Amazing to think that only this morning I was in that Army hospital in far-away California, and now, after riding all that way with those truckers, here I am, right back lying on a cot in the orphanage I grew up in. It gives me such a feeling of being home, I don't think I'll have any trouble sleeping tonight. There are no blankets on this cot, but I don't feel like getting back up and going clear across the room to the big old cabinet just to get a blanket. It's such a warm night, I shouldn't need one.

Chapter Four

"Move and I'll kill ya!"

What the hell? I'm feeling a bit groggy, but I'm pretty sure I'm awake, and there's a damn light shining in my eyes. And is that a knife blade I feel against my throat?

"What are you doing here, mister?"

A kid's voice. My sneaking in here in the middle of the night must have scared him. But putting a knife to my throat? Why would any of Father Saul's boys do something like that? "Hey, kid. What's with the knife? Think about what Father Saul would say."

"You crazy, mister? I got the knife, and I said don't move."

I grab his wrist to pull the knife away from my throat, and then I take the flashlight away from him. Keeping hold of the wrist that holds the knife, I shine the light on his face. He *is* a kid, a skinny little Pima kid. I'd guess him to be maybe thirteen or fourteen.

I sit up and take the knife out of his hand. It turns out to be only a little pocket knife. The kid is squirming to get loose, but I keep a tight hold on his wrist. He's a brave little boy. I have to give him that. He's not whimpering or crying at all. In fact, he starts yelling at me, calling me a son of a bitch and a damn bastard, and then sputtering as he tries to think up other insults. I wonder who taught him to cuss like that. When I was here in this orphanage, Father Saul would never have allowed such language.

I say, "Hey, kid, pipe down. Do you want to wake up all the others? What if Father Saul wakes up and comes in to see what the racket is all about?"

That stops him. He stares at me like I'm completely crazy, and then he turns to look into the darkness of the dorm.

I follow his look with the flashlight's beam and see that there's nobody else in the dorm.

What is going on here? Where are all the other boys? It hasn't been that long since I left here, so how could they all be gone?

The kid is still squirming to get loose. I keep a good hold on his arm and say, "Quit squirming, kid. What's going on here? Where is everybody?"

"What? Who the hell are you, mister?"

"I used to live here. Grew up here."

"Bullshit. You're not from the tribe."

"Maybe I am, and maybe I'm not, but I did grow up right here in this orphanage. I lived here from when I was a baby. I'll ask you again, kid, where did everybody go?"

"Nobody here. Gimme back my knife."

"I'll give it back to you when you calm down and tell me why nobody's here. Is Father Saul gone too?"

"How should I know? Wasn't nobody here when I came."

"But why would Father Saul leave? He started the orphanage a long time ago. He wouldn't just up and leave."

"Yeah, I heard some white priest used to be out here. They said he don't belong on our res."

"Are you saying the tribal elders kicked him off the reservation? After all the years? This orphanage is so far out in the desert, it's barely even on reservation property, so why would they care if he was out here?"

"Before my time on this res, but I heard the priest kept sayin' gamblin' was wrong."

I think I'm starting to understand what happened. Shortly before I left the orphanage, the tribe started a weekend bingo game. When the retired people from the nearby towns started showing up to play, it was making the tribe a lot of money. They started holding bingo every evening, and it got bigger and bigger. Father Saul was against it. He said it would change the tribe forever, said it would cost them their historical values. "Okay, kid, maybe I'm getting it. I guess you're saying Father Saul had a run-in with the tribe over the bingo games, and they kicked him off the reservation."

"Gimme my knife back, and I'll tell ya."

I let go of his wrist and give him his knife back, but I keep the flashlight. I half expect him to run, but he doesn't. He just rubs his wrist and stares at me.

"Well?"

"It was before I was on this res. They say the priest called the cops. Told the cops the tribe was breakin' gambling laws. Cops came and shut it all down."

"Sounds just like Father Saul. But he had run-ins with the tribal elders before. I can't believe they'd kick him off the reservation just for that."

The kid frowns. "Beats me. The tribe got some lawyers. Said under the old treaties, we're a separate nation, so the state has no ruling here. And now the bingo is back."

I can tell the kid is repeating something he heard the elders say. So that must be what happened. Lawyers. They must have thought Father Saul was making trouble for their gambling business, so they made him get off the reservation.

"I get it, kid. But where did Father Saul go?"

"Quit calling me kid. My name's Cody. It means bear in the old language."

I know the name Cody doesn't actually mean bear in the old language. I suspect he probably made the name up for himself, but I don't say that. I just say, "Okay, Cody it is. But you said it was before your time. Didn't you grow up on this reservation?"

"Naw. I grew up on another res. Down south."

I guess if I want to find out what happened to Father Saul, I'll have to talk to the tribal elders. But then, maybe I don't want to let them know I'm here, at least not until I find another place to live. If they kicked Father Saul off the reservation, they probably wouldn't want me living out here either. I guess I should have had a backup plan before I came here.

Cody turns away from me. "I'm goin' back to sleep."

Using the flashlight beam, I can see where he's heading. It looks like he's pulled together a couple of the old cabinets to wall off a little room for himself in the corner. I wonder how long he's been living out here. Well, if he wants to live out here all by himself, it's okay with me. I lie back on the cot and close my eyes. I've got to get some sleep. If the kid is still here in the morning, maybe I can get more out of him.

Chapter Five

The sun coming in through the open hole in the wall that was always our only window is so bright I can tell I've slept in well past dawn. I guess I didn't realize how tired I was.

I get up and look into Cody's little hideaway. He's still sound asleep.

I go outside and do some of the exercises they taught me in physical therapy. Everything hurts, but that's to be expected with all I did yesterday, my first day out of the hospital. But that's not my main problem right now: what's important now is to find some food. I haven't had anything to eat since I left the hospital except for the candy bar Mr. Foucher gave me. As much as I hate the idea of doing any more walking, I'd better head back down into town to find something to eat.

I hope while I'm gone, Cody doesn't go tell the tribal elders about some guy that showed up at the old orphanage in the middle of the night. But then, I suspect he's not supposed to be here either, so hopefully he won't do that.

I head across the desert toward Mesa, trying to imagine how I'm going to get some food without any money. Panhandling, I suppose. But will anybody give money to a young guy that looks as healthy as me? They'll probably just tell me to go get a job.

"Hey!"

I look back. It's Cody.

He runs to catch up with me. "Where you goin', mister?"

"I figured I'd better walk to town and try to scare up something to eat."

"But I got food. Come back, and I'll show ya."

He leads me back to his hideaway and pulls out a couple of bread rolls. Then, he brings out something wrapped up in a napkin. "It's cheese," he says, grinning. "You can make a sandwich."

I'm not sure I should be taking this kid's food. He's so skinny, I suspect he doesn't get all that much to eat himself. "Are you sure? Isn't this your food?"

"Hey, I got plenty. I get it at the bingo hall."

"I hope you didn't steal it, Cody."

He shrugs.

I'm so hungry two rolls and a little bit of cheese sounds pretty good, no matter where he got it.

He hands me the food and says, "Hey, while you eat, you can tell me what it was like growing up here in this orphanage."

I'm so hungry, I quickly start eating. Between bites, I say, "Not much to tell, Cody. Just a bunch of boys that didn't have any place else to go. I was the baby of the group, so they all kind of took care of me."

Cody grins. "A bunch of boys out here all together? Sounds like fun."

"It *was* fun being together out here. But it wasn't all fun. There was a lot of work to do around the place. And Father Saul taught us like it was a regular school. Still, if you had to go to school, this was a good place to do it. Father Saul taught us a lot of important stuff, and he made sure we learned it. He could be tough on us, when necessary."

Cody is still grinning. "Okay, let's do that. You stay here with me and do that."

"Do what?"

"Teach me stuff. About the world and all that. I'll get food for ya. Nobody'll ever know you're here. Nobody from the tribe ever comes out this far. All they care about is the bingo hall and makin' money."

"I'm not a teacher, Cody. And why do you want to stay out here anyhow?"

"I have to."

"Why?"

"Aw, no big deal. Let's talk about you teachin' me stuff."

"Don't you get lonely out here all by yourself?"

He looks away. "Naw, I do fine out here. Nobody likes me anyhow."

"Nobody likes you?"

"Naw. I didn't grow up on this res, so the other kids don't think of me as their cousin, even though I am. My mother was from here. And they don't like my old man either. Cause of what he did to her."

"What did he do? Did he beat her? Is that why she took you away from this reservation?"

"Aw, who wants to talk about that old stuff? Let's talk about what it was like growing up out here with a bunch of other kids."

"Okay. But first, why don't you tell me how you found this building."

He shrugs. "Just out explorin'. Lookin' at desert stuff. And here it was. Nobody around, so I figured why not use it as my hideout place."

"I can understand why you like to go out exploring the desert by yourself. I used to do that a lot myself."

"I bet you know a lot of cool stuff about the desert, don't ya? Stuff you can teach me."

"Like I said, Cody, I'm not a teacher."

"You said you went to school here. And you said the priest taught you good stuff. I bet you know a lot more than me. I ain't been out nowhere."

"Don't say ain't, Cody. Say I haven't been anywhere."

He puts his sly grin back on and points at me. "See there. You know all kinds of stuff I don't know. Before she took off somewhere with that weird guy, my mother told me I was really smart. But after she took off, they made me come back here to live with my old man, and he don't know shit about nuthin'."

"I expect you are smart, Cody, but your English could use some improvement."

"Oh yeah, like how?"

"Well, I can tell you one tip Father Saul gave us. He told us the use of swear words usually doesn't really contribute much to the overall meaning of a sentence."

"See there. You do know lots of good stuff you can teach me."

Is that a look of admiration on his face? That's definitely not something I'm used to. "Well, Father Saul did teach us good stuff, as you say. But he had his rules. If there was one thing sure to get us punished, it was the use of curse words."

"Okay, Teach. Got it." He looks down at his hands and says, "You know, Teach, I'm sort of doin' better now that I found this place. Even if I do get . . . like you said, lonely."

"What about your dad? What does he say about you not coming home at night?"

"Aw, he don't like me neither. Never did. Don't even want me around. He's got his job at the bingo hall. Sellin' the booze. Sellin' the booze and drinkin' the booze. It's his whole Goddam life."

"What did I tell you about that kind of language, Cody?"

"Oh right. Sorry, Teach." He grins at me.

"Cody, my name is Murphy. But you can all me Murph. In Vietnam, everybody called me that."

He stares at me wide-eyed. "You were in the war?"

"Yes."

"Geez. Some of the young guys from the tribe are over there. Some of 'em already got killed. One of 'em just got sent back and was buried in the reservation cemetery. They said he was a hero."

"Everybody who gets killed is sent home a hero."

"You don't think they really were?"

I shrug. "Yes, I suppose they were. They gave their lives."

The morning sun is getting hotter, so I suggest we go into the classroom building where it's always slightly cooler. Also, my injured back is killing me, so I'd like to sit down. But I don't tell him that. Maybe I really do like the idea of him looking up to me.

I sit down in a classroom chair, but Cody runs out of the room. He's soon back with an apple and two more rolls. Then, he turns another one of the classroom chairs to face me and says, "Okay, Teach. What's my first lesson?"

"Maybe I can at least tell you some things Father Saul taught us, but I can't keep on eating your food. I should go to town to get some for myself. Maybe I can get a job of some kind."

"Naw, don't do that. Stay here and be my teacher. I can even pay you. Look here. I got money." He reaches into his pocket and pulls out a roll of bills tied up in a rubber band. "How much you need?" He holds the entire roll of money out to me. "Here, take it. Take it all. I can get more any time I want it. It'll be the start of your pay as my teacher."

He really does seem to want me to be his teacher. Or maybe he's just so lonely he's bribing me with money and food to be sure I'm going to stick around. I say, "I'm not going to take your money, Cody."

"Why not? I can do some more errands at today's bingo game and earn a lot more. Then you can go buy yourself some better teacher duds."

I shake my head. "I won't be doing that, Cody. Actually, Father Saul showed me you don't need to wear special teacher clothes to be a teacher. He didn't even wear his priest clothes. But we all knew he was our teacher. That's for sure."

"That's the kind of teacher I want, not those idiots at the res school. Hey, wait a minute, Murph. I just had a thought. You say you don't know how to teach me. You should go learn how. My cousin June is goin' over to ASU, the university, tomorrow to learn how to be a teacher."

"So you think I should go to college to learn how to be a teacher?"

"Sure. Why not? You got somethin' else to do?"

"Actually, I might want to take some college classes. The Army said they'd pay for it, but I'm not sure I want to study to be a teacher."

Cody is all grins. "Okay. Go there and learn whatever you want. Then, you can come back here and teach it to me."

"That university is not exactly within walking distance, Cody. I went by it on my way here. It's over in Tempe."

"No problem. There's a bus that stops right out in front of the reservation entrance. That's how my cousin gets there. The bus goes over to Tempe. Stops right at the university entrance."

"I'd have to find out when the next semester starts."

"It's starting right now! This week. My cousin told me she's gonna go there tomorrow and register for her new term. That's why I mentioned it."

"I guess I could do that. I could at least go over to that university tomorrow and check it out."

"All right! You do that. Right now, I'm gonna go to the bingo hall. Make more money for us."

Before I can protest that I don't need his money, he jumps up and runs out the door.

After he leaves, I start thinking about what he told me. So the new term at the university is starting right now. That's interesting. The discharge officer back at the hospital, gave me a benefits pamphlet that said the Army would pay for me to go to college. I only looked through that pamphlet quickly, so why did I just happen to notice that one benefit? I wonder why those kinds of things are happening just when I'm trying to decide what to do with my life. I don't even know what day it is. If a term at the university is starting, it must be a weekday. How long has it been since I had to pay any attention to days of the week? Not at all at the orphanage. And not much in Basic Training. In Vietnam, I didn't know, or care, what day of the week it was. Did I subconsciously think I was going to die out there in that Vietnamese jungle, so what did days of the week matter?

But now that I survived, and I'm going to be "in the world," I need to start making my own decisions about what the next step in my life is going to be, and I suppose that means I should start thinking about everyday things, like the days of the week.

Chapter Six

The next morning, Cody leads me through the desert to the bus stop near the reservation's main entrance using what he calls his "secret way" that gets us there without going past any of the tribal buildings. As usual, the long walk is hard on my legs and back, but I don't mention it to Cody.

When we get to the bus stop, he forces some bills into my hands. "For the bus and other stuff," he says.

I accept it, but I again tell him I'll pay it back as soon as my Army severance check comes.

As we wait for the bus, two Pima women come walking toward us, a young one, maybe in her twenties, and an older woman who's carrying a baby that's maybe about a year old.

Cody whispers, "That's June and her grandma with June's baby boy. They say June is one of my cousins, but who on this res isn't? Let me do the talking."

When the two women arrive at the bus stop, Cody says, "Hi Granny. Going shopping?"

The old woman scowls at him and then leans forward so June can kiss her cheek. Then, she heads off down the street with the baby toward the nearby shopping area.

Cody takes my arm and pulls me forward to meet June. "This is my friend, Murph. He's also headin' to the university."

June smiles at me. "Oh, I haven't seen you here before, Murph. Do you live around here?"

"He sure does," says Cody. "I just met him. He was in Vietnam. Got wounded and everything."

"Oh," she says, "I'm sorry to hear you were wounded."

I'm not sure how I'm supposed to respond to that, but luckily, before I can decide what to say, the bus arrives. I let her get on first while I stay to say goodbye to Cody. I tell him I might not be over at the university very long, just long enough to check it out.

When I get on the bus, I'm happy to see that June has gone to the back of the bus where she joins some other young women. I sit up front behind the driver, grateful for the chance to sit down and rest my legs and back.

When we get to the university, I get off quickly and step to the side so I don't have to explain to June how I know Cody.

But I didn't need to worry because June and the other young women get off together and hurry onto the campus.

I let them get well ahead, and then I also go onto the campus. The first thing I notice is that a lot of the buildings look new. This must be a fairly new university, or else it's been expanding quickly.

There are a lot of students walking ahead of me on the broad sidewalk. Cody told me his cousin June came here today to sign up for the next term, so maybe this is the day everybody comes to campus to get registered.

I sit on a bench for a while to rest my aching legs and watch the seemingly endless stream of students flow by. I feel out of place. I'm not all that much older than they are, but they seem uh . . . lighter. I'm not exactly sure where that thought came from, but I suspect it's true. They're even dressed lighter, many of them in shorts and T-shirts. I wonder if any of them will notice I'm wearing Army fatigue pants.

The question is, do I really want to become one of them? If so, how would I go about doing that?

After a while, I get too curious to just sit and watch them go by. I get up and follow them. I soon find out that a lot of them are going into a large building. Should I follow them inside? Well, why not. What could it hurt?

I follow them inside the building. It's a very large open room, and students are lined up at several tables.

I guess they're engaged in the registration process, but I have no idea how it works. Should I try to find out? Might as well. At least I could learn how it all works. As a test, I could sign up for just one class.

That way, I could attend the class for a while and see if I like being a student before I decide if this is really what I want to do as the next phase of my life.

I stop a red-headed student with thick glasses and ask him how I would go about registering for a class. He looks at me in an odd way and asks, "You just starting? First time?"

When I nod, he does a kind of soft chuckle and says, "Follow me."

He leads me to a table where students are gathered around filling out some kind of form. I pick up one of the forms. It has lines for name and address and another for a major. I don't have an address, and I sure don't have a major, so I just write my name and leave the rest of the form blank. Then, I ask the red-headed guy, "What's next?"

He's busy filling out his form, so he just points toward a long line of students lined up at a table in the middle of the room. They're all holding the same kind of form I am, so I join in at the end of the line.

The line moves pretty slow, but I eventually reach the woman at the desk and hand her my form.

She says, "You didn't write down an address."

"I just moved here. I haven't got a permanent address yet."

"All right, but you should notify the university as soon as you get one, okay?"

"Will do."

She looks at my form. You also didn't declare a major. Do you want me to write down undeclared?"

"I guess so."

She begins to write on my form.

"No, wait. I don't think I want to be undeclared. From now on, I'm not going to be undeclared. At anything."

"Well, I have to write down something. Either the name of a major or undeclared."

"A major then. What are my choices?"

"Well, there are many."

"Can't you list them?"

"I'm afraid there are too many. And you're holding up the line."

I can tell she's exasperated with me. This is not turning out to be a very good start to my college career.

She hands my form back to me. "I suggest you get a university catalog and look at the list of possible majors."

I turn back to look at the long line of students waiting for their turn to talk to this lady. Why do they all look so young? I'm not really much older than they are. Maybe being in Vietnam and then in those hospitals for so long has aged me. I look for the red-haired guy. He's not far behind me in the line, and he's watching me. I say to him, "What's your major?"

He does his odd smile again before answering. "Philosophy."

Philosophy. I know what that is. Father Saul taught us a little about some of the old time philosophers. I ask him, "Is that like studying . . . uh, Plato and all that?"

He smiles again. Does he think I'm making jokes? More likely, he just thinks I'm an odd sort of person. Well, compared to all these fresh-faced young people around me, I guess I am.

"Yes," he says, still smiling. "Plato and all that."

I turn back to the lady. "My major is philosophy. Plato and all that."

"So, you want me to write down philosophy as your major? Are you sure about that?"

"Sure about what?"

"That you really want to study philosophy?"

"No, but I am sure I want you to write down philosophy as my major, okay?"

She shrugs and writes "Philosophy" on my form. She looks up at me and says, "You've never done this before, have you?"

"Nope. What do I do next?"

She points at a row of tables on one side of the large room, each of them with students lined up at them.

After she hands me back my form, I move aside, but I stay close, waiting for the red-haired guy to finish.

When he does, I say, "Where do we sign up for philosophy classes?"

"We?"

"Yeah, we philosophy majors."

He again gives me his odd smile. But then he says, "Follow me."

He leads me to a table at the far end of the big room. Sure enough, the sign on the front of the table says "PHILOSOPHY." There aren't as many students lined up there as at the other tables. I wonder why.

The red-haired guy starts to wander away, but I stop him and ask him what class I should sign up for.

He says, "Well, if you really are now a philosophy major, you can sign up for any philosophy class you want to. Whatever you're interested in."

"All I know about philosophy is Socrates and Plato. My old teacher told us about them."

"Ah, the history of philosophy. Well, there is a class about that."

"Okay, I'll sign up for that. How much does it cost?"

"You don't know?"

"Actually, I guess it doesn't matter. The Army is paying for it."

"Really?"

"Yes. I just got out."

He nods thoughtfully. "Vietnam? Or aren't I supposed to ask that?"

"Doesn't bother me. Yes, I was in Vietnam. Just got out."

"Is that right? Well, being as how I'm getting close to draft age, I think I'd like to ask you some question about that."

"I don't know what to tell you. There's a lot of jungle. It's hot, except when it rains."

That makes him laugh out loud. "I was actually referring to questions about how not to end up there."

"I don't think I can help you with that. I got drafted, and that's where they sent me."

"Oh. Well, I've gotta go sign up for some different classes. See ya."

I watch him go and then head for the philosophy table. I do what he suggested and sign up for the history of philosophy class. The woman behind the desk hands me a paper, but it only says the class number, Philosophy 301, and the room number. It says the class meets Mondays, Wednesdays, and Fridays at nine AM, but it doesn't say the starting date.

I ask, "When does the class start?"

She looks at me in an odd way, and says, "It started this morning. Didn't you know that?"

"No. I just got registered."

"Well, you made it just in time. Today is the last day of registration. But if you show up day after tomorrow, you'll have only missed one class."

"Oh. Okay. Uh, am I done with registration?"

She points at some tables on the other side of the big room, and says, "Final checkout over there."

I go there and while I wait in yet another long line, I'm thinking about how easy that was. Is that really all it takes to become a college student? Amazing how easy it is to completely change your life if you just do it.

But will it completely change my life in a good way? Although I loved being a student in Father Saul's ramshackled old school out in the desert, will I like being a student here in this big modern university? And what kind of teachers do they have here? Here, I probably won't be learning at the feet of a very unusual, but very wise, old priest. And what about who I am now? Maybe I'm not the same person that enjoyed being Father Saul's student. I know I've changed, but does that change mean I won't enjoy the same things anymore?

Why am I having these doubts? So far, since I left the Army hospital in California, just going forward seems to be working. That approach seems to be taking me into new situations with interesting possibilities.

By the time I get to the front of the line, I'm ready to go for it. I've gone this far, so why not just keep going and see where it takes me?

It turns out the next step in the process is to get a student ID. The woman behind the table asks for my driver's license.

I tell her I don't have one.

She says, "Come on. Everybody has a driver's license. You just don't want to show it to me because you want your student ID to say you're twenty-one."

"I grew up in an orphanage, so I don't really know how old I am. You can put any date on it you want to."

She frowns at me. "I can't do that. Don't you have any kind of ID?"

"No. I did have an Army health ID when I was in the hospital, but now all I have is my discharge papers. Do you want to see them?"

"Oh. You were in the Army? And in an Army hospital? Were you in Vietnam?"

"Yes."

"Oh, well, you're probably at least twenty-one then, and we'd better not hold up the line any longer. I'll just say today is your birthday and you're twenty-one." She types that on a student ID and hands it to me, still smiling. "Thank you for your service."

I wonder why she said that. Maybe it means she has a relative in the military. Or could it mean the opposite, that I'm the first person she's met who was in Vietnam?

The final step in the process is tuition payment. When I tell the woman at that table the Army will be paying my tuition, she says, "Okay, do you have your pre-authorization?"

I do my usual shrug. "Nobody told me about that."

"Well, you have to go to the cashier service. In the administration building. Get a pre-authorization, and then come back here. You don't have to wait in the whole line again. Just come back to me, okay?"

I stand at attention and salute her, but then I smile to let her know my salute was a following orders joke.

At first, she's not sure how to react, but then she also smiles and salutes me back. Despite waiting in line all morning, I'm actually starting to enjoy this process—a little. And why not, I'm learning a lot of new things about how universities work.

I go out of the registration building and find a bench in the shade so I can sit down after being on my feet for so long. I watch the students stream past. Nobody seems to notice me until a friendly-looking girl slows and smiles at me. I use the opportunity to ask her where the administration building is. She looks at me in an odd way and then points at the building right across the sidewalk. I laugh and say, "Got it." I salute her too, but she just frowns and walks away. Maybe I'd better quit doing that. Actually, I don't know why I've been doing it. I must be a little nervous. Now that I think about it, it's no wonder I'm a little nervous; this is the first time in my entire life that I've done anything like this. With no Father Saul to tell me how to be, and no Army officers to tell me what to do, I'm having to make up my own mind about everything. I might have expected that to be a freeing feeling, but surprisingly, it's turning out to be kind of stressful.

But actually, I'm feeling pretty good about how this is all going. Everybody seems pretty friendly, even when they find out I'm not really one of them.

At the cashier service inside the administration building, just showing them my discharge papers doesn't seem to be enough to get the required pre-authorization paperwork. They say they have to make a few calls, and that I should go back out and wait in the lobby.

I sit on a bench in the lobby watching the students come and go until eventually, they call my name. I guess it all got taken care of because they give me the pre-authorization paperwork.

With the paperwork in hand, I head back to the registration building, and the nice woman at the checkout table takes it and congratulates me on finishing the registration process.

I walk out into the midday heat and go back to that same bench in the shade to rest. My legs are hurting, but guess I should take this opportunity to walk around a bit to get the feel of this campus. After all, I am going to be a student here now, aren't I?

I walk around the campus for a short while, just to drink in the reality of what I've just done. I'm starting to feel even better about it. Only a few days ago, I walked out of that veteran's hospital in California without a clue what my next step in life would be, and now here I am, in Arizona, a real live registered student at a big university. Unlike how hard it is to get anything done in the Army, this wasn't very hard at all. In fact, when I got onto that bus this morning, I was just planning on checking the college thing out, but the momentum of it kept leading me on until I actually became a student. Is this what happens out here in real life when you don't have anybody to tell you what you have to do?

As I approach an older-looking building, I see a small group of students crowded around a large fountain in front. They're listening to a guy who's standing up on the concrete lip of the fountain. He's yelling at them using a bullhorn. As I get closer, I can hear that he's talking about the war in Vietnam. He's saying we shouldn't be in that war, that we never should have been there in the first place, that young men are dying for no real reason. He's saying it's a phony war, an illegal war. A few other young guys are with him, holding up hand-painted "STOP THE WAR" signs. The group of gathered students aren't clapping or cheering, but they are sticking around to listen.

I'm not sure what to think about what the guy with the bullhorn is saying. Nobody in my unit over there ever mentioned hearing about any anti-war protests back home. And now everybody in my patrol group is dead. My first reaction is irritation. Do these protesters think my friends died for nothing?

But that thought makes me remember Father Saul's often-repeated warning to us: think with logic, not emotion. Okay, I'll try to think logically about it. Why are these students saying the war is bad?

Maybe they're just worried about getting drafted themselves. I notice there are no female students among the protesters.

But then, the guy with the bullhorn was saying it's an "illegal" war and young men are dying for no reason. His words make me wonder how many have died over there. Odd that I never heard anybody in my unit talk about that number. There *was* some talk about a lot of our guys dying in big battles farther up in the northern part of Vietnam. Rumors mostly. But actually, nobody talked much about the war itself. Now that I think about it, that seems odd: we were in a real war, so why didn't we talk about it? When I first got to Vietnam, the enormity of it all was almost overwhelming. The air base where we landed was so huge it was hard to imagine how all those men, and all those planes, and all that military equipment could have been brought there in such a short time. But once I got sent to my jungle firebase, the days became a daily grind. What at first seemed so dangerous, eventually became boring.

Until it wasn't.

The guy with the bullhorn notices me. "Hey, you!"

I point to myself.

"Yeah, you, buddy. How come you're wearing them military-type pants and boots? Like to play soldier dress-up, do ya? Thinkin' about goin' over there to get yourself killed for nothing?"

I hurry away. I'd forgotten that I was still wearing my Army pants. It makes me remember how I had to trade away my Army shirt in LA in order to get anybody to give me a ride. As soon as I get my discharge money, I need to get some pants that look more . . . student like.

As I walk away, the last thing I hear from the bullhorn guy is him trying to convince the males in the crowd to come forward and burn their draft cards. As if that would do them any good. Unless they were isolated and unknown to the draft people, like we were out there in the orphanage, won't they still get drafted sooner or later?

I wonder how common that kind of anti-war talk is. Maybe Cody can tell me. Maybe he's been hearing about it on TV or something.

I use what's left of my walking strength to head for the bus stop. I wonder how excited Cody is going to be when I tell him I did what he suggested and signed up to be a student at the university. I'm not sure he'll be all that interested in philosophy, though. He probably won't even know what it is. In fact, I'm not sure I do either. I wonder if I'm going to like studying about old philosophers. Actually, there must be more to it than that. I guess I'll find that out when I go to my first class in a couple of days.

The first bus to arrive says it's bound for Mesa. Just before it leaves, I decide to hop onto that one instead of waiting for the bus that goes to the reservation entrance. In Mesa, I can find the post office and get a PO box so the Army will have an address to send me my discharge check. I can use a little bit of the money Cody gave me to pay for the PO box and pay him back as soon as the check comes.

Chapter Seven

As the bus rolls into Mesa, I keep my eyes open for the post office, and luckily, the bus goes right past it. I get off at the next stop and walk back. I sit down to rest on the steps in front. It's been a long day and I'm tired, but it's good to be alive and able to just sit here and watch the people go by. They're all just regular people, going about their business. It's surprising how much you can tell from the way they dress. Despite the heat, some of the men are dressed in suits. They must work in an office with air cooling. Other people are dressed in light shirts and shorts, ready for the hot day ahead. Surprisingly, even a lot of the women are dressed in shorts. I wonder if that's something new.

A police car coming up the street interrupts my people watching. Only one policeman is inside the car, and his window is rolled down. He slows down to look me over.

Maybe I shouldn't be sitting out here, doing nothing. I get up and hurry inside.

Inside the post office, the woman behind the counter tells me how much it costs to rent a post office box. It's not all that much. After I pay for it, I explain to the woman behind the counter that I need the mailing address so I can get my severance check from the Army. I tell her I need to make a call to tell the Army to send it here. She doesn't seem very sympathetic. She says her boss won't let anybody use the post office phone, but she does call back to him. When he comes out, I explain my situation to him. He immediately says, "Come right on back to my office, son. You can use my phone."

He seems very friendly. I wonder why. Maybe he was in the military too. So far, military veterans have all been nice to me.

He says his name is Frank Gibson, and he shows me where the phone is. I get the folded Army benefits pamphlet out of my pocket and dial the number the discharge lady wrote on it.

She answers, and I tell her my name and my new post office box address. I have the feeling she remembers me, but she pretends not to. She says she'll have to look my name up. I'm getting worried that I'm tying up the post office phone too long, but Mr. Gibson is busy doing other things and doesn't seem to mind. Finally, she comes back on and says my check should go out in a few days. I start to thank her, but she's already hung up.

I thank Mr. Gibson, and he says, "No problem, son. I thank you for your service."

Here's another person saying that to me. I don't know if I'm supposed to say thanks or what, so I just say, "Well, I didn't do much. I got hurt, and that was the end of it for me."

He gets a concerned look on his face and reaches out to touch my shoulder. "You were wounded? I noticed you were limping a bit. Are you still hurt? Why don't you sit down here and rest."

As soon as I'm seated, he says, "Me, I had no chance of getting hurt. I was in the Navy, but I was stationed at Navy Pier in Chicago. We trained pilots how to land on aircraft carriers."

"I learned about Chicago from my school teacher. It's in the middle of the country, and they have one of the biggest big rail hubs there. But how could they have had aircraft carriers there?"

He chuckles. "That's what everybody says, but we did. Sort of. During the war, they couldn't take a real aircraft carrier out of service to train pilots, so they built flat tops on a couple of old ships out on Lake Michigan, and we trained them there."

"That sounds like an interesting assignment, sir."

"It was, but I wanted to go overseas. It never happened. Never really got to be in the war. Just stayed stuck in Chicago. But enough about me, son. What happened to you in Vietnam?"

He's the first person who's actually asked me how I got wounded, so I haven't really thought though how to tell it. "To tell you the truth, sir, I'm not exactly sure what happened. We were out on patrol. In the jungle. Usually nothing happened on those kinds of patrols, but then one day something did happen.

There was gunfire and an explosion that knocked me out. Probably a mortar or something. Landed right behind me, I guess. When I woke up, a Vietnamese soldier was standing over me, pointing a rifle at me. He was wearing a uniform. I'd never before seen the enemy wearing any kind of actual uniform. I knew he was going to shoot me, and I couldn't do anything about it. I couldn't move at all. Another Vietnamese in a uniform, probably his superior officer, said something to him, and the soldier lowered his rifle and just walked away. I think they thought I was pretty much dead already, so they didn't want to waste a bullet on me. Later on, an evac helicopter came and somebody said I was dead, or might as well be, but they loaded me onto the chopper anyhow and flew me out. For some reason, I didn't die."

I begin to wonder if I'm taking up too much of his time, so I stop talking.

"That's an amazing story, young man. You're lucky to still be with us."

"Yes, sir, that's what they told me. I found out later they killed all the others in my patrol group. I was in a hospital in Saigon for quite a while, and then for a long time in another hospital back in this country."

"Sorry to hear you had such a hard time, son. Tell me your name."

"Oh, like I wrote on the PO Box form, it's Murphy. But back in Vietnam, everybody just called me Murph."

"All right, Murph. Well, is there anything else I can do for you? Do you have a place to stay?"

"Yes, for now, but thank you. Like I said, I just need to get my severance check in the mail, and then I'll decide what to do next."

I start to thank him for letting me tell him what happened to me in Vietnam, but then I decide that might sound strange. He doesn't know it's the first time I've been able to tell anybody about it. Instead, I just thank him for letting me use his phone.

He says I can stay there in his office where it's cool, but I don't want to take up any more of his time, so I tell him I've got things to do, even though I actually don't. I thank him again and leave.

Outside, in the growing heat, I sit on the steps in front of the post office. Even if the police do come by, I'm going to stay here in the shade for a bit. I need to think about what to do next. Should I ask around town about a job? Maybe I could get a job painting houses or something like that. Like I told that Army discharge lady, I don't have any special skills, but I can paint. I did a lot of painting at the orphanage. Despite my injuries, there's nothing wrong with my hands and arms.

But to do that, I'd need to buy work clothes, so maybe I should just hike back to the reservation and wait for my check from the Army to arrive before I decide what to do next.

I stand up, ready to start toward the orphanage, but then I think maybe there is one thing I could do while I'm here in town: I could look for Father Saul. I'm still wondering where he went after they kicked him off the reservation. Mesa is the closest town to the reservation, so maybe he came here. As far as I know, he'd been running his orphanage on the reservation for most of his life, so it's hard to imagine why he would go anywhere else. Maybe I should go to the local Catholic church and ask if they know where he is. After all, he is still a Catholic priest. Maybe the church found another job for him. That thought makes me wonder if the Catholic Church approved of him being out there running his orphanage on reservation property. Maybe the church didn't send him there in the first place. Did they even know he was out there? I don't remember anybody from the Catholic Church ever coming by.

I go back inside and ask the post office lady if there's a Catholic church around here. She tells me there's one just down the street.

"How far?"

"About eight blocks. That way." She points.

My legs and back are already hurting, but I guess I can walk eight blocks.

I thank her and head out in the direction she pointed. I stay on the shady side of the street, but with the heat coming up off of the pavement, even the shade of the buildings doesn't help much.

I soon see the Catholic Church in the distance. It's pretty fancy, and to my eyes, it doesn't quite fit in this dusty little town. But what do I know?

As soon as I get to the church, I go inside and see a priest sitting in one of the pews reading something. I go right up to him and ask him if he knows where Father Saul went.

He seems surprised at my question. "Father Saul? Isn't he still running his school out on the reservation?"

"No. I was just out there, and he's gone. The school's deserted."

"No kidding? That surprises me. I've never met him, but we knew he was out there. As far as I know, he's been out there just about forever. But then, I haven't been here in Mesa very long. Why did he leave the reservation?"

I'm not sure I should tell this priest that he got kicked off the reservation because of a disagreement over gambling, so I just say, "I'm not sure. That's what I'm trying to find out."

The priest looks closely at me and says, "Why are you looking for him? Do you know him?"

"Yes, I was a student in his school. I lived at the orphanage from when I was a little kid."

"Oh, so you're a Pima Indian."

"I guess so."

He looks at me in an odd way. "You guess so? I didn't think there were any kids out there but Pimas."

I don't want to get into explaining why I'm not sure what I am, so I just say, "Well, I never knew who my parents were, but I was at his orphanage since I was real little."

"Well, son, if Father Saul has been transferred to another church or school, the archdiocese in Phoenix will know. Do you want me to call them?"

"Yes, if you wouldn't mind, sir. I'd really like to see him again."

The priest tells me to wait while he goes to his office to make the call.

He leaves me standing there, and I'm not sure what to do with myself. I've never been in an actual church, so I'm not sure if a person is supposed to sit in the pews if they aren't a member. I decide to remain standing, even though my legs are hurting.

Thankfully, he isn't gone long. When he comes back, he's got a puzzled look on his face. He says, "The orphanage out there wasn't sanctioned, but they knew about it. They were surprised to learn he was no longer there."

"So nobody knows where he went?"

"I'm afraid not. But if you'll give me your phone number and I hear anything, I'll let you know."

"I uh, don't have a phone yet, sir. I'll let you know when I get one."

"All right, son. If you find out anything about where he went, be sure to let me know. You've got me curious. And the archdiocese also needs to know where he is."

I leave the church and head back up Main Street.

I'm almost back to the street that heads north toward the orphanage, when I think I see what looks like a Pima boy. I think it's Jimmy, one of the boys from the school. But if it is him, he's gotten a lot thinner. Has he fallen into hard times?

I yell at him, "Hey, Jimmy!"

He keeps walking away as if he didn't hear me. Is he trying to avoid me? I hurry to catch up with him. "Jimmy, don't you recognize me?"

He turns to look at me. It's like he can't believe it's me.

"Junior?"

It takes me a moment to remember that's the name he would know me by. At the orphanage, Junior was the nickname Father Saul gave me, so that's what everybody called me.

"Yeah, it's me. I'm back."

"Back? From Vietnam? Brent heard you got killed over there."

He must be referring to the Brent that was one of the older boys at the orphanage, the only kid who was even a little bit fat. He was a bully who liked to pick on the smaller boys. "You say Brent heard I'd been killed? Who told him that?"

"He ran into some guy who was just back from Vietnam. When he heard Brent was from Mesa, Arizona, he asked if he knew a kid named Murphy from Mesa that had got killed in a jungle ambush."

"Well, that's almost true, Jimmy. I did get wounded in an ambush. Pretty bad. And for a while, they didn't think I was going to make it. But as you can see, here I am."

"Jesus, Junior. It's like I'm talking to a ghost. Brent and I talked a lot about how you might have gotten yourself killed over there. He thought you shouldn't have been there in the first place. That you were too young."

"Well, when I couldn't tell the draft board exactly how old I was they inducted me right away. They thought maybe I was older than I was admitting. That I was a draft dodger."

"Draft dodger. That's a laugh. As if Father Saul would have let any of us get away with something like that." He turns and looks down the street. "I'd like to talk to you more, Junior, but I'm late for a job interview. Gotta get there quick. I need the job bad. Hard to find work these days."

"Okay, Jimmy. But how can I get in touch with you? I'd like to talk to you about what happened to Father Saul. I just went to see the priest at that Catholic church." I point back up the street. "He didn't know where Father Saul had gone. He even called the archdiocese in Phoenix, and they didn't know either. Do you have any idea of where I can find him?"

"Nope. As far as we knew, he just up and left. After you left, the tribe got even heavier into their bingo games, and Father Saul called the cops on 'em. Called it illegal gambling. After that, they didn't want Father Saul on their reservation anymore, so maybe that's why he left."

"Yes, I heard Father Saul was against the bingo games."

"Right. They didn't want him interfering, but Father Saul wouldn't back off."

"I heard that too, Jimmy. Were you still there when he left?"

"Yeah. The orphanage started to fall on hard times, so Father Saul began looking for foster parents for us. Pimas mostly. But later, anybody who would take us."

"So, he was in the process of shutting the orphanage down."

"Yeah, and by the end, there were no more young boys left. Father Saul made sure they all got adopted. But nobody wanted to adopt Brent and me. We were too old. So we knew it was only a matter of time before we'd have to leave. And then one day, when we came back from trying to catch some fish for supper, he was just gone. When he didn't come back after a few days, we assumed the lawyers had brought in the cops to take him away, just like they'd been threatening to do. After that, Brent and me had to leave and go find jobs. For a while, Brent kept in touch, but now I've lost track of him. He said he was gonna go up to Canada. Said he'd heard there were jobs up there. But listen, Junior, like I said, I gotta run."

"Just one more thing, Jimmy. You're still calling me Junior. I haven't heard that name since I went into the Army. And I always wondered why you older boys called me Junior. Was it because I was the youngest."

"Well, that was part of it. But also because you had the same name as Father Saul, Saul Murphy, and we didn't want to call you that. Besides, what if you really were Saul Junior?"

"Saul Junior? What do you mean by that, Jimmy?"

"Well, we heard your mother was a Pima, but it's obvious just from looking at you your father must have been a white man."

"Are you suggesting Father Saul could have been my father?"

"Well, he gave you his name, didn't he?"

"That was only later, when I needed a legal name. I didn't have one, so he gave me his."

"And what about him treating you like a son? You were always his favorite."

"He couldn't have been my father, Jimmy. He would have told me. And he was a priest, right? Priests have to take a vow of chastity."

"Well, that's the story they all tell, isn't it? But he was still a man. And maybe screwing a squaw might not be the same as . . . well, you know what I mean."

"Yes, I do know what you mean, Jimmy, and I don't like you saying it. Father Saul took care of us and protected us. Took care of us all, not just me."

"Yeah, you're right. I probably shouldn't have said anything. It's just what we were all thinking back then. Anyhow, I gotta get goin'."

"Okay, Jimmy. But tell me how to get in touch with you if I find out anything more about where he went."

He hesitates, but then he takes a small pencil and a piece of paper out of his pocket. "Here, I'll write down the address of the apartment where I'm staying. A friend. Over by the university. He's letting me sleep on his couch until I can find a job."

I put the note in my pocket and say I'll come tell him if I find out anything more. But he's hurrying away so fast I'm not sure he even heard me.

I'm left standing there on the hot sidewalk thinking about what he said about my father maybe being Father Saul. Why didn't I ever think more about who my father might have been? I did ask Father Saul once if he knew. He said he didn't, but I got the feeling there was something he wasn't telling me. I couldn't figure out why he didn't want to talk to me about it. Could Jimmy be right? Could Father Saul really have been my father?

No, that couldn't be. Father Saul would never do what Jimmy suggested.

As I walk out of town to get back to the orphanage, I think about what Jimmy told me about the orphanage's last days. So Father Saul didn't even get the chance to say goodbye to the last two boys that were still living at the orphanage. Damn those tribal lawyers. They must have got the police to come and take him away. They probably wanted to make sure there was nothing that might interfere with the tribe's new gambling enterprise, their wonderful new way to make money. But the police couldn't have kept Father Saul in jail for long. Did they run him out of town? Or maybe Father Saul was in ill health and had to go somewhere to get treatment. After all, he was a pretty old man.

Even though my legs and back are hurting like hell, I make it out of Mesa and onto reservation property in pretty good time. As I continue toward the orphanage, I try to ignore the heat, but I guess I'm not as used to it as I used to be. I stop and rest under a palo verde tree, in what little shade it provides. It still has a few of the nice yellow blossoms with the red centers left on it. I remember how much I liked waiting for the late spring when those spindly green-bark trees would burst out with those dramatic blossoms giving the desert some much-needed bright color. The bees would soon show up to sip their nectar, even some of the larger digger bees that Father Saul told us live underground. I once got stung by one of them. My own fault: I was trying to examine it too closely. It didn't hurt too much though.

I look out across the desert remembering how much I always loved being out here when I was a kid. When I told a guy in my unit in Vietnam I'd grown up in the desert and how much I liked it, he asked me how I could stand being in a bone-dry place with no plants. He said he'd grown up in Missouri where everything is green. I tried to explain to him that the desert is actually a beautiful place with lots of interesting plants. He still didn't get it.

But now that guy is dead, and here I am, somehow still alive and back in that same desert I was trying to describe to him. Back then, I knew I loved the desert, but I don't think I did a very good job of explaining why.

Now, sitting here looking at the familiar Arizona desert, I'm not sure if I could explain it any better. That Missouri guy seemed to think the desert was just flat sand with no plants, but it's not like that at all; it's actually alive with all kind of plants, low-lying prickly bushes and spine-filled cactuses. In fact, vegetation spreads out in all directions, mostly low to the ground, in marked contrast to the tall saguaro green cactuses standing so stately above it all. When I was a kid, I imagined those saguaros were tall green guards, watching over the quiet desert, watching over me.

I'd prefer to just sit here and enjoy the desert, and let it relax me, but I can't stop thinking about why nobody knows where Father Saul went. The Catholics knew he was running his school out here, but apparently it wasn't in any official Catholic capacity. So if they knew he was out here, why don't they know where he is now? You'd think the archdiocese in Phoenix would know. If he was forced to leave the reservation, you'd think the first thing he'd do would be go to the archdiocese. Maybe to get their help, or to get a new assignment. Even if he'd decided to retire, you'd think he'd of told them. The more I think about it, the more puzzling it seems.

Chapter Eight

By the time I get to the orphanage, I'm hot and my legs are really hurting.

There's no sign of Cody, and that brings me down a bit, because I was eager to tell him the news about how my day at the university went. He'll be sure to say that now I really can be his teacher. But I'm not so sure he'll be all that excited about me teaching him philosophy, especially if I tell him I'm not even sure myself what it is.

I decide to lie down in the dorm to rest my aching back and to think about what it actually will mean to be a university student.

But when I try to think about my day at the university and the registration process, my thoughts keep returning to those anti-war protesters. That guy with the bullhorn standing on the edge of the big fountain, and the others with him, seemed so sure the war in Vietnam was wrong. Were they a group of pacifists? Father Saul taught us about pacifists. He said they thought *all* war was wrong, and therefore, they refused to fight in the second world war.

No, the sign those guys at the university were holding up said stop *the* war, not all war. And the guy with the bullhorn was shouting that the war in Vietnam was an "illegal" war. What did he mean by that? If the government declares a war, doesn't that make it legal?

Father Saul taught us about the "Cold War." He said it was a war against Communism. He said the Cold War wasn't like a shooting war against a specific country, not like the war the allies fought against Germany and Japan.

But the War in Vietnam *is* a shooting war, and it is *in* a specific country. And what do I think about those students saying young men like me should burn their draft cards and refuse to go?

I guess they have a right to express their opinion, but what does it say about me and what I did?

I sit up. I don't want to think about that anymore. I feel like going for a hike in the desert, exploring some of my old haunts, but it's too hot, and my legs are too tired.

Instead, I go into the classroom and sit in one of the rickety old school chairs. Sitting here brings back so many memories: Father Saul standing up there in front of us, often writing his lessons on the blackboard to emphasize them. There are actually still a few faint traces of writing on the blackboard. I wonder what they say. A last message from Father Saul?

I get up to take a closer look. The only words I can make out are "Never" and "Remember."

I go back to the student chair and sit down to think about what those words might mean. Never do what? Never allow gambling to come to the reservation? And remember what? God's message to us?

But maybe it's only part of a lesson he was teaching and not a final message. It could mean anything.

I'm still thinking about that and the kind of teacher Father Saul was when Cody comes in. He's happy to see me, and starts telling me about how many people showed up for today's bingo session. He says it's always big on Mondays, and he doesn't know why.

I say, "I registered as a student at the university, Cody. And now, sitting here in the classroom like I did for so many years, makes me remember how much I enjoyed being a student."

"So, ya think you're gonna like being a college student?"

"Yes. At least I liked learning here. Father Saul was pretty strict with us boys, but he was really a smart person, and he taught us a lot. Even though we worked hard, it really was a lot of fun being here."

"So, why'd you leave?"

I look out the open window. There's a slight breeze coming in, which reminds me of the many times I felt that welcome breeze come through that open window on hot days.

"I didn't leave, Cody. Father Saul made me go register for the draft, and I ended up in the Army. I didn't mind. I was ready to go out and learn about the world. I hadn't seen any of it. Father Saul wouldn't even let me go into town. It seemed like he was trying to protect me from what he saw as the evils of the world out there."

"So, did ya learn what you wanted to learn out there in the world?"

I laugh. "Not really. All I saw of the world was the Army base where I got my initial training, and then it was off to Vietnam. Over there, all I learned about the world was the jungle and the everyday work to maintain the small base I was in. Later on, I did learn a lot about Army hospitals though."

"Yeah, it's too bad you got hurt. But I bet it was fun livin' over there in the jungle with a bunch of other young guys."

I smile at his idea that risking your life in a hot and sticky and dangerous jungle with other draftees who didn't want to be there was fun. "I'm not sure fun is the right word, Cody. For fun, the other guys used their R and R to go into town to get girls and drugs. I wasn't there long enough to get any R and R."

"So, you never got to meet girls or try any drugs?"

"No. But I did see what happened when the other guys got into drugs. They didn't just get into marijuana. Some of them got into other stuff too. Heavy stuff. I learned some of those drugs can really mess you up."

"Tell me about that."

"About what? Drugs?"

"No, about Vietnam. Like I said before, some of the young guys in the tribe got sent over there. Seems like most of 'em didn't make it back alive."

"Yeah. I guess a lot of guys are getting killed over there. Everybody in my patrol group got killed."

"But you didn't get killed. Why not?"

"Well, I think it was because I was so torn up they didn't think I was worth wasting a bullet on. But for some reason, I lived. I was in hospitals for a long time. I had a lot of surgeries on my back and on my legs. Especially on my legs. I've got so many metal screws and bolts inside my one leg it's a wonder I don't clank when I walk."

That gets a laugh out of Cody. "Maybe you do. Maybe other people hear it, but you don't."

"Could be. Want to go outside and try it?"

He looks puzzled. "Try what?"

I laugh and wave off his question to show him I was just kidding. "Hey, Cody, now that we've talked about all that bad stuff, how about we go for a walk. You said you wanted to learn about the desert. The shadows are getting longer out there, so it'll be cooling off, and I'd like to go check out some of my old secret places."

He jumps up. "Secret places? Oh boy! Let's go!"

I lead him out into the desert and point out the names of the plants and cactuses as we go along. He seems to be paying close attention, so I keep doing it until he raises his hand like a student and asks, "Uh, what about the secret places?"

I say, "We're getting there." When we come to the deepest ravine on the reservation, I lead him down into it and say, "Check this out. It was our secret dugout." I rap on the old worn wooden door. "We boys made it. It's a cave. It took us a long time to dig it out of the shady side of the ravine wall. I don't remember where we got this wooden door, but the deep hole and the solid door to cover the opening make it a lot cooler inside. It was a perfect hideout for us boys. We always tried to convince ourselves that even Father Saul didn't know about it, but he probably did."

I clear away the weeds and pull open the door, and I'm surprised to see that it's pretty much the same inside as it used to be: assorted junk and a couple of patched-up wooden chairs. The old wooden crate we used as a table is still right where we left it. I remember the older boys playing a lot of penny-ante poker on that table. The crate is now pretty dusty, and it seems to be half filled with what I suspect is nesting materials.

Cody leans down to look inside. "Somethin's been living in here."

"Yeah. Let's hope he's moved on."

But as soon as we start pulling out the nesting material, we discover that he hasn't moved on: a cute little furry brown and white pack rat sits back in the corner staring at us.

I remember pack rats. They used to prowl around the orphanage all the time, often sneaking into the dorm at night to steal just about any small thing they could carry away. This one continues to stare defiantly up at us. He seems to be guarding a hoard of little red seeds. I say, "Looks like he isn't about to give up his home. It probably took him a long time to gather all those seeds."

Cody gets the giggles. "We should let him stay. He's cute."

I shrug. "Okay with me."

"And we should name him Gregory. Gregory Pack Rat."

"Why Gregory Pack Rat?"

"After Gregory Peck."

"Who's that?"

Cody stares at me. "You never heard of Gregory Peck? He's a famous old time movie star. He was in a great movie called Moby Dick."

"Father Saul didn't let us go to movies. But you can name him whatever you want to."

We carefully stuff Gregory's nesting materials back into the box and leave him be.

Cody starts looking around the dugout. "You kids dug all this out by yourselves? It's like a little house in here. And it's not near as hot as outside."

"Yeah. It just kind of evolved over the years. We kept on digging it out more and more until it got this big. To furnish it, we hiked over to an area that people use as a dumping ground. That's where we found the chairs and the other stuff. See that metal barrel?" I point. "On cold days, it was our wood stove."

"Pretty smart."

"Well, we can leave now. I just wanted to be sure it was still here."

All of a sudden, Cody gets more serious. "It's a cool hide-out, Murph. Maybe I might have to use it some time. If you don't mind, that is."

"Sure. Why not?" I wonder why he thinks he might need to hide, but I decide not to ask him. At least not right now.

Back at the school, we go back into the classroom to get out of the heat. Father Saul's clever placement of the school in the shade of the only hill in the area keeps it cooler than anywhere else, at least until late in the afternoon when the sun is at its hottest. I remember that really hot summer when Father Saul had us boys build a false ceiling in the classroom to make it a bit cooler. Even so, I'm sweating from the walk in the desert, so I find a piece of cardboard and use it to fan myself.

"You hot?" asks Cody. "Why don't you go out to the well and dump a bucket of water on your head. That's what I do."

"You know, Cody. That's a good idea. I haven't bathed since I left the VA hospital in LA. I must stink. It's a wonder nobody has mentioned it."

"Well, I woulda mentioned it, but I didn't wanna embarrass ya."

I look at him and see that he's kidding me. "Tell you what, Cody. I'm going to do what we used to do every Saturday night. Did you see that big old tub out by the well? Once a week, Father Saul made us all line up for a bath, whether we wanted to or not. He provided the soap, and the old boys were assigned to watch us to make sure we all washed up good, even behind our ears."

"All of you in one tub?"

"As many as would fit. As you might imagine, there was a lot of splashing and playing around, at least until Father Saul came out and yelled at us to knock it off."

"Sounds like fun. Let's do it."

"Okay."

We find a bar of soap, and I lead him out to the well. Together, we pull up enough buckets of well water to partly fill the old wooden tub. I'm happy to see that the old tub still doesn't leak, at least no more than it ever did.

Once it's full, Cody quickly rips off his clothes and jumps in. As I think about getting undressed, I hesitate. After being in the Army, of course I'm not shy about being naked in front of other men, but I have to wonder what would happen if somebody came along and saw me naked in the tub with this young boy.

But Cody is already having fun squealing and splashing water at me, so I have no choice but to get undressed and join him in the tub. I get busy soaping myself down, but Cody is more interested in splashing and yelping. The water is really cold, so I ignore him and focus on getting my washing done. When I'm done, I get out and dry off and get dressed. Cody continues to play in the water. I stand there watching him, remembering how much fun we little boys could have doing what the older boys dreaded, washing ourselves once a week in ice cold water.

I go back inside to the classroom and sit in one of the student chairs to rest.

Soon, Cody comes in, still wet and dressed only in shorts. Not a bad idea in the mid-day heat. It again reminds me that I need to get some different clothes as soon as I get my Army severance money.

Cody goes immediately to sit in a student desk in the front row. He demands I go to the front of the room to be the teacher.

"I told you before, Cody. I don't know how to teach."

"Yes you do. You already taught me some things. You taught me about Vietnam and what it was like to be out in the world."

"That wasn't teaching, Cody. That was just telling."

"Okay, then, tell me some more things."

"But what about the kind of lessons you learn in school? Aren't you supposed to be in school?"

"Naw, we're out for the summer."

"So, you'll be going back to school soon. You don't need me. You'll get some real learning there."

"Aw, we're supposed to go back next week, but I don't wanna go. I didn't go before, and nobody cared."

"The school didn't care?"

"Well, they talked to my old man about why I wasn't attending, but he doesn't care."

"Whether he cares or not, you should go. What you learn in school will help you later in life."

"Okay then, you teach me."

"And as I keep saying, Cody, I don't know how to teach."

"Well, now that you're gonna be learnin' stuff at the university, you'll have lots to teach me."

With that, he says he's going back to the bingo hall to "make us some more money."

It's cooling off a little, so I decide to lie down in the dorm and rest.

As soon as I'm lying down, I start thinking about what I might be going to learn at the university. Like Cody said, I expect I will be learning a lot of new things, but I'm not sure it will be the kind of learning Cody is looking for.

Chapter Nine

I wake up with a start and realize I must have fallen asleep. It's dark outside. How long did I sleep? I must have been really tired.

I get up and look inside Cody's little hideout space. He's not there. He must still be at the bingo hall. I realize I'm really hungry. I look for any leftovers from the food Cody brought back from the bingo hall, but I can't find any. Cody must have gotten hungry and eaten it all. I guess I'll have to wait for him to get back from the bingo hall and hope he brings some food. I guess I could have used some of the money he gave me to get something to eat over there at the university, but actually, despite all the time I spent there today, I never once thought about getting something to eat. There were times in Vietnam, when we were out on patrol, that we went quite a long time without thinking about food. Other than that, back at base, food was always available. Now I have to hope that Cody again manages to bring some from the bingo hall.

That thought makes me laugh at myself. Quite a weird situation I've got myself in: here I am, a grown-up person, a veteran back from a foreign war, entirely dependent on a young boy. He gives me money and brings me food. I'm even depending on him not to tell the tribal authorities I'm staying out here at the old orphanage. But if I wasn't staying here, where would I be? Would I have ended up like those men I saw under the freeway in Los Angeles, living on the streets?

Despite my aching legs, I decide to go for a short walk in the desert to keep myself from thinking about food.

And it works. As soon as I'm out walking, I'm no longer hungry, and all the memories of doing this kind of nighttime walking in the desert when I was a kid come flooding back. Just like back then, I don't even need to wait for the moon to come up —I can walk in whatever direction I want to and still be confident I can find my way back.

Soon, without really thinking about how far I've gone, my aching back and legs tell me I've walked quite a ways from the orphanage. I sit down to rest. But soon, I get an itch to do more nighttime exploring. My legs are feeling a bit better, so I get up and continue walking. I go over small hills and down into shallow ravines, not really paying much attention to where I'm heading. But I know I won't get lost; it's the same familiar desert I wandered through while I was growing up here. Even the ravines, the one thing that does change in the desert, getting gradually wider and sometimes deeper when the springtime rainstorms create runoff, feel more or less the same.

I keep going, heading mostly uphill toward the mountains. I know I've walked quite a ways, but my injured back and legs don't feel too bad. I must be getting stronger. I keep going, "feeling" my way along in the darkness.

I bump into a cactus, but no harm done because, from memory, I knew to stop the moment I felt them touch the front of my pant leg.

I keep walking until, ouch! I instantly realize I bumped into some chollas. The sharp pain in the front of my legs reminds me that cholla stickers, unlike those of other types of cactus, do hurt. As I sit down to pick the stickers out of my legs, it comes back to me that chollas grow in groves, and are light colored, so if I keep my eyes open, even in the dark, I should be able to see them in time to detour around them.

As I go back to walking, paying more attention now, I'm reminded of another thing: most cactus plants, other than the chollas, are solitary. I wonder if they put out some kind of chemical that keeps their cactus cousins and most other plants away. That would make them sort of like I've always been, solitary by choice. I was even that way in Vietnam—mostly staying alone with my thoughts, despite always being around other soldiers.

I hear a car go by on the distant highway, and then it's quiet again. Another thing I always liked about walking in the desert is how extraordinarily quiet it is. The occasional car going by in the distance only emphasizes how silent the desert usually is.

Something scurries away in front of me. Probably some kind of rodent.

A little way farther on, I hear something else moving, something bigger this time. Probably a coyote.

And then I see him, a large coyote, undoubtedly a male. I'm upwind from him, so he hasn't picked up my scent yet. But he must know there's a human around because he seems nervous. His head is up, and he's looking in all directions, checking the air for scents. I stay still to watch him.

But then he must pick up my scent because, just like that, he's gone. When I was a kid walking alone out here, I always felt a bit of a thrill whenever I'd come across a coyote. I'd always stopped to watch them nose around. I don't know why I liked them so much back then. Most of the other boys didn't like them, were somewhat afraid of them. I never understood why. As far as I knew, they never hurt anybody.

As I walk, I think of another reason why I like the desert so much: you don't need a path. The sandy desert soil and the overall lack of rain means it's mostly wide-open. There's not much to deter my walking in whichever direction I feel like going. That gives me the feeling of freedom that I haven't felt since the last time I did this, just before I got drafted. I wonder why I didn't miss it more. After I left the orphanage, I suppose I just got caught up in doing whatever I was told to do in basic training. And then it was the same in Vietnam. It's amazing how easy it is to get caught up in whatever you're doing and forget the really important stuff like this wonderful desert.

I stop when I sense an indication of light in the sky ahead, up over the mountains. I know what it means: the moon is about to come up.

I sit down to watch it creep up over the distant mountain peaks. It reminds me of the few times the usual Vietnam nighttime cloud cover would dissipate enough for me to see the moon. Although I knew I was supposed to be watching for any sign of enemy movement out past the wire, I would sometimes lie back and just stare at it.

I often thought about the possibility that Father Saul's boys might be out in the desert at that very moment looking at that very same moon. Of course, it would have been a different time of day there. Maybe it would have been daylight in Arizona when it was nighttime in Vietnam. I should look that up at the university library. In fact, now that I think about it, there could be a lot of new things like that I can look up at the university library.

My aching legs are starting to tell me it's time to head back to the orphanage. I stop to get my bearings. Even with the moon rising up behind me, I know the need to avoid cactus patches, and the frequent dropping down into shallow ravines, could make me wander a widely zigzaging path on my way back. The trick is to always keep the same distant point in view.

Using that old familiar method, it doesn't take me long to get back to the orphanage building.

Cody is still not there. Maybe he's not going to show up at all tonight. I hope he's all right. It's not like him to stay out all night like this.

If Cody's not coming back tonight, there's no point in my thinking about being hungry. I should just go to sleep and worry about finding some food in the morning.

But as soon as I lie down, I know sleep is not going to happen; I just stare up into the darkness, wide awake. I remember doing that a lot back when I was a student here, lying awake, listening to the breathing—or snoring—of the other kids. Back in those days, I thought of myself as really smart. I wanted Father Saul to think I was smart, too. Once, when I was still pretty little, I asked him if I was smart. He said I was, but he also said he saw something in me that told him I was bound to get myself in trouble. I think he was referring to my endless curiosity. He was probably worried that eventually I'd start doing what some of the older boys did, sneaking off to town where they sometimes got themselves in trouble. I admit I was curious about what they were doing in town. I overheard some of their whispered secrets about girls and booze—and sometimes drugs.

Actually, now that I think about it, maybe I was lucky to get drafted before anything like that happened to me. Maybe Father Saul was thinking about that when he said I had to go to the local draft board and register. He said it was my patriotic duty. I did what he told me to, and they immediately inducted me into the Army. I guess with the war raging in Vietnam, they were under orders to induct as many men as possible. The weird thing is if I hadn't voluntarily walked into that draft board office, they would have never known about me. Growing up in the orphanage since I was an abandoned baby, they couldn't have had any record of me.

I wonder what kind of life I would have had if I hadn't been drafted. I guess I wouldn't have stayed at the orphanage much longer; pretty soon, Father Saul would have made me leave. He didn't like older boys hanging around. He said they were a bad influence on the younger boys. I suppose I would have gone off to find a job. And that probably would have meant that, sooner or later, the draft board would have found out I existed, and I'd of gotten drafted anyhow.

Or maybe I would have gone to college back then.

No, there's no way I would have been able to afford going to college, not without the Army paying for it. Interesting how things turn out.

But I guess none of that matters now. I did get drafted, and I did get sent to Vietnam. I didn't die, not quite, and here I am, back in the US, a genuine registered student at Arizona State University. I wonder what Father Saul will say when I tell him about that. That's assuming I ever manage to find him.

I'm finally starting to feel sleepy. But now I hear a noise. Is it Cody? If it is, I sure hope he brought some food.

A flashlight is in my face. "Is that you, Cody? Get that light out of my face."

The light turns away. "Yeah, it's me. I'm goin' ta bed."

I see him and his flashlight heading to his little cubbyhole.

But there was something odd about his voice. What was it? It was like he was upset about something, but trying to hide it. And he didn't ask me about my day at the university.

I call after him, "Hey, Cody, don't you want to hear about what happened to me at the university today?"

As first, I don't think he's going to respond, but then he says, "Oh, sure. But I'm in bed. Can't you tell me from there?"

"What's wrong, Cody?"

"What makes ya think something's wrong?"

"This morning, you were all excited about me going to the university. Now it's like you don't care."

"Oh sure, I do care. I wanna know all about it. But can't you tell me from there?"

He must not want me to look at him. "Cody, you might as well tell me. What's wrong?"

Again, he doesn't respond right away, but then I see the flashlight coming my way. He comes to sit down on the cot next to mine. He shines the flashlight in my eyes.

"Don't shine that light in my eyes, Cody. Shine it on yourself so I can see you while we talk."

"No!"

"No? You don't want me to see you? What's wrong?"

"All right," he says, "I'll show you, but you can't ask me any questions."

He shines the flashlight on his own face, and right away, I can see why he didn't want me to look at him: he's been beaten. He has bruises on both sides of his face that are already darkening, and there's a bit of red under his nose, as if it's been bleeding. He probably doesn't want me to ask him about it, but I know I have to. "What happened, Cody? Did you get into a fight?"

"No! Nobody can get the better of me."

"So who's been hitting you?"

"Nobody. Just tell me about the university."

"Was it your father?"

"Don't wanna to talk about it."

Maybe I should let it go, but I know I can't. In the orphanage, when I got a little older, I was never able to stay out of it when one of the other older boys started picking on some little kid who couldn't defend himself. Sometimes my intervening led to me being the one that got hit, but I eventually learned how to give as good as I got.

I say, "Listen, Cody, he may be your father, but nobody should be allowed to hit a child. Maybe I should go talk to him. What's his name?"

Cody shakes his head, hard. "No. It's my problem."

"It's not just your problem when a child is being hurt, somebody has to—"

"I'm not a child. I can take care of myself."

"You are a child, Cody. Like it or not. And I'm not going to stand by and see something like that go on. Why don't some of the other adults protect you?"

"Aw, he takes me out back behind the building so nobody can see. Says he has to teach me a lesson."

"Why? What did you do to deserve being taught a lesson?"

"Nothing. He just saw me making money running errands for the bingo players, and he wanted it. He said any money I make automatically belongs to him because he's my father. I wouldn't give it to him, so he dragged me out behind the building. But before he could get his hands on my money roll, I threw it as far out into the desert as I could. He punched me a bunch of times, and then he went stumbling off into the darkness to try to find the money. When he couldn't find it, he came back and started hittin' me some more. He said I had to go find the money and give it to him. I did go find it, but then I kept on runnin'. But don't worry. I ran off in the opposite direction so he couldn't follow me here."

"I'm not worried, Cody. I can take care of myself. In fact, like I said, I think I'd better go have a talk with him. I'll ask you again, what's his name?"

Cody reaches out to grab my arm. "His name is Jake, but don't go there. If he finds out you're out here, he'll get the tribal leaders to come throw you offa res land. And besides, he only gets like that when he's real drunk. Tomorrow, he probably won't even remember he did it."

I wonder if a father really can get so drunk he won't remember beating his own child. Maybe I'd better not interfere right now. But if this kind of thing ever happens again, I think I'll have to. But I wouldn't want to get kicked out of here, especially not if Cody needs somebody here to protect him.

"Really," says Cody, "I'm all right. I can take it. Now tell me about the university. So you sign up to be a college student. Did you get some things to teach me?"

"Well, I registered as a philosophy major."

"Philosophy? What's that?"

"Well, I'm not exactly sure, but that's what I signed up for. I just signed up for one class to check it out. I think I'll be studying Plato and the old philosophers. I'm sure I'll learn a lot, and then I'll come back here and tell you all about it."

"Cool."

Cody is all smiles, at least I'm pretty sure he's smiling even though his lower lip is so swollen it's a little hard to tell if it's a smile or a grimace on his face. Maybe it hurts him to smile. 'You know, Cody, why don't you go to bed. I'll go out to the well and get a bucket of cool water. I'll find a rag to get wet. That'll feel good on your face."

"Naw, I don't need it."

"Yes, you do. It's what Father Saul always did for us when we boys got into a fight and somebody ended up with a black eye. You go to bed, and I'll be right back."

By the time I get back with the bucket of cold water and a clean rag, he's already asleep. Nevertheless, I still put the wet rag on his poor swollen face. He doesn't even wake up.

I go back to my own cot and lie down. I'm still damn hungry, but I decide against hiking all the way into town to try to find something to eat.

No matter how hungry I am, I'm not going to leave Cody alone here in case his father comes looking for him.

But then, as I start to get sleepy, I'm pretty sure his father will be sound asleep somewhere. In Vietnam, I saw guys fall into that kind of drunken sleep, and they don't easily wake up. Maybe Cody is right; maybe his father won't even remember beating his son. But I have the feeling that sometime in the future, it may be up to me to go remind him not to ever do it again.

Chapter Ten

The rising sun wakes me up, and I immediately go to check on Cody. He's still asleep, and the damp cloth has slipped off. I dip it into the bucket of cool water, ring it out, and carefully place it back on his forehead.

He's doesn't even wake up. Poor lad. No kid should have to suffer a beating like that.

I got into some tussles at the orphanage, but nobody ever hit me as hard as Cody got hit. Father Saul did sometimes give us "hard lessons," as he called them. He had a hand-carved paddle he used for such lessons, but we only got hit on the butt. I never thought it hurt all that much, and he always claimed it hurt him more than it hurt us.

I'm still feeling really hungry, so while Cody is sleeping, this might be a good time to hike back to town to get something to eat. I still have a little money left from what he gave me.

Outside, the rising sun is low in the sky. I hope I can get to town and back before Cody wakes up. He might try to go to the bingo hall to make money.

I hurry as fast as my injured legs will let me, and I soon find it actually hurts less to do a slow jog than to walk. I must be getting stronger.

I make it to Mesa in good time, and I soon find a small store. But when I go inside and look at the sandwiches in their glass case, nothing looks very appetizing. I give up on that and look at the items on the shelves.

Finally, I decide on a box of crackers. I take the crackers to the checkout counter. The young man behind the counter has a bad case of facial acne, and he seems nervous. Is there something about me that makes him nervous? Maybe he thinks I'm an Indian from the reservation.

I'm about to pay for the crackers when I notice a colorful sign encouraging people to buy soft drinks to go along with whatever they're getting to eat. The paper cups next to the soft drinks dispensers are huge.

Those big cups give me an idea: ice might help take down the swelling on Cody's face. I point to them and say, "I don't need a drink, but can I get a cup of ice?"

The young man seem confused by my request, but he finally says, "Well, I guess. But you gotta pay for the cup. They keep track."

I pay for the crackers and the cup which he fills with ice from a dispenser. I also ask him for a lid for the cup. He begrudgingly gives me one, and thankfully, he doesn't charge me for it.

On my way back to the reservation, I detour down a neighborhood street and pick up a couple of oranges from under a tree that overhangs the street. The older boys at the orphanage, who seemed to have gotten to know the town of Mesa pretty well, claimed you can pick as many oranges as you want in Mesa because the trees owners already have so many they don't care. I don't believe that, but I doubt the tree's owner will mind me picking up a few off the ground.

I pocket the oranges and start eating the crackers as I walk. They're dry, and they seem a bit stale, but I'm so hungry they actually taste pretty good. After I've eaten all the crackers, I start on the oranges. They taste even better, and as I hurry out of town, I'm feeling a little less hungry.

I'm going to have to hurry back to the reservation before all of the ice in the cup melts. As it melts, I sip the cold water, and the feel of it in my dry mouth makes me realize how thirsty I am. I scold myself, just like my sergeant in Vietnam used to do, for letting myself get dehydrated. It's an especially dumb thing to do here since there's no reason for it; the well water at the orphanage is really good.

I feel a sense of relief as soon as I'm on reservation property and walking through the desert. I wonder why. Is it because I grew up wandering around this very desert?

Do we get something stored in our brains as kids when we're doing something we love that stays hidden away, ready to be rekindled later in life? Maybe I'll learn more about that at the university.

By the time I get back to the dorm, my legs and back are really hurting. I'm glad to see Cody is still asleep. I'd like to let him sleep, but I want to get this ice on his swollen face.

I pack the ice into the wet rag, and as soon as it touches his face, he wakes up. He stares at me, blinking. His left eye is swollen almost clear shut, and because he's not quite awake yet, his sleepy mind is probably wondering why he can only see out of his right eye. I guess it means his father is right handed and threw roundhouse punches to hit the left side of Cody's face. I'll have to remember that if I ever have to fight that man.

"Keep this on your face, Cody."

"What is it?"

"It's ice. Wrapped up inside this rag. It'll help take the swelling down."

He moves it onto his hurt eye, and from the way he winces, I can tell that just the rag touching his face really hurts.

He notices the big paper cup in my hand. "You went out and got a drink?"

"No. Just a cup of ice to help take down your facial swelling. But I did use a little bit of the money you loaned me to get something to eat."

He stares at me. "You walked all the way into town to get me some ice?"

"Well, I was going there anyhow. Like I said, to get something to eat."

"But you got the ice for me? Without me even asking for it?"

"Well sure. That's what friends are for, right?"

"Is that . . . what we are, friends?"

"Sure. Aren't we?"

"I guess so. My old man says I don't know how to make friends. He says I've always been a loner because I'm selfish."

"Are you?"

"Aw, he just says I'm selfish so I'll give him my tip money. But maybe there is somethin' wrong with me. When I was real little, some of the older boys picked on me. I guess 'cause they thought I was uh . . . different."

"Is that right? Different in what way?"

He shrugs. "I don't know, but it turned me into a fighter. If anybody made fun of me, I'd punch 'em. My old man liked that. He was always teaching me how to box. How to fight, actually. He taught me how to fight dirty if the other guy was bigger than me. Poke 'em in the eye,' he said, 'kick 'em in the knee.'"

I'm not sure how I should respond to that. I was a loner too, but I wasn't much of a fighter. I did learn how to fight, and how to protect myself, but mostly I stayed out of the way of the bullies. I guess I'd better try to explain that to Cody. "Listen, Cody, I saw a lot of tough guys when I was in the Army. But sooner or later, they always ran into somebody tougher. I think it's better to learn how to get along. There are better ways to solve things than fighting."

"Yeah, well, after a while they mostly left me alone. If any of the older guys picked on me, they knew they might be able to beat me up, but they knew they were going to get hurt some too."

I can see my lesson about getting along isn't going to work, at least not right now when he's hurting so much.

Before I can say anything else, Cody sits up and tries to hand the ice back to me. "I got to go. The night session's good for making money from the out of town people."

I make him put the iced rag back against his face, and then I say, "Listen, Cody, are you sure you should go there today? Won't everybody be asking about why your face is so beat up?"

He waves my words off. "Sure they will. But they seen it before. I just lie and say I got into a fight. Some of them don't believe me and blame my old man. But that's good because they feel sorry for me and give me bigger tips."

"That may be, Cody, but I don't think you should go back to the bingo hall today. Why don't you stay here and rest. We can start your lessons."

"Okay. Let's do that first, and then I'll go to the bingo hall."

He gets up and heads for the classroom. I follow, bringing the cloth-wrapped ice.

After he sits in one of the front-row seats, I make him put the ice back against his face. Then, I go to the blackboard and turn to face "the class," just as I saw Father Saul do thousands of times. But then I'm not sure what to say. Do I really have anything to teach this boy? "Listen, Cody, I'm not sure what I have to teach you. I did sign up at the university, but I haven't even been to any classes yet."

"Well, how 'bout you teach me about what it's like out there."

"Out where?"

"Out there in the world. You've been places, seen things. I haven't ever been anywhere. Tell me about that."

"Not much to tell you, Cody. The only place outside of Arizona I've ever been is to an Army base in Oklahoma where I did my Army training. It was out in the middle of nowhere. Then I got sent straight to Vietnam."

"Okay, tell me about that. What was it like being in a foreign country."

I'm not quite sure what I can tell him about that. But if he really hasn't been anywhere, maybe he'd like to hear just about any of it. "Well, we landed at a huge air base. There was some orientation, and then I was sent to what they call a firebase. A small one. Not many of us were out there. And it was entirely surrounded by jungle. Do you know what a jungle is?"

"Sure. Green. Wet."

"Well, that's pretty much it. Hot, but not like here. Very humid. And it rained a lot."

"That must have been different for you. Coming from here, I mean."

"Yes. It took me a long time to get used to it. Your toes rot."

"Really?"

"Well, not exactly rot. But it's like that. They call it trench foot. Caused by your feet being wet inside your boots all the time. It can get real bad."

"Did you get it?"

"Yes. I got it. Just about everybody gets it if you're out on a long patrol in a wet area."

"Geez. What did you do?"

"You have to get your feet warm and dry. But you can't let them warm up too quick. No hot water or anything like that. And you have to keep them dry after that. Hard to do in the jungle. Mine got better after a while, but some guys didn't. They had to be sent to the hospital."

"What about shooting? Did you shoot lots of Gooks."

"Don't call them that, Cody. It's disrespectful."

"Well, that's what they call 'em on TV. And they're the enemy, aren't they?"

"Yes, and a lot of the guys over there called them that. But Father Saul taught us not to disrespect anybody. He said, in the long run, it hurts you more than the ones you disrespect."

Cody frowns. "I don't get that."

"He told us using disrespectful terms marks you as a narrow person who doesn't try to understand the position of others, someone who just follows the herd. He told us to think things through ourselves, be an individual."

Cody thinks about that for a few moments, then says, "You know what, Murph, I think you really are a good teacher."

"I don't know about that. I'm only telling you what Father Saul taught us."

"Well, isn't that what a teacher does? Passes on what he learned from others?"

"I guess that's part of it."

"Okay then, how 'bout you teach me what you learned in Vietnam. Did it make you different, like you are now?"

His question makes me stop and think. He sees me as different. Is that how everybody sees me? Am I different? If so, is it because of what happened to me in Vietnam? "Well, Cody, it's hard to say how much Vietnam changed me. But I guess I do feel different about life and death now, and about other humans."

"Humans? You mean like . . . everybody?"

"Yes. Over there in Vietnam, human life didn't seem to mean very much. Father Saul taught us to respect everybody, even people that were not like us. But over there, nobody seemed to care very much when they killed somebody."

"Well, sure, but they were the enemy, weren't they?"

"Not always. I mean . . . well, let's not get into that."

"Get into what? Is it like they say on TV, that they're shooting innocent people?"

"Is that what they're sayin on TV? Well, all I'm saying is that sometimes you can't be sure who's the enemy and who isn't. If they're not wearing a uniform, how can you be sure?"

"So, did you shoot somebody who wasn't wearing a uniform?"

"Not that I know of. The only shooting I ever did was in what they call a firefight. Somebody was shooting at us, so we shot back. And then, usually, whoever was shooting at us just disappeared into the jungle, so we never knew who it was. Afterwards, if we found dead bodies, they weren't wearing any kind of uniform."

"You said nobody cared if they killed somebody."

"Unfortunately, that's true. To most soldiers, it was just part of their job. Others seemed to uh . . . like it. I never understood that."

"Sounds like you didn't enjoy being in a war. Because of what the priest taught you?"

"I don't think fighting in a war is something we should enjoy. But if somebody is shooting at you . . . well, let's talk about something else, Cody."

"No, I want to learn about that. What does it mean if somebody seems to like to hurt you?"

I can see that Cody is actually looking for answers regarding what is going on in his own life, answers about why anybody would want to hurt him, especially why his father hurts him. I'll have to be careful what I say about that.

Cody raises his hand like a student in a class would. "You stopped talking. Did I say something wrong?"

"No, Cody, you didn't say anything wrong. I was just thinking about how to explain it. There's not much about the war that I like to remember."

"Okay. How about now? You came back to where you were before you got sent over there. Does it feel different to be back here?"

I look around at the old schoolroom and think about his question. "I do feel different, Cody, but this place feels pretty much just like it always did. So I'm glad I decided to come back here. When I got out of the hospital, out there in California, it felt like the world had changed. There were men living out of doors, on the streets, and some of the people I met were . . . mean."

"Mean?"

"I was trying to hitchhike from California to get here, but nobody would give me a ride. One lady called me a baby killer and another one spit at me."

Cody raises his hand again. "I know why they did that. It's like I said, the TV's sayin' our soldiers in Vietnam are killing innocent civilians."

"I never heard anything like that. But then, where I was, out in the jungle, we didn't get much news."

"And on the TV news, they're sayin' a lot of our guys are getting killed over there. Everybody in the tribe is upset that our guys are getting killed. And the ones that come back alive seem kind of freaked out. Different than when they left. I asked one guy about what it was like over there, but he said he didn't wanna talk about it. It was like he was mad at me for asking."

"I can understand that, Cody. Vietnam is a different kind of war. It's . . . complicated."

"Complicated? In what way? Because we invaded their country?"

"I guess that's part of it. Father Saul said Vietnam is part of what they call the Cold War. He said we're fighting against the Communists."

"Yeah, I heard that too. Some old bingo player guy was talkin' about it real loud. He was sayin' the Cold War is only politicians makin' the commies the enemy to get themselves elected."

"Well, Father Saul didn't say it like that. But he did say all humans do whatever works best for them."

Cody again, points at me, grinning. "See there. Like I said, you got lots to teach me. You can teach me all the things that old priest taught you."

"I guess I could do that, but right now, I think you need to rest. Why don't you go back and lie down. And keep that ice against your face,"

"Naw, I'm gonna head for the bingo hall. People'll feel sorry for me and give me lots of dough."

I try to protest, but he's out the door before I can stop him. I guess a kid his age thinks nothing can hurt him.

After he's gone, I wander around the classroom and then into the dorm, trying to decide what to do with myself. When I was a kid Cody's age, Father Saul would notice if I was ever idle and quickly find me some little task to do. He always said, "Idle hands are the devil's tools," and he was serious about it.

Thinking like Father Saul, it doesn't take me long to find plenty of things that need fixing. The place really is always falling apart: boards are coming loose, and I can see holes all over in the roof. There's nothing I can do about the roof right now, but that's not a big problem because it'll be some time before the rains come. I guess I might as well get a hammer out of the tool shed and get busy doing some fixing.

For the rest of the day, I keep myself busy fixing things as best I can, and when Cody gets back, I'm happy to see that his face is less swollen.

He shows me a big roll of money and says his looking beat-up "worked great." He says he got "tons of tips."

I'm also glad to see that he brought back a large sack full of food, and as we eat it, he jabbers on about how many people showed up at today's bingo session. He says a busload of people came all the way from Phoenix, and they were especially big spenders.

Thankfully, there's no indication that he's had any more trouble with his father. Maybe his father is also making money, so he's leaving Cody's money alone.

Chapter Eleven

The next morning, I wake up at sunrise. It's going to be a big day, my first day at my university class.

Before I go, I check on Cody and find him still sound asleep. Thankfully, much of the swelling in his face has gone down.

I take the usual roundabout route through the desert to the reservation bus stop, and I'm glad to see that Cody's cousin June is not there waiting for the bus. I still wouldn't know how to answer her if she asked me how I met Cody. I can't let her find out the two of us are living out at the old orphanage.

I'm one of the few passengers on the bus, and when we get to the campus stop, I'm the only one that gets off.

The first thing I need to do is figure out where the philosophy building is. I have the room number, but that's all.

I ask several students where the philosophy building is, but they all say they have no idea and walk on. Don't any of these students ever take philosophy classes?

I catch up to a man that looks like he might be a professor and ask him. He tells me the philosophy department doesn't have their own building. He points at a modern-looking three-story building and says their classes meet in that building.

I go into that building and wander the silent halls until I find the correct classroom. The door is open, but I'm a little nervous, so I walk past as if I'm going somewhere else. As I pass by, I take a quick look inside. It's a small room, and the students are seated around a large rectangular wooden table. A man in a suit is seated at the near end of the table, and he's the one doing the talking. He must be the professor.

Okay, if you really do want to be a university student, it's time to do it. After all, you signed up for this class, so walk right in and get started.

I turn around and go straight into the room and sit down in one of the empty chairs. The professor stops talking and frowns as if he's not too happy about me coming in late and disrupting his lecture. But he doesn't say anything. He will probably also be aware that I wasn't here for his first class. I hope he doesn't think I'm going to be a troublemaker.

When he goes back to lecturing, I take the opportunity to check out the other seven students, six males and one nice-looking girl with long dark hair. She's wearing blue jeans and a white boy's shirt with the top button unbuttoned. I don't think I've seen a girl wearing jeans before, but I like it. She's obviously not worried about dressing up to go to class.

The professor has written his name on the blackboard, Dr. Schmidt. He's also written the name of a philosophy textbook, and it says the book will be on reserve for this class at the university library.

When the professor goes back to lecturing, I notice all of the other students are taking notes. I didn't even think about bringing a notebook. Not a very good start to my college career. But then with no money at all, I don't know how I would get a notebook anyhow. Before my next class meeting, I should look around the orphanage classroom; there should still be some note-taking paper there.

The professor is saying philosophy is not just what university professors talk about, it's something all of us do all the time. He says, "It's simply thinking about who and why we are. It's thinking about the reality of the world around us."

Makes sense to me. Actually, it sounds a bit like what Father Saul used to say to us. If that's the way this class is going to go, I think I'm going to like it.

The professor goes on. "We humans can't help but wonder about why we are here and what our role in the world is. It's a normal function of our human brains. We are not only thinking animals, we are wondering animals."

He pauses, and then adds, "The very first philosophers, back in early times, were thinkers who were not satisfied with the explanations they were given. In their day, they were supposed to believe the world around them had been created by the gods. But for some men, that didn't seem logical, and they began to search for other explanations."

The other students are still taking notes. The professor is not talking about very complicated stuff, so I wonder what they're writing down. Are we going to be tested on this material, or are they just trying to impress the professor, showing they are paying attention? I expect he'll be sure to notice I'm the only one not writing anything down. I hope that first impression of me doesn't turn out to be his lasting impression.

The professor says, "Those early philosophers discussed their ideas with each other, and some of them wrote down their ideas. Believe it or not, after thousands of years, some of those writings have come down to us today. In this class, we will be discussing the ideas presented in those early writings, and how they led to the foundations of modern philosophy. When you read the writings of those early philosophers, you may think they came up with their ideas all by themselves. Nothing could be further from the truth. Their ideas emerged through discussion and analysis with others. Discussion and analysis is the essence of philosophy, and in this class, we will be discussing and analyzing the historical foundations of our modern philosophical ideas."

As he goes on, I'm beginning to think I'm going to enjoy this class. Thinking back on it, I remember thoroughly enjoying it when Father Saul encouraged us to discuss our ideas. Coming into the orphanage as a baby, for a long time, I was the youngest of his students, but he always encouraged me to test my ideas against the ideas of the older boys. I think I did pretty well at that.

The professor says, "Perhaps the best known of the early philosophers was Socrates. He didn't leave any writings. In fact, he claimed to *know* nothing. He encouraged his students to make that same assumption, to approach any argument as if what they held to be true was not true."

The professor looks at each of us. I think he's making sure we understand that he's talking about us. Then he goes on. "One of his students was named Plato. He was the one who wrote down what they were discussing, usually in the form of what he called dialogues. Dialogues were the presentation of ideas and the examination of arguments for and against those ideas. Students were to present counter arguments as forcefully as their own arguments. The point being was to accept that there is no one truth. In fact, one of Plato's best-known students, Aristotle, held very different views from Plato on fundamental philosophical questions. We will be discussing their differences, and the process that brought them to differing views. In this class, we will be doing our own dialogues, examining the arguments of those old philosophers, and newer arguments, and learning how to argue both sides of the question. That process will help you learn how to come up with entirely new ideas of your own."

Is he saying I should be examining and reexamining what I believe personally? It's as if he's telling me that if I want to think like a philosopher, I should foster doubt about everything I currently believe. I don't remember Father Saul telling us anything quite like that, but I think he'd approve of the idea.

After the professor dismisses the class, I leave the building and find a bench in the shade of a big palm tree. I need to sit down to think about the lecture I just heard. I'm feeling like Professor Schmidt was talking to me personally, telling me that, at this point in my life, it's time to examine what I believe and what my life means.

So, what do I believe, and why do I believe it? I guess I should first think about where I am right now and how I got here. I came out of Vietnam, somehow alive, and when I walked out of that hospital in California, I felt very unsure of what was next for me. Until then, I hadn't ever taken the time to wonder what my life was about—I was just living it. Now, sitting here, thinking through all that, I'm starting to think that from the moment I was standing there undecided on that busy street in Los Angeles, I've been making exactly the right choices, seemingly accidentally.

But were those choices accidental? What was it about my life up to that point that made me decide to become a college student, and made me choose to sign up for, again almost accidentally, what is apparently turning out to be exactly the right course of study, philosophy. I don't think my choices were predetermined, but I can now see how my past history, in some odd way, led me to make them.

Whatever the reason for my choices, I'm starting to feel like being here as a student at this university, studying philosophy, is just what I needed at this point in my life. All my life, I never felt as sure of things as other people seem to, and I always kind of thought that was a liability. Now, it feels like Professor Schmidt is telling me that fostering doubt about those beliefs, until I've examined them carefully, is exactly the right approach.

I should go to the university library right now and start reading the textbook the professor put on reserve there.

Chapter Twelve

I jump up, ready to go find the university library.

But as soon as I'm on my feet, I feel a little unsteady, and I have to sit down again. Why do I feel so unsteady? I'm not dizzy. It's more like I'm suddenly aware of the starkness of reality all around me. Am I feeling like this new life I'm undertaking is going to be too much for me?

No, that can't be. It's just what I want, what I need in my life right now. It's probably only that I haven't been eating much lately. I should spend a little bit of Cody's money and find someplace on this campus to get something to eat.

I get up and start looking for a place that might have food.

Nothing looks promising until I come to a building identified as the Student Union, and on its directory plaque, it says there's a cafeteria in the basement. I go down the stairs and see that the entire large room is a cafeteria. It's fairly crowded at the tables, but there aren't many people in the food line, so I get a tray and push it along the chrome railings looking at the food and the prices. The food doesn't seem to cost much, so I think I have enough of Cody's money left to get a little something.

When I come to deep metal trays of hot food, they look a little too much like the bland stuff they fed us in basic training, so I skip that section and push my tray along until I get to a rack of packaged sandwiches. They aren't labeled, so it's hard to tell what's inside of them. I pick them up, one after the other, but I can't decide.

"Go for the cheese. It's the safest."

I turn to see who spoke to me. It's the thin, dark-haired girl who was the only girl in the philosophy class. "Okay," I say, "I'll bow to your expertise."

She chuckles at that and puts a wrapped sandwich on my tray. "If I'm an expert," she says, "it's only from making mistakes."

"Best way to learn," I say, hoping that sounds at least a little bit philosophical.

After we push our trays on down the rails, I'm ready to go to the cashier and pay, but as we pass the desert section, she grabs two small plates with what looks like some kind of pie. She puts one of them on each of our trays. "Apple pie," she says. "It's not half bad. I think they must have a little old lady stashed in the back baking them."

All I can think to say is, "Undoubtedly."

After I pay, I wait for her, hoping she wants to sit with me.

Apparently, she does because she leads us to an empty table in a corner and starts taking the food off of her tray.

I sit down across the table from her and take the food off of my tray too.

She quickly starts eating. "Sorry to eat so fast," she says between bites. "Got another class soon as I'm done eating. Takin' a full load this semester. Cheaper that way. Same tuition, no matter how many classes you take." She takes several more bites from her sandwich before swallowing. Then, she pauses eating long enough to mumble, "Name's Clara."

"Oh, hi, Clara. My name's Murph. At least that's what everybody calls me. From my last name, Murphy. Uh, I don't think I ever met a Clara before."

"Yeah, I know it's a weird name. Blame my mother. She liked an old-time movie actress named Clara Bow. Ever heard of her?"

"I don't think so."

"No, probably not. She was pretty famous in her day, but I've never seen any of her movies. You probably haven't either."

I try to remember if Father Saul ever talked about movies. I don't think so. Maybe he didn't approve of movies. I guess it's another big hole in my knowledge of the world. I should be honest and tell her that. "Actually, Clara, I've never been to any movie."

She stops eating and stares at me.

Maybe I shouldn't have admitted that. It probably makes me seem like a weird person.

"You've never seen a movie? Ever? Where'd you grow up, under a rock?"

I smile and say, "Well, that wouldn't be far off from the truth of it. I grew up out in the desert. We didn't . . . uh, get to go into town."

She's still staring at me. "Out in the desert? Here in Arizona?"

"Yes. A ways out east of Scottsdale."

"East of Scottsdale? There's nothing out east of Scottsdale but an Indian reservation. Are you an Indian? I guess you do look a little like a Native American. You've got those dark eyes."

"Supposedly I am. My mother was. At least that's what I was told. But I'm not sure. I was an orphan."

"No kidding. Last year, I took a psych class, and we went to a reservation. It was out south of Phoenix. Did you grow up on a reservation like that?"

"Uh, sort of."

"Sort of? I guess you're saying it's more complicated than that. Okay, maybe we can get into that more later. Like I said, I've gotta run to my next class. But I should at least ask you how you liked the philosophy history class."

"Uh, good. So far. Actually, I think I'm going to like it a lot."

"Are you a philosophy major?"

"Yes. At least that's what I signed up for."

"That's interesting. Don't think I ever met a philosophy major before. I'm a psych major."

"Well, Clara, I never met a psych major before. Are you studying to be a psychologist?"

She goes back to eating. She finishes her sandwich and starts on her piece of pie. Between rapid bites, she says, "Aw, who knows what I'll grow up to be. But since I was little, I've been trying to figure people out. People didn't make sense to me. So now I'm studying them."

I think about that for a few moments, and then say, "Uh, do they now? Make sense, I mean?"

She looks up at me and grins. "Are you kidding?"

I think by that she means people never will make sense, but I guess I'd better not ask her if that's actually what she meant.

As if she anticipated my thought, she says, "So, far, after one year of taking psych classes, the only thing I know for sure is that we humans are far too complicated for anybody to ever figure out. Maybe studying philosophy is a better approach. Have you philosophers figured out why we humans do what we do?"

"Uh, it's my first class."

"Your first philosophy class or your first university class?"

"Both. I'm just starting college. I just got out of the Army."

She's finished eating, but now she doesn't seem quite ready to get up and leave. Did my mentioning the Army make her curious about me?

"I thought you looked a little older than most of the students here. See any action?"

"Do you mean, did I see any fighting?"

"Yeah. Were you in Vietnam?"

By now, after having people in LA spit at me and call me a baby killer, I'm not sure if I should answer that question honestly. But if I'm going to be in the same class with this young woman all this semester, I guess I should be honest with her. "Yes, I got drafted and sent right over there."

"Well, you seem to have come through it unscathed."

"Not really. I spent a lot of time in hospitals."

Her smile immediately goes away. "Oh, I'm sorry, Murph. I guess I didn't really expect that answer. To me, it all seems so . . . far away. I mean, here I am blithely going about my life, taking university classes and all, and there you are, a person who got hurt in combat. Risked your life for us."

I'm not sure how to respond to that, so I just shrug, which was probably the dumbest response I could have come up with.

"But what do I know about that war?" she says. "All I know is what I see on TV, and they make it look pretty scary. I hope it wasn't as bad as they're making out."

Again, I don't know what to say. I guess I'm going to have to figure out some kind of response for these kinds of encounters. Father Saul always said when in doubt, honesty is the best policy. But people here are so far away from the war, I'm not sure how they would take it. From now on, maybe I'd better not even tell people I was in the Army.

"Uh oh, you got quiet, Murph. Sorry if I upset you."

"Oh, no. You didn't upset me. It's just that I haven't quite learned how to . . . uh, talk about it. Like I said, I just got out."

"Okay, Murph. Tell you what. I'd like to talk to you more about your experiences. If you don't mind, that is. You may be by far the most interesting person I've met so far at this university, and I'm sort of a collector of experiences. Psych major, you know. But right now, I've gotta run to class." She stands up. "How about we make this a regular thing? Lunch after the philosophy class, okay?"

I stand up too and say, "Sounds good to me." Then, for some reason, I find myself reaching my right hand out to shake on it.

But she doesn't shake my hand; instead, she lightly squeezes it with her left hand. Then, she hurries away.

It gives me a chance to see that's she's light on her feet. Athletic, I'd say. I watch her all the way until she goes up the stairs and out of sight.

I sit back down and slowly eat while I think about what just happened. I went to my first university class, and I actually understood it. And then a young woman named Clara ate lunch with me and told me a little about herself, and she said she'd like to meet with me again. That's for sure the first time anything like that has ever happened to me. Growing up in an orphanage for boys, I never once was around any girls. I guess it shouldn't be a surprise that I don't know how to be around them.

The older boys at the orphanage would come back from town with tales of how they met girls and "got them into bed." But I don't want to be like that with Clara. I just want to get to know her. Then, maybe other things might evolve from that.

But maybe I shouldn't even be thinking about things like that. She seems like a nice person, and that should be reason enough to spend some time with her.

I finish eating and leave the building. It's getting hot, and I should head for the bus stop. I think about going to check out the anti-war protesters at the big fountain, but I decide against it. I still don't know what to think about them. Their chants against the war make me think what the soldiers I served with in Vietnam —the few that are still alive—would think of those students yelling that they're fighting in an "illegal" war. What does that say about them? What does it say about me?

As I walk to the bus stop, I force myself to stop thinking about those anti-war protesters and just look at the interesting, very modern university buildings. I guess I'm going to be spending a lot of time here from now on. Years? Maybe. One thing for sure, I really am now a university student. How did it all happen so fast? From being in a military hospital in far-away California, to end up here in Arizona as a university student. Amazing how fast life can change.

Uh oh, as I approach the bus stop I see that June is there waiting for the bus. I think about turning away and waiting for the next bus, but it's too late; she sees me coming and waves. I hope she's not going to ask me how I know Cody. I wave back, and continue toward her, but before I get there, the bus pulls up. She gets on, and so do I. I take my time paying, and I see that she's gone to the back of the bus.

Good I'll sit up front. I start to sit down, but she waves for me to come back and sit next to her. I do that, and she says, "Murph, isn't it? My young cousin, Cody, introduced us at the bus stop the other day, remember?"

I say, "Sure, I remember. June, isn't it?"

"Yeah. I said Cody was my cousin, but I'm not sure of that. He claims to be. He hasn't been living at the reservation all that long, but he's getting pretty well known. I'm told he shows up at most of the bingo games. Makes tips running errands for the players. That's what I heard anyhow."

I'd better be careful not to let on how I know Cody, so I just say, "He seems like a nice boy."

She stares at me. Is she suspicious that I know more than I'm saying?

"They say he's a sharp boy, but they also say he can be stubborn. Last spring he was refusing to go to school. And they say he runs wild. His old man doesn't pay any attention to him, and nobody even knows where he sleeps some nights. Not always in his old man's trailer. That's what my grandmama said anyhow."

Before I can think how to respond to that, she blurts out, "Cody said you were in Vietnam. How was that?"

Now there's a question nobody has asked me. How am I supposed to answer that?

"Oh, sorry," she says. "Maybe you don't want to talk about it."

"No, no, it's not that. It's just that I wasn't there all that long. And I was in one place. Until I got . . . uh, injured."

"How did that happen?"

Does she really want to know? I decide to give her the summary version. "Well, it was some kind of explosion. I don't remember much about it. Got torn up pretty bad."

"Bad? You seem okay now."

Maybe she actually does want to know. "Yes, I'm okay now, but I was in hospitals for a long time."

She stares at me for several seconds. "That must of been hard."

Again, I'm not sure how to answer that.

"Maybe you really don't like to talk about it. I'm too nosy. I'm a teaching major, but I'm interested in other stuff. Makes me too inquisitive." She looks out the bus window.

I stare at her. She's nothing like what I thought she would be. She's a mother, has a young child, but here talking to me, she seems more like a regular college student. But what do I know about how women are? The only women I've ever met in my entire life were the nurses at the hospital. Until I met Clara, that is. June also seems like a smart, interesting girl.

June turns back to me. "Sorry to be so nosy. It's just that I don't have anybody to talk to. I live with my grandmama, and she's only interested in talking about the baby and what a bastard his father was to run off and leave us."

"It's okay, June. It's only that I'm still learning how to talk about Vietnam. Most people don't want to hear about it. It's like they've already made up their minds, one way or the other. It's taking me a while to figure out how to fit back into the world."

"I understand. The other reason I'm being so nosy is that one of my classes is called War, Psychological Trauma, and Resilience. But our reading is mostly about survivors of combat in World War Two. If you can tell me about Vietnam, I think I'll be the only one who got to interview an actual Vietnam survivor."

I smile at that. "Is that what I am, a survivor? I guess I hadn't thought about it like that."

She's not smiling. "Of course you are. Most of the boys from the reservation who got sent to Vietnam ended up dead. That makes it seem like anybody who comes back is a lucky survivor."

I smile to let her know I don't mind her questions. "Okay, June, if you need to interview a Vietnam survivor, I'll be that for you. What do you want to know?"

Now she seems confused. "Well, I'm not sure. I guess to start, what was it like? Scary?"

I shake my head, but I do think about her question. "I'll tell you, June, most of the time you don't think about it being a dangerous situation. You just do what you're supposed to do, things like stacking sandbags all day. You're working hard in the heat and looking forward to when it's time to knock off for the day and get some chow."

"But you got wounded. Bad, you said. That must mean sometimes you were in scary situations."

"Well, going out on patrol is kind of nerve-racking at first. But after you've done it a number of times with nothing happening, you get used to it. Mostly you focus on dealing with the heat and the wetness and the bugs and taking care of your messed up feet. Trench foot, they call it."

"So, the time you got wounded was an unusual situation."

"Right. At least I think so. Actually, I hadn't been out on that firebase all that long before it happened. And then it all happened so fast, I didn't quite know what was going on. The explosion must have knocked me out, so I didn't experience all of it. Later, the doctors told me I'd suffered a concussion, and that was what caused my memory loss. The first thing I actually remember was waking up to see the enemy . . . uh leaving. Eventually, the dustoff came and picked me up."

"What's a dustoff?"

"Oh, it's a medevac. A type of helicopter they use over there to haul away the wounded. I found out later I was the only one from my group that made it alive to the aid station. Lucky, I guess."

June seems a bit stunned by my story. Maybe I've done it again, given more details about the war more than anybody really wants to hear. I say, "But maybe that's not what you need for your class."

She shakes her head. "No, it's exactly what I need. My classmates are going to be jealous of me for being the only one to get the real story of a wounded soldier."

She glances out the bus window. "But it looks like we're about to my reservation. It's where I get off. Can I talk to you more later? I bet even my professor will tell me to ask you more questions."

More questions? What other questions could there be? But I guess I wouldn't mind talking to this nice young woman again, so I just say, "Sure. Anytime."

"Okay, what's your phone number?"

"Uh, I don't have one yet." I hope that didn't sound suspicious. She's the last person I want to start questioning where I'm living.

She just gathers up her books and stands up. She says goodbye and leaves the bus quickly. Does she want to avoid talking to me anymore? I hope I didn't upset her. But she said what I told her was just what she needed. Maybe she's just late for something.

Chapter Thirteen

As I start the long walk from the bus stop through the desert to the orphanage, it gets hotter. I stop a few times to rest. When I finally get to the orphanage, the sun is high in the sky, so the first thing I do is go to the well. I pull up a bucket of water, and then I take off my shirt and drape it over the edge of the well wall. I have to be careful not to get it wet or dirty; after all, it's the only shirt I've got. I'll be glad when my discharge check from the Army comes so I can buy some clothes that look more like what the other students are wearing. I splash my face and my shoulders with the cool water, then I go into the dorm to rest my aching back and legs.

But I'm not sleepy. Not at all. Too much happened to me today to just go to sleep.

I get up and go outside to sit in the shade of the building, and it isn't long before I see Cody coming from the direction of the old secret dugout. I hope he didn't have to go there to hide from his father.

Then, I see he's not alone; a little black dog is with him.

When Cody gets closer, he sees me and yells, "Hey, Murph. Look what I found. He was in your secret hideout."

I think I recognize the dog. Can it be Blackie, the pup that used to come around the orphanage every once in a while?

When Cody and the dog get closer, I'm pretty sure it is the same dog, only looking a bit more tired and beat up. He's limping. I wonder if he's been in a tussle with a coyote.

"He's friendly," says Cody. "Can I keep him? Can I?"

"His name is Blackie, Cody."

"Blackie? You know him?"

"Sure. He's been coming around the orphanage for years."

"Oh. It seems like his foot is hurt. I think we should keep him and fix his foot."

"Okay with me, but when he's better, he'll just wander off again. In the past, he'd show up, but after a few days, he'd disappear again. We always assumed he lived out in the desert somewhere and only came around when he got hungry. Father Saul had a rule against pets, but once he learned Blackie wasn't going to stick around for long, he decided he wouldn't count as an actual pet. Every time Blackie showed up, us boys would feed him, and then we'd spend a lot of time pulling porcupine quills out of his mouth. At mealtime, we'd sneak food off our plates for him. In time, even Father Saul took a shine to him and quit scolding us for wasting food on a dog. Blackie was such a mangy mutt, Father Saul jokingly made up a fancy name for him, Stygian Mark Royal. But we all just called him Blackie. Eventually he started to answer to that."

"So I can keep him?"

"I'm afraid it's up to him, Cody. He'll stick around for as long as he wants to."

"Okay. Keep him here. I'm gonna run over to the bingo hall to get some food for him."

After Cody leaves, I sit down on the floor to check Blackie out. He's gone gray around his mouth. I wonder if that means he's getting old. Blackie scoots forward and lays his head on my lap. That proves to me that it's the same dog, even though he's in rougher shape than the last time I saw him. "Where you been, boy? You don't have any porcupine quills in your mouth this time. Given up chasing porcupines, have you?"

He looks up as if he's asking me a question.

"If you're asking for food, I don't have any. But stick around for a while and Cody will bring you something back from the bingo hall."

As if he understood me, he closes his eyes and seems to go to sleep.

I gently move his head off of my lap, and even that doesn't wake him up. He must be really tired.

I go into the classroom building to look for an empty note-book. When I open the big cabinet, I see that Father Saul's stuff is still there on the shelf. Everything of his is still there, his hair-brush, even his toothbrush? I look at the cot he slept on. The depression in the middle of it makes it look like he could have just gotten up and left. Nothing about his disappearance makes sense. Why would he have left so hurriedly that he didn't even take time to collect his personal possessions?

On the shelf below his stuff, is a stack of notebooks. Maybe there's some usable paper in them. But when I look through all the notebooks, I find them mostly filled with student writing. But there is one notebook that's only half filled with notes. Reading through the carefully handwritten notes of that one, I don't recog-nize the writing. But I recognize the first topic: it's one of Father Saul's lectures about how a young gentleman should present him-self to the world. Whoever was taking these notes was carefully transcribing what Father Saul was lecturing about. Unlike the notes I used to take, there are no personal thoughts about what Father Saul was saying. I wonder what happened to my note-books. I haven't thought about them since I left. After I left the orphanage, they probably got used to start the morning fires in the wood stove.

I start to tear the handwritten pages out of the partial-ly-filled notebook, but then I hesitate. What if the student comes back someday looking for these notes? But I know I'm going to need a notebook for my classes at the university, so I continue to tear out the filled pages, and when I'm done, I neatly stack the torn-out pages back into the cabinet. I decide to read some more of the notebooks, and I'm amazed at how clearly those notes bring back memories of Father Saul. He was a wise old man, and knew how to talk to young boys in a way that would get their attention and hold it.

I'm still reading through the old notebooks when Cody comes back. He's got a sack that I assume is filled with food from the bingo hall. The first thing he does is go inside to find Blackie.

I follow him in to see how the dog is going to react.

Cody removes two hot dogs in buns from the sack and puts them down on the floor in front of Blackie. The dog noses the buns aside and wolfs down the hot dogs. Cody tries to get him to eat a cupcake, but he's not interested. He lies down and stares at us.

I suspect it means he wasn't all that hungry. It can only mean somebody else is also feeding him. Maybe he even has an actual home to go to somewhere. It means he won't be hanging around long this time. Now that I think about it, because he's a wanderer, it's possible he might actually have multiple homes to go to, places where people feed him whenever he shows up. They might even think he's their dog.

Cody sits down on the floor to pet him, and the dog lies back to allow it. Soon, Cody is fully involved in picking burrs out of Blackie's coat. He looks up at me and says, "Hey, Murph, what did you learn today at the university? Teach it to me."

"I don't know that what I learned today is the kind of thing I can teach you, Cody. The professor just introduced the old philosophers he's going to teach us about."

"Well, what was it like? Was it a big class?"

"No, it was actually pretty small. Only eight students, counting me."

"Did you talk to any of them? Were they nice?"

"I talked to a girl. She's the only girl in the class."

Cody grins at me. "So you went right after her. I should have known you'd be the one to get the girl."

"I didn't go after her, Cody. Actually, she approached me. She's a psychology major. She said she was a collector of experiences."

"Oh yeah? What does that mean?"

"I guess it just means she thought I was unusual."

"Was she pretty?"

"Yes, I'd say so, but what I liked most about her was that she's really smart. She said she thought I was a Native American."

Cody kind of wrinkles up his face. "Yeah, that's what some outsiders call us."

"I was surprised she said that. In the Army, I never told anybody about my background. But one guy in Vietnam called me Geronimo."

"Geronimo? Ha! You don't look Apache at all."

"Yes, but the guy was from Chicago. He was the type who liked to make fun of everybody. Gave everybody a nickname. He probably never even suspected I really did have some Indian blood in me."

"I hope you taught him a lesson."

"No, Cody, I didn't go around in Vietnam teaching anybody lessons. In the Army, you're better off getting along. There were a lot of tough guys there, guys from places like Chicago and Pittsburgh or Atlanta. They got into a lot of fights."

"So you backed down from 'em."

I hesitate. Maybe this is not the right moment to try to teach Cody a lesson about getting along in the world. I just say, "Those guys mostly left me alone, and that was fine with me."

"Okay. What about your class at the university? Did you like it?"

"Yes, I did. I think I am going to learn some interesting new things."

"Good. Then you can teach me. Except right now, I'm gonna go to the bingo hall to earn some more money."

He leaves, but he's only gone for a few minutes before he comes back, leading Blackie. "You gotta keep him here, Murph. He keeps tryin' to follow me."

"Okay, come here, Blackie. You can stay with me."

Cody takes off again, and when Blackie again tries to follow him, I manage to get ahold of him and take him into the dorm with me. It's hot and it's been a long day, so I decide to lie down for a while. Blackie lies down next to my cot, and I let my arm hang down, touching him, to make sure he doesn't try to follow Cody.

Surprisingly, I must have fallen asleep, because when I hear Cody come in, it's already dark. He comes to collect Blackie and leads him into his hideout in the corner of the dorm.

I'm still feeling sleepy, so I turn over and try to get back to sleep, but my mind wants to go back to thinking about my day at the university. I went to my first class, and I feel like I can handle it fine. Not only that, I met a nice-looking girl who seems to like me. She said she wants to spend more time with me. I sure hope that works out. I know I've got a lot to learn about that kind of thing, but I'm ready to try.

Chapter Fourteen

I feel somebody shaking my shoulder, and there's a bright light in my eyes. I'm instantly on guard. I'm ready to jump up and grab my rifle. But then I remember I'm not in Vietnam anymore. I must have been having a dream about the war.

The light in my eyes must be Cody's flashlight.

As soon as I push the flashlight away and see Cody's face, I can tell something's wrong.

He says, "Get up quick, Murph. Blackie found a man."

"He found a man? What man?"

"Yeah. Come quick. It's a dead man. Blackie dug him up."

Outside, Cody leads me away from the dorm building. There's no moon and the big dipper is standing on its tail, which means it's still the middle of the night. I'm trying to imagine what dead man Cody could be talking about. When I was still pretty young, a couple of the older boys were trying to start a garden out here in the desert, and in the process, they dug up a skeleton. Father Saul said it was probably an old Indian burial ground. He said a prayer over it and made them cover the skeleton up again. So, is that what Blackie dug up? But Cody said it was a man. There's no way he could know that if it was only a skeleton.

When we get to the place he's leading me, Cody shines his flashlight, and I see a hand sticking out of the dirt. It's a recognizable human hand, not a skeletal hand.

Cody says, "That's what Blackie dug up. I dug a little more and found a face. The dead guy wasn't buried too deep. He's lyin' on his back, and he stinks."

He shines the light on the dead man's face, and although the cheeks of the face are dark and sunken, and the eye sockets are just dark hollows, probably eaten by bugs, I know exactly who it is: it's Father Saul.

I have to sit down to recover. How can this be? Father Saul is dead? The man who took care of me for many years, the man some of the other boys suspected might be my real father is dead? None of this makes any sense. I'm seeing Father Saul's face right in front of me, but my mind doesn't want to accept it. Previously, I had the thought that he might have gone away because he was ill. Because he was old. But this? Dead and buried out here in the desert? I saw some dead bodies in Vietnam, but this is completely different. This is Father Saul. How could this have happened? Did he die and want to be buried here? If that's what happened, why doesn't anybody know about it? Somebody had to bury him here. But who?

"What's wrong?" asks Cody. "Do you know him?"

It takes me a minute to get the words out, but I finally say, "Unfortunately, I do, Cody. It's . . . it's Father Saul."

"The priest that ran this place?"

"Yes."

"But everybody said he left."

"That's what I thought too. After you told me the tribe was unhappy that he opposed gambling, I thought he'd either left on his own or was run off. And when I was in town, I ran into Jimmy, a boy who was in the orphanage. He said there were only two boys left in the orphanage when Father Saul disappeared. He said one day the two of them came back from fishing, and Father Saul was just gone. He assumed the tribe had sent in the local cops to kick him off the reservation."

"They wouldn't do that. The tribe don't get along so good with the local cops. They don't want 'em nosin' round the res, 'specially not at the bingo games."

"I understand. Now we know he didn't leave on his own, or get kicked out. He's been buried out here all the time."

"So if the boys in the orphanage didn't bury him here, who did?"

Cody's question is important. I need to pull myself together and try to understand how Father Saul died and why he was buried out here.

Although this is Father Saul, the man who was so important to me growing up, he is now a dead body, like the dead bodies I saw in Vietnam. I need to be calm and unemotional and try to figure this out.

"What're ya thinkin', Murph?"

"I'm trying to think it through, Cody. I think I'll dig up a little more of him. To try to figure out how he died."

Cody backs off, holding up both hands. "No way. I'm not gonna touch a dead person. Are you?"

"I touched some dead bodies in Vietnam. Enemy soldiers. We had to pick up what was left of them after our beehive rounds ripped them to pieces in the night."

"Yuck. Okay, you do it then."

"All right. You keep Blackie away while I take a closer look at him."

Cody gets ahold of Blackie and pulls him back.

Using Cody's flashlight to see, I carefully brush away more of the dirt from Father Saul's face. Other than the damage from insects, he isn't in too bad a shape. I wonder how long ago he was buried here. The fact that he still smells means he couldn't have died all that long ago. On the other hand, the dry desert air might have preserved him somewhat.

But now I see a problem with the side of his head, toward the back. I use my fingers to dig away a little more of the dirt, and that's when I see it—the back of his head has been bashed in. I turn and call to Cody. "Somebody killed him."

Cody says, "What? How can you tell?"

"It's pretty obvious. The back of his head has been caved in."

"Oh no. What should we do?"

"We have to call the police."

Cody shakes his head, hard. "No way. They'd kick you off the res, and I'd be back with my old man. And he'd take this out on me."

"Why would your father take something like this out on you, Cody? You didn't do anything wrong."

"Oh yeah? If I have anything to do with bringing in the cops, he'll beat the shit out of me. And like I said, they'd kick you out of here right away, and then how will I ever get to learn anything about the world? Especially now when you're gonna go the university to learn new stuff to teach me. We should just cover him back up and try to figure this out ourselves."

He has a point. I'm not worried about myself, but what about Cody? Once the word got out that Cody was the one who found Father Saul's body, he could be in danger, not only from his abusive father, but also from whoever killed him. "I understand the problems, Cody, but there's been a murder. That means we have to tell the police. Maybe I can keep you out of it. What about the reservation? Don't they have a police force?"

"Yeah, but they're just volunteers. They mostly just break up fights when people get drunk. And what if they were in on it?"

Cody has a point. We probably shouldn't trust anybody in the tribe.

Cody is still shaking his head. "Come on, Murph, please. We can't tell nobody. At least not right away. After all, he's obviously been dead for a long time, so there's no hurry to report it. We should try to solve the murder ourselves, and then we'll call in the cops."

He's right about Father Saul having been dead for some time, and if the police take the body away, what would they do with it? Examine it for evidence? And then where would Father Saul end up? Buried in some town cemetery? I'm sure Father Saul would much rather be buried out here in the desert he loved. "You know, Cody, you may be right. Maybe we should investigate a little before we call the police."

"Right. I bet we can solve this ourselves. It'll be fun."

"I'm not sure fun is the right word, Cody. But I guess it wouldn't hurt to check out a few things before we tell the police. I have the address of that other orphanage boy I mentioned, Jimmy, the boy that was here the day Father Saul disappeared. Maybe he'll have some ideas about who'd want to kill him."

"Right. Should we bury him better so Blackie doesn't dig him up again?"

"Good idea. Why don't you and Blackie go get a shovel from the shed."

After Cody and Blackie take off, I sit down in the dirt to stare at the sadly distorted face of Father Saul. Somehow, despite the damage the insects have done to him, he looks oddly peaceful. Maybe he didn't see whoever was about to hit him from behind. But that wouldn't be like Father Saul. Despite his advancing age, he was as sharp as any of us boys. So there's no way an enemy could sneak up on him. That means it must have been somebody he knew, somebody he didn't suspect was about to strike him from behind. But I can't imagine that he had any enemies, except maybe somebody from the tribe. They must be making a lot of money from their bingo games, and it was obvious that they didn't want him interfering with that. But why would they think they needed to kill him? They had the right to kick him off their reservation.

But maybe he had problems with some individuals in the tribe. I can't think of anybody else who could have done it. Who else had access to him so far out here in the desert?

Also, it seems like he was buried hurriedly. That must mean it wasn't planned. Maybe somebody from the tribe came out to try to talk him into leaving the reservation, and there was some kind of argument that got out of hand. Then, maybe, after they'd killed him, they panicked and did this quick burial before any of the boys from the orphanage could come back.

But is there any chance it could have been a stranger? Could somebody from outside the reservation have come by? Maybe thieves that thought the orphanage had something worth stealing. I know Father Saul would have fought them. He was like that.

I lie back and stare up at the sky. It's still dark in the east, meaning the sun's not even close to coming up over the distant mountains. It'll be hours before sunrise.

I sit up and again use Cody's flashlight to look at Father Saul's sadly misshapen face. I don't think he'd like being buried here so close to the orphanage where people might come and walk on him. Maybe when Cody gets back with the shovel, we should bury him in a better place. Farther out in the desert, in a place he'd like better.

No, that's not a good idea. It's better to leave him here, close enough to the orphanage so I can keep an eye on his grave in case whoever killed him comes back to see if he's been found. Maybe they'll come back to bury him better.

I see Cody coming back with the shovel, closely followed by Blackie. I know he won't talk about this, but if he starts asking questions, trying to "solve" the murder himself, it might tip the killer off. If it was someone from the tribe, it could put Cody in danger.

Cody hands me the shovel and stands back. It's clear he doesn't want to have anything to do with a dead body, and that's okay with me. Better that he has nothing to do with it.

After I finish burying Father Saul as well as I can, I break a branch off of a weed and use it to smooth out the whole area, including getting rid of our footprints.

"Why are you doing that?" asks Cody.

"I don't want anybody to know we've been here. Especially not the killer if he comes back."

"You really think he'll come back?"

"Depends on who it was."

"I get it. You really are thinkin' it might have been some-body from the tribe. Maybe even my . . . ."

Cody stops in mid-sentence, but I know what he was about to say. Does he really think his father is capable of killing? I guess it's possible. Could Cody's father have come out here and gotten into a fight with Father Saul? The fact that he severely beat his own son shows he is a violent man. But did he even know Father Saul was out here?

I turn to Cody. "By the way, Cody, when you came here, was anybody around?"

"Nope. I didn't even know this place was out here. I never heard anybody in the tribe ever talk about it. After they moved me to this res, I started exploring the desert. It was a surprise when I came across this empty old place."

"So you started sleeping out here."

"Not for a while. Not until I learned what my old man was like when he gets drunk."

"Did the place look like it had been deserted very long?"

"Not really. In fact, it sort of looked like whoever lived here might have left all of a sudden. I thought maybe they'd come back. But I kept on coming out here and never saw anybody, so I just kind of moved in."

"How long ago was that?"

"Couple of months I guess."

"I wonder how long he'd been dead and buried out here before you discovered the abandoned orphanage building."

"How can we figure that out?"

"Well, it's hard to tell how long he's been dead, but his body is still recognizable, so it couldn't have been too long."

"Can't you tell? You said you saw dead bodies in Vietnam."

"I did see a few of the enemy dead, but they hadn't been dead very long. And they were really torn up. Maybe I can look for a book at the university library that will tell me how long it takes bodies to deteriorate after death."

As we walk back to the orphanage building, I warn Cody not to try to solve this murder by himself. In other words, I tell him, don't do or say anything that might tip the killer off that we found the body. He agrees, but says he'll keep his ears open and listen for anything that might give us some clues.

With that, he says he's going back to bed, and he's going to make sure Blackie stays with him.

I also go back to bed, but there is no way I'm going to get much sleep. I've got to try to figure out why somebody would kill Father Saul, and why he was hurriedly buried close to the orphanage? I'm not sure I'll ever be able to figure it out, but I think I should at least try. I owe it to Father Saul.

Chapter Fifteen

The next morning, I get up quietly to be sure I don't wake Cody. I want to get to the university early and try to find some books at the library that might help me figure out how long Father Saul has been dead.

It's a warm morning as I head for the bus stop, meaning it's going to be another hot day. How well I remember that Arizona sun. By the end of the long hot summer, I expect most of the adults in Arizona had come to hate that sun, but to us kids, it was just the normal summer sun, really hot, but we were used to it. To us, summer meant no rain, and that meant not as much work for us to do repairing the orphanage building. Summertime was outside play time, at least as soon as our classroom studies were done. We'd often go to our secret hideout out in the desert, and if Father Saul knew about it, he never showed up to bother us.

Father Saul. How could he be dead? And why was he hurriedly buried in the desert?

I wonder where I would have been buried if I had died over there in Vietnam. Would they have sent me back here? I had no next of kin to write down on my enlistment papers, but maybe they might have found out where I grew up. If so, would I have been buried in the reservation cemetery? Not likely. Not knowing who my parents were, the tribe probably wouldn't claim me. More likely, the military would have put me in one of the huge veterans' cemeteries, along with all the others that are being killed in this new war.

Or maybe Father Saul would have claimed my body and found a way to bury me out here in the desert. He knew how much I loved it.

But maybe he was already dead by the time I got wounded. I guess that's the first thing I've got to try to figure out—how long ago did he die?

But why am I having thoughts about being dead and buried? I should be grateful to be alive and out here in the desert again. The truth is, there were times in Vietnam when I thought I'd never see the desert again. I often had to fight off the feeling that the dense jungle surrounding me would be the last place on this earth I would ever know. I hated to think I might never see the desert again.

Now, I'm feeling like if this place, this wonderful desert, is the last place I'll ever know, it's all right with me. Maybe I too will end up buried out here somewhere.

As I walk, I'm thinking about what I might find at the university library. Will there actually be any books that tell about how dead bodies deteriorate? And maybe I should also look for books that might teach me how to solve a murder. Are there any such books? Not likely, but I've got to start somewhere.

The bus comes soon after I arrive at the bus stop. There are only a few other passengers, but they don't look like students. Probably early morning agricultural workers.

As we go on, the bus picks up a few more passengers, but none of them look like students. And then, when I get off at the main university entrance, I notice that there are very few students walking around. I have no idea what time it is, but it must be too early for classes. Maybe the library won't be open either. I bet the other students would think it's weird that I don't have a watch or any other way to know the time of day. I guess I didn't need a watch when I was growing up at the orphanage, and I didn't think I needed one in Vietnam either. Maybe it's another thing I need to get if I'm actually going to learn how to fit into the real world. When I get some money, that is.

As I walk around the campus looking for the library, I again notice how new most of the buildings look. It must mean the university is growing. In fact, about the only old building I saw on registration day was the one with the big fountain in front, where I saw those anti-war protesters. I wonder if they're here this early in the morning. Probably not, and I don't have time to go check anyhow. I need to get to the library.

When I find the library, it is open. As soon as I get inside, I realize I have no idea how to find the kind of books I'm looking for, so I just stand there near the entrance and watch. The other students probably think I look confused standing here. Well, I am. I don't even know how to start looking for a certain type of book.

I keep watching what the other students do. As soon as they walk into the library, most of them head down a wide hallway that heads deeper into the library. But a few of them stop at a large cabinet with small pull-out drawers before they head off to where the books are. That cabinet must be where they keep a record of the books in the library.

I wait until there are no other students using the cabinet, then I go to it and start by looking up the word "bodies." I pull out a "B" drawer, and looking through the little cards, I find several books listed with the word "Bodies" in the title. But none of them seem to have anything to do with the deterioration of bodies after death. Nevertheless, I do find one about medical examinations, so I take note of the number and go try to find that book section. I go farther back into the library and wander through long rows of metal book shelves until I find the number I'm looking for on the end of a bookshelf. Sure enough, when I go down that row of books, they are all about medical topics.

I soon find one that's for coroners. I learned in Vietnam that dead bodies were sent to a coroner in Saigon, so I pull that book off the shelf and take it to one of the small desks that are at the end of the bookshelf rows.

As I go through the book, I find a chapter on body decomposition. It says there are three phases, early, advanced, and skeletonization. It says in the early phase, there is skin slippage and hair loss. It says these changes start from the first day after death to up to five days after death. It also talks about maggots invading the body almost immediately. It's hard to think about maggots being inside Father Saul, but I need to be logical and unemotional if I'm going to figure out who killed him.

The book goes on to say that after about ten days, the skin gets "leathery," and that process continues until it forms a hardened leathery shell that covers the entire body. Although I could only see a small part of Father Saul's body, it did seem to have a leathery look. That could mean his body is in that second stage. The book says further decomposition depends on temperature and humidity. In a hot place with high humidity, it says the body could move rapidly into skeletonization, the phase in which the internal organs and soft tissue have been completely eaten by maggots and other types of bugs and worms, leaving only bones and bits of dry skin. Father Saul's body hadn't turned into a skeleton, so that must mean he hasn't been dead all that long.

I look up from the book and try to think what it's telling me about how long ago Father Saul was killed. Although the dry desert air might have changed the decomposition rate, he must not have died all that long ago. Cody said he'd discovered the abandoned orphanage a few months ago, and he said the building had the feel of being recently abandoned. So I know Father Saul has been gone at least that long. So maybe he was killed shortly before Cody found the orphanage. But I didn't get the feeling from Jimmy that Father Saul had gone away that recently. I need to go find Jimmy and get him to tell me exactly when Father Saul disappeared.

I sit back to think about it. If Father Saul's body hasn't been buried out there all that long, then I'm even more sure we did the right thing in leaving his body buried right where it is. Maybe the killer did a quick burial, planning to come back later and do a better job of it. That would mean the killer would have to be someone who planned to stick around, and that makes it even more likely the killer was someone from the tribe. But who? And would they really kill Father Saul just because he was interfering with their gambling business? There must be more to it than that, maybe there was some other kind of trouble between him and somebody in the tribe. Maybe it only started with somebody trying to get him off reservation land, and it escalated.

Or could it have been a planned killing? Maybe Father Saul had something on someone in the tribe, something more significant than the gambling issue.

I put the coroner book back on the shelf and think about what my next step should be. I doubt if there are any books in this library about how to solve a murder mystery, but then I didn't think I'd find a book about how dead bodies decompose.

I head back to the cabinet with the little cards that list the books and look under M for murder. All I can find are novels. Murder mysteries. I don't see how they could help me solve Father Saul's murder, but I've got nothing else to go on, so I might as well at least look them over.

I find the murder mystery bookshelf, and take several of those novels to a desk. As it turns out, even though the books are fiction, after scanning through several of them, I realize they do tell me how someone goes about solving a murder.

The stories almost always feature a clever person, either a professional detective or just a smart amateur, who solves murders with brain power. By logical thinking. The detective usually begins by questioning people, and that provides him with clues that eventually lead to the killer.

So, should I begin by questioning people? But who? Who might have information that would help me figure out who would want to kill Father Saul? So far, nobody even knows he was murdered except for me and Cody. And the killer, of course.

The detective in the novels also analyzes the way the victim was killed. Unlike most of the murders in the novels, Father Saul wasn't killed with a knife or a gun. However, I know that most of the men in the tribe do have guns. I know that because Father Saul often complained about them wandering around the desert shooting stuff. They called it "target practice," but they were drinking booze as they did it, and Father Saul worried that their drunken shooting might accidentally hit the school. He said bullets can travel a long distance.

Father Saul wasn't shot, and he wasn't knifed. He was hit in the head with something hard, and he was hit with enough force to kill him. It seems like somebody would have to be really angry to do that. And it indicates that it wasn't a planned killing. Maybe it was some kind of argument that got out of hand.

But that doesn't really make sense either; Father Saul's face hadn't been hit, only the back of his head. That means somebody hit him from behind when he wasn't expecting it. That means it wasn't an argument.

It also means he probably knew his killer. But would Father Saul turn his back on somebody who was threatening him, even if he knew the person? Father Saul *was* trusting of other people, but he was also smart. Who could get behind him while holding a club? But maybe it wasn't any kind of club. It could have been a rock. There are rocks lying all over out there. Maybe somebody got behind him, picked up a rock, and hit him with it.

I have no way of figuring that out, and another thing I'm learning from reading these murder mystery novels is that the detectives in those stories, whether they're professionals or amateurs, have resources. If they're police detectives, they have a whole department of people to do tests and help gather information. They call it forensics. If they're private detectives, they also usually have people to help them, smart people who know how to find out things. I don't have any such resources. Maybe I *should* just turn it over to the police, no matter what Cody wants. I know it might get him in trouble with his father, and it would undoubtedly get me kicked off of reservation property, but the killer needs to be found and the police have the resources to do it.

But would the local police want to spend those resources on the murder of an old man, a murder that happened on an Indian reservation some time in the past? In several of the books I looked through, a private detective is solving crimes that the police are not interested in. And the fact that it happened on reservation property could result in the local police just turning it over to the reservation police, and Cody reminded me that the reservation police are only volunteers that could be in on it.

Finally, I give up on reading murder mysteries. I don't think they have anything more to tell me. I should take a break from thinking about who killed Father Saul and do what I'm supposed to be doing, being a student. I should find that textbook Professor Schmidt put on reserve for us and start reading it.

Chapter Sixteen

I go to the main desk and the friendly woman there tells me where to find reserved books. Turns out they are in a special section of the library. I go there and the somewhat grumpy woman behind the counter says I have to sign it out. She makes me show my student ID, and she says I can only keep the book out for an hour. That seems like a silly rule when I'm the only student here. But I don't mind her being grumpy. Maybe she's been having a bad day.

The book is titled, "The History of Philosophy." An obvious textbook title for a class on the same subject. I take it to a table and get out my pencil and notebook.

The first chapter of the book says there are several distinct periods of philosophical history, each period related to the cultures that embraced them. The first period the book discusses is the Greek period. It talks about the philosophy of a Greek named Herodotus, who in 600 BC was the first to use the word "philosophize." But the practice of what we know of as philosophy goes back even earlier, to a Greek named Pythagoras who described himself as a philosopher. When anybody asked him what that was, he said it was the investigation of the nature of things. That's pretty much what Professor Schmidt said in his lecture.

The book then goes on to cover the more famous Greeks, Socrates and Plato, describing them as men who "loved wisdom."

I put the book down to think about that. So, is my study of philosophy going to be to investigate the nature things, or will it be a search for wisdom? It must be both. Professor Schmidt said the most important thing to remember about philosophy is that it's simply thinking about who we are and why we are.

But doesn't everybody spend time thinking about that? I know I do. Maybe I think about things like that because Father Saul taught us to think about such things. He always said a thinking person is a good person.

He also talked about God, but not a lot. One thing I remember him saying our search for knowledge should be to understand why God had made us the way we are. But then, at other times he'd get in a strange mood and tells us to imagine what the world would be like if God didn't exist. It was as if he wasn't quite sure himself about whether God existed or not, or at least he wanted to think beyond normal ways of thinking about things.

I'm pretty sure he did believe in God, at least in his Catholic version of God, but he wanted us to imagine other possibilities. And he often talked about all the terrible things that go on in the world, like the wars in which huge numbers of people suffer and die. Then he asked us to wonder why God would allow such things to happen. After allowing us to think about that for a while, he said it was because God wanted us to have free will, even if that freedom resulted in terrible things happening.

So, do I think about such things just because I had Father Saul for a teacher? Was I studying philosophy at a very young age, Father Saul's Catholic version of philosophy? Does that make me unusual? I don't think about such things all day long; it's only when something happens that I don't understand, and that makes me start wondering why. I thought about that a lot in Vietnam, but for some reason, I didn't spend much time thinking about why I was there, or why I was participating in it. I guess I just didn't understand what it was all about. But I did think about the war. I knew we were fighting an "enemy," and I saw big airplanes flying over us all the time, heading north. I assumed they were going up there to drop bombs on people. But I didn't know why they were doing that. I did wonder how dropping bombs on people up north helped us defeat the enemy soldiers we were fighting there in the jungle. I guess my problem was that I didn't feel hatred for the people who were going to die from those bombs being dropped on their homes. But I got the feeling the other soldiers, and maybe even the people back in the United States, did feel some level of hatred for those "gooks" as they liked to call them.

There in the jungle, watching those bombers go over, I knew Father Saul would want me to think about what it all meant. And I did. I thought about it a lot. He would have wanted me to wonder if those so-called "enemy" people up north had to die because it was what God wanted. And if so, why did He want that?

That thought leads me to start thinking about why a good man like Father Saul had to be murdered? Did God want that too?

I stare at the book lying on the table in front of me. Is it this book that's making me have such thoughts? I look around at the huge library. I keep having the same thought: how did I end up as a student attending a major university when only a short time ago I was in an Army hospital, recovering from the wounds I got in a foreign war, a war that's still going on.

"Daydreaming?"

It takes me a moment to realize it's Clara. I say, "Oh hi, Clara. I guess I was." I touch the book. "This book's got me thinking."

She smiles at that and says, "Well, I suppose that's what a philosophy book's supposed to do, isn't it?"

"I guess so. This book says the study of philosophy involves investigation into the nature of things. Do you think that's really what philosophy is all about?"

"Beats me. I'm a psych major, remember? I'm here at this university to try to figure out why humans are the way they are." She hesitates and then says, "But I'm also at this university to learn other things, maybe to learn about learning."

"Isn't that why all the students are here? To learn more?"

She shakes her head. "I don't think so. I haven't met a single student here at this university that wants to talk about philosophical things. A lot of the students are here to learn about *things*. Like electronics, or making pottery. Or painting. Or playing the piano."

"I hadn't thought about signing up for anything like that, but I guess it would be interesting. Studying how to make pottery or learning to play piano would be more doing and less thinking."

She grins at me. "That's very good, Murph. You've broken down university studies into the thinking majors versus the doing majors. Not bad for an Army guy."

"Oh, are Army guys supposed to be dumb?"

She smiles at me and points toward the library entrance with her thumb. "Well, that's what those anti-war protesters at the fountain would have us believe. I was just there. They're out there right now badgering any male student that walks by. They're saying going to fight in a war of invasion is wrong, and I'm pretty sure they think anybody who would participate in it is dumb."

"So, what do you think? Was I dumb to go over there to Vietnam?"

She's still smiling, so I guess my challenging her isn't about to drive her away. I wouldn't want that.

"Hey, Murph, I'm a girl, right? We don't get drafted, so we're not supposed to have any opinion about it, right?"

"But I bet you do have an opinion about it, don't you?"

"I always have opinions, but when it comes to that war in Vietnam, I'm not sure what to think. My parents are all for it. They think we have to stop the Communists before they take over the world. But I'm not so sure determining who controls the jungle in some far-away country is going to determine who takes over the world. Seems to me, countries like Russia and China, and this country we happen to live in, are busy seeing who can make the biggest hydrogen bomb. If they actually use them, there probably won't be much of a world left to take over."

I'm not sure how to respond to that. None of the guys I served with in Vietnam had those kinds of doubts about the war we were fighting in. At least none of them mentioned anything like that to me. I suspect they were just trying to stay alive for another day, like I was. But I decide not to say that to her. Instead, I ask her, "So, are you here to read this book Professor Schmidt put on reserve? If you are, you can take it."

"No, I bought it. Ordered it, but it hasn't come yet, so I wouldn't mind taking a quick look at it. That's why I came by before I had to go to a class."

I push the book toward her, and she sits down next to me and starts quickly leafing through it. Is she that fast a reader, or is she just trying to get a feel for what's in it? Father Saul once told me I was the fastest reading student he'd ever had, but I wasn't sure if he was telling me I was smart, or that I should take more time.

Clara pushes the book back in front of me. "Okay, I got the gist of it. By the way, when I said I ordered the book, I should have said my parents ordered it for me. I'm a kept woman. That is, my parents keep me living at home, and they pay for everything. I guess that would seem odd to you."

"No. I understand. Actually, I guess I'm kept in a way too. The Army is paying for my education."

"Not the same thing, Murph. But never mind about that. Do you think the book is any good?"

"It seems pretty good. Interesting. To me anyhow. But I haven't got very far into it. It keeps on making me stop to think."

"Hey, that means it *is* good. That's what textbooks are supposed to do, right? Make us think?"

"I guess so, Clara. But I have no background in this philosophy stuff at all."

"Who does? My English teacher in high school, my favorite teacher, said they don't teach the two most important subjects in high school like they should. He said psychology and philosophy should be taught from the time kids are little. His words were the main reason I signed up as a psych major when I got to college, and why I'm taking the philosophy class."

"I had a good teacher too. He taught us to think about things logically, but he didn't call what he taught us philosophy."

"I thought you said you grew up in an orphanage, on an Indian reservation."

"Yes, but our teacher at the orphanage was a Catholic Priest. And he was a really good teacher."

She stares at me a me for a few moments, and then says, "I think I'd like to hear more about that. Like I told you before, I'm a collector of experiences. But I just came by to take a quick look at that philosophy book before I have to go to another class this morning. Tell you what, Murph, how about I go to my class and then we meet up in the cafeteria again so we can talk more. Deal?"

"Sure. What time"

"My class will last until eleven-thirty. I'll meet you then."

"Okay,"

Clara stands up and gently touches my shoulder before she hurries away.

I go back to reading, trying to concentrate, but I keep thinking about that touch on my shoulder. What did that mean? Was it just a friendly gesture, or did it mean something more? How do you tell how much a girl likes you? I suppose a guy should have learned such things as a teenager. But when I was a teenager, I was only around boys, isolated out in the middle of the Arizona desert. And then there was the firebase in the Vietnamese jungle —again, only males. There was a lot of talk about girls, and magazines with pictures of half-naked girls being passed around, but I was never part of those conversations. They treated me like a kid, and I guess in their eyes I was. Since then, the only females I've been around were the nurses in the hospitals I was in.

I guess I have to just stick with what I'm feeling. I know I like Clara. She's a smart person, friendly and talkative.

But what do I mean to her? How do you tell?

I should stop thinking about it. I shouldn't be hoping for anything more that just being friends.

But then I have to laugh at myself. More than just friends? What am I thinking? That she could be my girlfriend? I barely met her. The one thing I know for sure is that I'd better stop thinking about Clara and get back to reading this assigned textbook.

I have to reread the next few paragraphs before I can get my mind to focus on what it's saying. It's saying the really important thing about those original Greek thinkers was not *what* they thought but *how* they thought. Instead of sticking to the kind of mythological thinking that characterized that era—that the causes of all things should be attributed to the realms of the gods —the early philosophical thinkers took a more scientific approach; that is, they began to look for the causes of things in the earthly realm. The book says that even though those early philosophers didn't have any actual scientific knowledge of the world they lived in, it was important that they undertook a way of thinking that would eventually lead to such knowledge. In their attempt to understand the world around them, they looked for basic principles. For example, the book says a Greek philosopher named Thales attempted to explain the world in materialist terms, focusing on water as the primary stuff of nature, while another Greek philosopher, Anaximenes, speculated that air is the source of all things.

I think I'm beginning to get what this author is implying: he's saying that to us, the early Greek philosophers might seem to have been completely on the wrong track, but the important thing is that they were on *a track*. That is, they posited explanations for things around them in the world and invited other philosophers to build on, or refute, their positions. Although they were only spec- ulating, the important thing is that they were not depending on the traditional explanations the priests were giving them; they were daring to move away from the explanations they were given. They suggested that it was not the gods that were running the world, but that the world had it's own operating rules. I can see how that led to modern science. Today, we tend to think of science as being something done by scientists in labs, but what this philosophy book is telling me is that it's *the approach* that's important, that gaining knowledge turns us away from traditional ways of accounting for things in order to look for alternative explanations. For that reason, the book is saying we should honor those early philosophers and study their ways of thinking.

I put the book down. Ways of thinking. I like that. The *way* we think about things is as important as *what* we think. After reading just the start of this textbook, I think I'm going to really like being a philosophy major.

Chapter Seventeen

I look up with a start. Did I get so involved in reading about philosophy, I'm going to be late for my meeting with Clara at the cafeteria? I turn the book back in, and then I go looking for a clock. When I find one, I'm frustrated to discover I'm already late.

As I hurry toward the cafeteria, the heat of the day again makes me think about Father Saul lying out there in the hot desert. Even though I want to solve his murder, I know the desert is exactly the place he would have wanted to be buried. That may be the main reason against turning the matter over to the police. That and protecting Cody. Also, I doubt if the tribe would want a white man buried anywhere on their reservation, even if he had been taking care of their kids for many years.

As soon as I enter the cafeteria, I spot Clara. She's eating a sandwich at the same table we ate at after the philosophy class.

I hurry to join her, and before I can even apologize for being late, she says, "I got you a sandwich. Same as last time. Okay?"

As I unwrap the sandwich, I say, "How much was it? I'll pay you back."

She waves away that idea. "No need. Have you been at the library reading that philosophy book all this time?"

"Yes. Well, actually, I had some other research to do."

She says, "Is that right? What kind of research?"

I guess she's wondering what kind of library research a person would be doing in his first week as a college student.

"Oh, just learning about . . . uh, murder mysteries."

"Murder mysteries? Why, are you thinking about writing one?"

"You mean am I writing a murder mystery novel?"

"Yeah. Why else would you be researching them?"

"Well, I might write a murder mystery. What do you think?"

"You bet. I love murder mysteries. Tell me about it. What kind of detective? And who gets murdered?"

"Oh, I'm not sure. I'm just getting started."

"Okay, let's think about it. Last semester, I took a creative writing class on how to write a novel. Got an A in it, so maybe I can help you. Here's what I learned in that class. First off, you should make the detective be like yourself. That way you don't have to make up what they call the *voice* of the character. Make him a young man, just out of the Army. Hey, maybe he couldn't find a job after he got out, so he decides to start a detective business."

"Well, I guess that could work."

"And then comes the murder. Every murder mystery has to start pretty quick with the murder. What's the murder going to be?"

"Well, I was thinking of uh, finding a body out in the desert. Like I said, I grew up in the desert."

"Great. Make the setting a place you know. Is the body a young person or old?"

"Uh, I was thinking maybe it should be an old man."

"Okay, good. Young detective gets hired to find out who killed some old man. They told him where to find the body."

"Uh, I was thinking he might find the body himself."

"Okay. Yeah, that could work. He could get a tip about a dead man in the desert, and he goes out to find him."

I'm not sure where she's going with this, but I decide to play along. She may give me some good ideas about how to find the real killer. "Okay, what kind of tip?"

She waves away my question. "Doesn't matter. We can work that out later. Okay, let's say he does find the body. It would be best if he doesn't know who the victim is. Then that becomes part of the detective's job, to figure out who the old man is, and why somebody killed him. Now, how shall we say he died?"

"Well, in the murder mystery books I read today, a lot of them died from what they call blunt force trauma. To the head."

"Good. And your detective doesn't find the club or whatever it was that killed the old man. The murder weapon. So he has to figure that out too."

I can tell she's thinking about it as she goes back to eating her sandwich, so I start eating mine too.

She looks up and snaps her fingers. "I have it. Most murders are related to money. The old man turns out to be a rich man, an important figure in the community. But he made some enemies getting all that money, So plenty of people might want him dead. Your detective's job isn't going to be easy. He's got to investigate all the suspects. By the way, how long has the old man been dead? That will be another important clue."

"Uh, I'm not sure."

"Okay, he'll have to figure that out too." She glances at her watch. "But right now, I've gotta get a move on. Another class. Taking a heavy load this semester, like I said before. Why don't you go back to the library and see it you can find any books about how to tell how long someone's been dead."

I don't want to tip her off that I've already done that, so I just say, "Oh, right."

She quickly finishes her sandwich, and then she picks up her books. She leans down close to my ear and whispers, "This is gonna be fun, Murph. I think we'll like doing things together."

She hurries away, leaving me to wonder what she meant by that last statement. Is she just liking the idea of creating a murder mystery novel, or is it because she wants to do something with me? I don't want to get my hopes up, so I just finish eating my sandwich and head for the bus stop. As I walk, the more I like the idea of playing along with Clara's plan for us to write a murder mystery together. Not only would I get to spend more time with her, but she might actually be able to help me solve Father Saul's murder. And there I go again, hoping she wants to be more than friends. I like her, a lot, but maybe I shouldn't be thinking of anything more.

Chapter Eighteen

While I wait for the bus, I'm still thinking about Clara.

But then, I tell myself to stop thinking about possibilities that might never happen, and get back to thinking about what I learned reading those murder mystery novels. One of the main things they taught me was that the detective needs clues. So, how does he get clues? Often, he gets them by questioning people. But I don't have anybody to question. Nobody even knows Father Saul is dead.

But in those murder mysteries, the detective often questions the last person to see the victim alive, and I do know who that is. Jimmy said Father Saul was alive when they left to go fishing, and when they got back, he was gone. But now I know he wasn't gone, he was dead. And he was buried in the desert. I wonder how long Jimmy and Brent were away fishing? Overnight? Longer? I should ask Jimmy that. Now that I'm here at the university, I wonder how close the apartment is where Jimmy is staying.

I pull the note he gave me out of my pocket and look at the address. Of course I don't recognize the street name; I've never been in this town before. But if it's close by, I should go there and talk to him. He was in a big hurry when we met on the street in Mesa, maybe if I can talk to him when he's got more time, he might remember more about the day Father Saul went missing.

But how can I find this address? Maybe if I go back on campus, I can ask somebody. Or maybe I can find a city map.

I go back to the student union. I'm looking around for somebody to ask, when I notice a map on a large bulletin board. It marks the locations of off-campus student housing opportunities. Luckily, one of the apartment buildings listed is the same address Jimmy wrote on his note. I'm glad to see that it's only a dozen blocks south of campus. I think I can walk that far, despite my aching legs. I memorize the map and start walking south.

When I get to the address on Jimmy's note, I see that it's a one-story building next to a small swimming pool. But there are four apartments. All Jimmy wrote down was the address. There's no way to know which apartment he's staying in, so I guess I'll have to check each apartment.

I knock on the door of the first apartment, and a young guy in undershorts and a T-shirt with a picture of a car on it opens the door. He says, "Yah?"

"Uh, is Jimmy here?"

"Jimmy who?" The guy yawns and scratches the back of his neck.

I wonder if I woke him up.

I realize I don't know Jimmy's last name. At the orphanage, we never knew any of each other's last names. Maybe Father Saul wanted it that way so we would feel like equals. I say, "Actually, I don't know his last name, but I went to school with him. Over in Mesa." I point over my shoulder with my thumb. I show the guy Jimmy's note. "He said he's been sleeping on somebody's couch here."

The guy looks at the note, and then turns to look at his couch. I can see that the room is a mess, and the couch is littered with books and empty candy bar wrappers. It doesn't look like anybody has been sleeping there. The guy turns back to me. "No, nobody sleepin' on my couch."

"Oh, sorry to have bothered you. Do you remember anybody named Jimmy staying in this apartment building?"

"Nope, but I haven't lived here too long. Try next door."

I do try the next apartment, and after the young guy opens the door, I explain the situation to him. He looks at the note and nods. "Yeah, there was a guy named Jimmy stayin' next door. An Indian? Skinny? Bout this tall?" He holds up his hand.

"Yes, that's him," I say.

"Yeah, he was staying next door for a while, but it's been quite a while since he left. Before the new guy moved in. Jimmy just up and left. I heard he never did pay any of the apartment rent like he was supposed to."

I thank him and head back toward campus. Why did Jimmy write down that address when he hadn't lived there for a long time? Didn't he want me to find him?

By the time I get back to the campus bus stop, I'm still trying to figure it out. The only possible explanation is that Jimmy didn't want me to find him. Why not? Did he write down an old address all the way over here in Tempe, hoping I wouldn't go that far to find him? Did he suspect I'd be coming back to him with more questions about Father Saul's disappearance? In those murder mystery novels I read, people were often disappearing just as the detective tried to find them and question them.

Does it mean I should consider Jimmy a suspect? No, there's no reason Jimmy would want to kill Father Saul. And I'm sure I know him well enough to be sure he would never do something like that. Jimmy was always a kind of scattered boy, but he's actually a very gentle person. I never saw him ever once get into a fight.

There must be some other reason Jimmy didn't want to talk to me anymore. Maybe he doesn't have the kind of fond memories of the orphanage I have, and he doesn't want to even talk about it. After all, he was still there when it was falling apart. And It seemed like he's been having a hard time since leaving it.

As I get on the bus and take a seat in the back, I'm thinking there is one thing for sure, solving a murder is not as easy as those detective novels make it sound.

Chapter Nineteen

Back at the orphanage, I find Cody with hammer in hand, trying to do some minor fixing up of the loose boards in the schoolroom. He's trying hard, but he's not very good at it.

As soon as I walk in, he turns to ask me where I've been for so long.

I say, "I didn't want to wake you this morning, Cody. I had to go to the university library to do some reading."

"Well, I was getting worried. Did you take Blackie with you. He's gone too."

"No, I didn't see Blackie when I woke up this morning. But that's the way he is. He never stays around for long."

"Does it mean he's gone for good? Won't we ever see him again?"

"I'm sure we will. As long as he's still alive, he'll be back sooner or later."

Cody seems upset by my words. "Alive? You think he might be dead?"

"Well, he is getting old. But he's a survivor. As long as he doesn't run into a pack of coyotes out there somewhere, or a mountain lion, he'll be back"

Now Cody seems even more upset. "Coyotes? I hear them howling out there in the desert almost every night. Maybe we should go look for him."

I shake my head. "Blackie isn't a house dog He's a desert dog, as much as those coyotes are. I used to wonder how he survived out there, but after all these years, he must have some kind of agreement with the wild critters."

"Agreement?"

"I know it seems strange. After all, Blackie isn't a very large dog. We boys used to speculate about it all the time, and sometimes we'd even go out looking for him. Our best guess was that he has other houses to go to."

"Other homes?"

"Yes. He probably has an established route, as if he knows which set of humans will always have food waiting for him. They all probably think he's their dog."

Cody doesn't seem all that happy with my explanation.

But then he cheers up. "You said you went to the library to read. What'd you find out?"

"I read a book for coroners about dead bodies. From what I read, Father Saul might have only been dead for a few months. Maybe he was killed not long before you found this place."

"No kiddin'? He was buried out there when I was out explorin'? I'm sure glad I didn't find him before you got here."

"I also read some other books, Cody. Murder mysteries. But about the only thing I learned from them is that solving a murder mystery is hard."

"Okay, but we have to solve it, don't we?"

"I don't think there's much either one of us can do. Like I said before, sooner or later, we're going to have to turn it over to the police."

Cody shakes his head. "No, no, no. We can't do that. I keep tellin' ya that'd get me in big trouble, and it'd get you kicked out of here."

"I don't see why you'd have to get in trouble. I wouldn't even need to tell them you were the one who found him. I'd just say I found him."

Cody shakes his head again. "That's no good either. The police might think you did it."

"No, I was in an Army hospital at the time he died."

"Well then, they'd think it was somebody from the tribe. It'd mess everything up."

"But Cody, what if it was somebody from the tribe? Shouldn't they be brought to justice?"

Cody stares off into the distance. Then, he says, "How would that help? Father Saul would still be dead."

"That's true. In some of the books I looked through at the library, that kind of reasoning was stated by some of the detectives in the stories. But I think there are two issues we have to think about. First, there is the idea that if somebody kills a fellow human being and gets away with it, what's to keep him from doing it again? And before you say that probably wouldn't happen in this case, what about the idea of justice? In some of the books I read, there was often a detective who didn't much care about the person who got killed. In fact, sometimes the detective thought the victim deserved it. But the detective still thought the killer shouldn't be allowed to get away with it."

"Is that what you think, Murph? That they shouldn't get away with it?"

I have to think seriously about his question. I do feel angry and upset that Father Saul had to die like that. So am I really trying to play detective and solve his murder, or am I only out for revenge?

Cody says, "What are you thinking about, Murph?"

"I'm thinking about your question. And the answer is that I'm not sure how I feel about it. But I do feel we need to find out who the killer is. Then, we'll know better what needs to be done about it."

"Okay, but we can't let the police get involved. Besides, I bet they wouldn't be able to figure it out either. So, it would just get us in trouble for no reason."

"Now, Cody, we don't know how good the local police are at solving crimes."

"I do. I hear some in the tribe talkin' about 'em. One guy said the local cops couldn't find their own ass with both hands."

I'm still deciding if I want to tell Cody that I was also wondering if the local police would be any better at solving the murder than we might be, when he says, "Besides, I bet they wouldn't even wanna do anything about a supposed murder out on the res. The tribe doesn't want 'em around, and I've heard the cops feel the same. They don't care what happens on this res. They'd just say it's Indian business."

"Even so, Cody, I'm not sure we can figure it out our-selves."

"Hey, why don't I do some asking around at the bingo hall? See what I can find out?"

"I don't think that's a very good idea, Cody. If the killer hears you've been asking questions about Father Saul, you could put yourself in danger."

"Okay, then why don't you come in and do the asking? Tell them you used to live around here when you were a kid, and you're wondering what happened to the priest that ran the orphanage out here."

"I could do that, Cody. But would anybody talk to me, an outsider?"

Cody thinks about that. Then, he says, "I have it. They need to get to know you so you aren't an outsider. How about if you start coming in to play bingo? Until they get to know you."

"That might work. But I don't have any money. It'll have to wait until I get my discharge check from the Army."

"No, you could start tonight. I'll give you the money. You could play bingo. I'll show you how. You could act like you're just gettin' to know me. Then, I could introduce you to the others. Tell them you just got out of the Army, and you're a student at the university."

"I'd probably just lose all your money, Cody."

"That don't matter. It'd be funny. Players giving me their money and you giving it back to the tribe. How about it?"

"Actually, it doesn't sound like a bad plan, Cody. In some of those books I read, the detective asked questions and watched to see how people reacted."

"Oh boy! Now we're gettin' somewhere."

"Hold on, Cody. Are you sure you can pull this off? Can you really act like you just met me. Are you that good an actor?"

Cody grins. "You bet I am. You should see the actin' I do pretendin' to like all those crazy people so they'll give me big tips."

"Okay, but you have to promise me you'll be very careful. We don't want anybody to figure out we've already found Father Saul's body."

"Right, right. I'll let you do the askin'. I'll just tip you off who to talk to. We'll start at tonight's bingo game. Now lets get a piece of paper out, and I'll fill you in how it all works."

Chapter Twenty

At the time Cody told me the bingo games start, I take the roundabout route through the desert so I can go into reservation property from the main entrance as if I'm coming from the bus stop. The bingo hall is fairly large, but it looks like it was thrown up quickly. The sign over the entrance that says "BINGO" seems to have been hand-painted with a paintbrush.

I hesitate before going into the building. I need to get into the right frame of mind to be the kind of detective I read about in those murder mystery books. Mainly, I think I just need to focus. I need to watch every little detail, looking for any sort of clue. But no sooner do I have that thought than I realize I probably don't actually know how to go about doing it. I'm no detective. Besides, what kind of clues am I likely to get in a bingo game? Oh well, I guess I've got to do something. Cody is expecting me, so I might as well go ahead and do it. But I do need to be careful and keep on reminding myself that there may be a murderer in there.

I go into the building and stay just inside the door to look the place over. There's nothing in the building except a lot of long tables with lots of chairs mostly already filled with players. There's a bingo game underway. A middle-aged Pima man is standing at the front of the room, and he's spinning a metal cage filled with numbered ping pong balls. As the guy spins the cage, every so often, one of the ping pong balls falls out into a tray. He picks it up, looks at it, then speaks into a microphone, "Under the G, forty-seven."

The players heads all go down, looking to see if they have that number on their bingo cards.

I begin to worry that somebody might notice me standing here watching, so I do what Cody told me to do and go to the table where they sell the bingo cards. Using some of Cody's money, I buy two cards.

I look around for Cody and spot him at the far end of the hall. He nods to me slightly, and as planned, he touches an empty chair and walks away. The chair he's picked for me is in the corner, away from most of the other players. I hurry to that chair and sit down.

As I wait for the next bingo game to start, I look the place over, trying to notice everything. The most obvious thing is that all of the bingo players are intensely focused on finding the called numbers on their bingo cards. I see why it takes so much concentration: most of them are playing at least four cards at once. The players are all sitting close to each other, and they often comment about the numbers as they are drawn, things like, "Damn, only missed me by one," or "I should have got a card with a six on it. He's calling B-6 every time."

It gives the room an odd repeated sound pattern, very quiet as everybody waits for the next number to be drawn, and then widespread murmuring right afterwards.

I look around the room. There's a refreshments table run by a Pima woman. It looks like she's selling food and soft drinks. That must be where Cody gets the food he brings back for us. Does he pretend to buy it for bingo players and then hide it somewhere? Or does that woman give it to him?

The most noticeable thing in the room is the four Pima men standing against the wall on the far side of the hall. Are they the ones in charge? They seem to be keeping a close eye on everyone. I guess they're the watchers. But what are they looking for? Trouble? One of them, a short stout man in a dark suit, catches me looking at him. I quickly turn away. Did that make him suspicious of me? I need to be more careful. Maybe he was already watching me. But why would he be watching me out of all the players in the room?

I look over the crowd and see I'm much younger than any of the other players. In fact, they're mostly elderly people. Maybe this isn't going to work. I think I stand out too much here to be a good spy. Maybe I should just get out of here before anybody starts asking me what I'm doing here.

The bingo announcer says it's time for a new game, and then Cody is suddenly there standing next to me. He says, "Hi there, mister. Your first time here?" He says it fairly loud. He obviously wants the other players to hear his words.

I say, "Yep. Thought I'd check it out. But I don't even know how to play."

"No problem," he says. "I'll help you." He points to a bowl of dried beans that's on the table in front of me. "Whenever a number is called that you have on your card, you put a bean on that number. If you get them all in a row, up and down or across, you raise your hand and yell out bingo!" He nods toward the four Pima men standing against the far wall. "One of those men will come to check your card and you'll win the bucks for that game."

"Okay," I say. "I get it."

As the caller goes back to spinning the metal cage, Cody hurries away to help other players. As he previously told me, his job is mainly getting drinks or food for the players because they don't want to leave their cards for even a moment, but he also seems to be helping some of the very old people.

I watch him take some money from an elderly man and hurry to a booth at the back of the hall. A burly, tough-looking man with a pockmarked face is inside the booth. That must be Cody's father. I can see why Cody would be afraid of him; he looks mean, and he already seems to be drunk. I wonder if he drinks up all the booze profits. Why would the tribe let him get away with that? Is he some kind of tribe elder? Or does he have something to hold over them? Now that could be a clue; he might know something about Father Saul's murder. On the other hand, what I learned from reading all those murder mystery books is to not jump to conclusions: the first suspect is never the real killer. But maybe that's only the way it works in books. Maybe in real life, the most likely suspect really is the killer.

I'm not marking some of the numbers called, but that doesn't matter; I don't want to win any bingos anyhow. No use calling even more attention to myself.

Cody comes back and loudly says, "How're ya doin', sir?"

I whisper, "I can't get much information just sitting here. Sooner or later, I'll need to talk to people. Ask them questions."

He points at my bingo cards, as if he's giving me bingo advice. "Well, you can't. Someone already asked if I knew you. He thought you were pretty young to be in here playing bingo. I told him I'd never seen you in here before."

I look at my bingo cards and point to a number, as if I'm asking about it. I say, "Maybe this isn't going to work. I didn't realize almost all of the players would be elderly."

Cody looks up at the number caller and then points at one of my bingo cards, as if he's reminding me to put a dried bean on that number. After I do it, he says right out loud, "How about a beer, mister. Maybe that'll help your luck."

I whisper, "I don't drink."

"Never?"

"I tried it a few times in Vietnam, just to fit in, but I didn't like it all that much."

"Okay then, I'll just bring you a can of beer. That way, they won't be able to tell if you're drinking it or not."

He hurries away, and I go back to pretending to play the bingo game, still only marking an occasional number.

That game ends before Cody comes back with the can of beer. He puts it down in front of me and hurries away. Good. We wouldn't want anybody to notice that he's spending too much time with me.

One of the watchers comes from his place on the far wall. He goes to the player that called bingo and reads out the numbers. The bingo is verified by the number-caller, and the watcher pays the player, in cash. A disappointed murmur comes from the crowd as they clear their cards. They're jabbering about the game that just completed, most of them complaining about how close they came that time. It makes me wonder if that's the appeal of the game—if you play enough cards, you at least come close to winning every time.

The announcer says the new game will start soon. Even the players who didn't win seem excited.

No wonder the tribe is making so much money off these bingo games. Lots of money coming in, and only one winner at a time means not much money going out.

"No luck so far?"

I turn to see who spoke to me. It's the watcher from the far wall, the man in the dark suit who was watching me earlier.

I quickly clear the beans off of my two cards and shake my head. "No. Guess I'm not so lucky at this game."

"Your first time?"

"Oh, yeah it is."

"Didn't think I'd seen you in here before. Young guys your age are usually out woopin' it up somewhere else."

"Well, I didn't have anything else to do tonight, so I thought I'd check it out."

"You live around here?"

"No, I'm a student over at the university."

He looks surprised. "And you came all the way over here?"

Looks like he isn't going for my just-happened-by story. Instead of keeping a low profile, I'm making him even more suspicious. Thinking fast, I say, "Actually, I'm looking for a part-time job. I was hoping . . . "

"On this reservation?"

"Well, you never know. Looks like you've got a going bingo business here. I thought maybe you could use some help."

He shakes his head. "Only Native Americans can work in gambling. That's the rule."

"Well, that's me. Half anyhow."

"You're half Native American?"

"Don't I look it?"

He looks me over closely. "Maybe. Where you from?"

I'd better not tell him I was at the orphanage, and the only other place I've been in my life besides Vietnam was when I did my basic training in Oklahoma. I know I'd better not hesitate, so I quickly say, "Oklahoma."

"Oklahoma? Is that right? Which tribe?"

I shrug. "Not sure about that. I got adopted out. When I was a baby. But I was told my mother was from a reservation that was southwest of Oklahoma City."

"So, you're from Oklahoma, but you're a student here in Arizona? Why's that?"

"To tell you the truth, after the Army said they'd pay for me to go to college, I figured why not go somewhere warmer."

"You were in the Army?"

"Yes. Just got out."

"Lucky you didn't get sent to Vietnam."

"Well, actually, I did."

"Really? And you came back in one piece?"

"Sort of one piece."

"You got wounded?"

"Yes, but I'm okay now."

He stares at me for a long moment. "The Army pays for you to go to school, but you're looking for a job."

"They only pay my tuition. Nothing to live on."

He again stares at me for a few moments, then says, "Maybe we can find something for you after all. What's your name?"

"Murph."

"Okay, Murph, can you come back tomorrow morning?"

I say, "Sure." But then I remember tomorrow morning is the next meeting of my philosophy class. "Actually, I have a class in the morning. But I can come back in the afternoon."

"I'm going to be gone tomorrow afternoon. Do you have a class the next morning?"

"No, sir."

"All right. Come see me then. My name's Bob."

I say, "Okay," and as he walks away, I figure this is a good time to get out of here. Now that I've lucked into a much better way to learn more about this reservation, I'd better make sure Cody doesn't accidentally reveal that he knows me.

After I walk back to the orphanage, I go into the classroom where it's a bit cooler. I realize I didn't learn much at the bingo game, but I did learn that all the employees are Pimas. The ones in charge were the males. The only woman I saw was the one manning the food table. The place was pretty busy with bingo players, but none of the players were Pima. Maybe they're not allowed to play. Or maybe they're too smart, knowing the odds against winning.

With that many bingo players, it's obvious the tribe is making quite a bit of money. It does make it seem possible that Father Saul's death could have had something to do with his being against bingo as illegal gambling. In those murder mystery novels I looked through at the library, the murder almost always had something to do with money. Either that or love. Or revenge.

Chapter Twenty-One

By the time Cody returns, it's getting dark, and I'm again keeping myself busy doing a few repairs on the building. He hurries in loaded down with food and says, "Come on, Murph. Lets eat. I got lots of good stuff."

"I saw there was a refreshments table, Cody. Did you buy all that food?"

"Naw. After the last bingo session of the day, they give it all away to the us workers. I make sure I get my share."

"Don't they ever get suspicious about why you grab so much?"

"Maybe. But they probably figure I'm gonna sell it." He grins. "They know me."

"So they think you're a little conniver."

He grins again. "I suppose so. But so what. The food would just go to waste if I don't grab it."

"Wait a minute, Cody. Are you telling me there are no people on the reservation that need food?"

He shakes his head. "Naw. Used to be, but not anymore. Everybody gets their cut of the bingo money, and free food too. And with bingo growin' all the time, everybody's gettin' new trailers and all kinds of other shit."

It's all starting to make sense. With so much money coming in, protecting it would be what the murder mystery books call motive. I can see why they wouldn't want an outsider like Father Saul messing things up. It also means that if I really do get a part-time job working at the reservation, and if the killer is there, I'd better make sure I don't let it slip that I had anything to do with the orphanage and Father Saul.

Cody is staring at me. "You're always thinking, Murph. What're you thinkin' about now?"

"Oh, just thinking it all through. By the way, a man named Bob said he might be able to get me a part-time job."

That makes Cody smile. He says, "Yeah, I saw you talkin' to him. Good goin'. He's one of the top dogs on the res."

"Is that right? What kind of job do you think he might offer me?"

Cody shrugs. "Who knows. With all the bingo money coming in, they can probably afford to hire just about anybody they want."

"Well, maybe. I'm going back to meet with him day after tomorrow."

"Great. Then you'll be an insider. Just what we need. Hey, let's eat I'm starvin'."

At the big table, Cody makes a big show of spreading out all the food. I can't believe how much he brought this time. He'd better be careful or someone might start to wonder what he's doing taking away so much food.

Even though I'm suddenly feeling very hungry, I leave him there spreading out the food and go out to make sure Father Saul's temporary grave hasn't been disturbed. I'm determined to check it at least once every day. After reading all those murder mysteries, I have the strongest feeling that the killer will eventually come back.

At the gravesite, I look over the area carefully. There's no sign anybody has been there, so I go back in.

"Where'd you go?" asks Cody.

"Out to check on Father Saul's grave. I'm going to keep a close eye on the gravesite to see if anybody has been out there. The killer might come back."

"Oh, yeah. "Good idea. Have you had any more ideas about who might have killed him?"

"Well, I'm still thinking about what I read at the university library. In those books, the murder victim usually gets himself involved in something that leads to his murder. But Father Saul wasn't involved in anything except trying his best to teach us boys here in the orphanage."

Cody frowns at that. "Yeah, but this place is still on reservation property, even though it's way out in the desert. Sometimes when I'm walking back from the bingo hall, I see ATV tracks. Now that people in the tribe are buying things like new ATVs, they're a lot more likely to come out this far, so who knows who might have come out here to make trouble for the priest."

"But Cody, even back when I was living here, the tribe knew Father Saul was out here running this orphanage. And back then, he was already making trouble about the idea of them getting into gambling."

"Yeah, I'm sure the tribe leaders knew about Father Saul, but maybe not the ones that aren't the leaders. I'm thinkin' about the hunter types. They parked their house trailers quite a ways away from the tribal headquarters building, and they're not interested in tribal matters as long as they get their monthly checks. They might not have known about this orphanage until they came across it on their ATVs."

"Are you saying those types might not have liked the idea of this orphanage being out here?"

"Who knows. I don't know much about them. They keep to themselves. But I do know their reputations. Tough guys. The tribal police get called out to their trailers all the time. Wife beating and such."

We go back to eating, but as I eat, I'm thinking about those he called "tough guys." I guess I'm going to have to add them to my list of suspects. If I had such a list, that is.

"You know, Cody, I think we should make up a list of suspects."

He looks up at me. "Okay. Who should we start with?"

"I'm not sure. Who would you put on such a list?"

He looks down at his food and doesn't respond. I have the feeling he's thinking about his father, and I can see why he'd feel that way. He's already undoubtedly put his father on a list of the tough guys in the tribe. I've seen with my own eyes how badly he beat his own son.

And Cody told me he also used to beat his mother, and that's why she left. But should he really be on our list of suspects? Why would he want to kill Father Saul? But maybe I shouldn't discount Cody's opinion. "All right, Cody, tell me straight out. Who would you put on such a list? Not that you think the person actually did it, but who should we consider might be capable of such a thing?"

Cody frowns. "Are you trying to get me to say my father should be on our list?"

"Well, should he?"

Cody looks away. "I wouldn't put it past him. When he gets drunk, he can be a real bastard He . . . "

Cody looks away again. I can tell this conversation is making him really uncomfortable. Even though he doesn't like the way his father treats him when he gets drunk, he probably doesn't want to think of his own father as a murderer. "Okay, Cody. Let's leave him off the list for now. But we'll add those other guys, the ones you called 'tough guys.' Now who else."

"The leaders."

"The tribal leaders?"

"Yeah. They got a good thing going with all those bingo games. And the slot machines in the back room too."

"So, you're saying money was the motive?"

"Sure Why not?"

"But they could have just forced him off the reservation, so why kill him?"

Cody shrugs and looks away. "I wish Blackie hadn't run away. I miss him."

"I'm sure you do, Cody. But don't worry. He'll be back."

Cody says, "I sure hope so," and goes back to eating.

As I watch him eat, I can see that despite his bravado, Cody is actually a very sad little boy. I shouldn't push him to tell me more about the tribe. I'll be able to learn enough on my own if I really do get a job at the bingo games.

For the rest of the day, I busy myself around the orphanage and don't talk to Cody any more about solving the murder. But I do continue to think about it. In those books I read at the library, the detective always came up with a list of suspects, and in several of the stories, the detective gathered all of the suspects together in one room to announce who the killer was. Now that I'm involved in trying to solve a murder myself, I can see how contrived and unlikely that is. But if that isn't the right approach, what is? Maybe tomorrow after class, Clara will have come up with some useful ideas for the murder mystery we're supposedly writing. If not, I'm stuck.

Chapter Twenty-Two

As usual, I wake up early, and I again decide to head for the university without waking Cody. Before it's time for my philosophy class this morning, I want to go back to the library and finish reading the first chapters of the philosophy book Professor Schmidt assigned. Yesterday, I got so involved in reading murder mysteries and talking to Clara about it, I never did finish the assigned reading.

Before I head for the bus stop, I slip into the classroom to grab a stub of a pencil and the partially-used notebook so I can take some notes in class.

As usual, this early in the morning, the bus is nearly empty, only a Mexican couple with a young boy and a young girl in the back. All of them are dressed for work, even the kids. The family must be citrus pickers, and it appears that even the youngest children help. They are as tanned as their parents, and they too are carrying gloves. The parents don't look at me, but the children do. I wonder what they would have thought if they saw me when I was their age. I think about what their hard lives must be like compared to the relatively easy, and fun, life I had growing up in Father Saul's orphanage.

Father Saul taught us that the citrus season is year round, but lemons and grapefruits have two harvest times, spring and fall. I wonder how he knew so much about that. Did he grow up in Arizona? That thought makes me realize how little any of us knew about him except as our teacher. Could something from a past in Arizona have something to do with his murder? If so, I'll probably never find out who did it.

When I get to the university library, I know I have to stop thinking about Father Saul's murder and concentrate on philosophy, at least for the time being. I go straight to the reserve desk and check out the assigned philosophy textbook.

Soon, I'm completely engrossed in the book, not so much in the details of what the early philosophers thought, but in the way they thought. They didn't have our modern advantage of a body of science to draw from; they just had to draw conclusions from pure thought and observations of the world around them. From that, they asked questions. For example, the Sophists thought about concepts that might seem basic to all life, such as *what is truth*? They questioned whether it is even possible for humans to find any real truths, and that led them to think about laws and who has the right to make laws. They asked from where do laws derive their authority?

That thought stops my reading. Am I making up my own law by not telling the local authorities about finding Father Saul's body? Am I protecting myself and Cody from their laws. Am I denying their legal authority over us? That leads to the natural follow-on thought that if we can defy one law, what's to keep us from defying other laws? Or all laws? Maybe I should ask Professor Schmidt that question.

No, he's a smart person; it might lead him to suspect that I'm not referring to a hypothetical situation. Still, if I asked the question in exactly the right way . . .

The next part of the book is about the Stoics, the Epicureans, and the Skeptics. Together, they took philosophy to a new level. They said we should think of philosophy in terms of ourselves. They wanted to nail down what makes a man "wise."

The Stoics wanted to live life according to nature, while the Epicureans focused on how to live a life as pleasantly as possible. The Skeptics, on the other hand, took a whole different approach: they said we should live indifferently. They felt that if we expected nothing, we would never be disappointed.

That's an interesting idea, but only in the abstract. How could anyone actually live like that? Maybe when I meet Clara for lunch, I should ask her what she thinks. I should ask her if they talk about things like that in her psychology classes.

All of a sudden, that makes me worry that I might be late for my own class. I was late to class the last time, and I could tell the professor wasn't happy about that. I don't have a watch, so I'd better go find a clock to make sure I'm not late again.

I turn in the reserved book and go to find a clock. When I do, I'm happy that I looked because it's almost time for the class. In fact, I'm going to have to hurry.

As I hurry out of the library, I'm thinking about how fast the time can pass when you're deeply engrossed in something. Maybe I should ask Professor Schmidt about that too. Or is that the realm of psychology? The more I learn, the more questions about psychology I have for Clara. Maybe next semester, I should take a psychology class.

When I get to the classroom, I'm relieved to see that despite the fact that it's just about time for the class to start, I'm still the first one to arrive. I take a seat closer to the front of the room; the professor will see that this time I do have a notebook, and I am taking notes. Maybe I should ask some questions to show I've already been reading the reserved textbook. Or would that be taken as showing off? I don't know what's normal in a college class. The fact is, I've got a lot to learn about how to be a college student.

The other students straggle in, mostly talking about sports and their other classes. Am I the only student taking just one class? Well, there's nothing I can do about that now, and it's probably good that I'm only taking one class; it's not only my first time being a college student, it's my first time being a student in any kind of school other than the teaching sessions Father Saul gave us at the orphanage. Besides, I need time to work in order to make money. Maybe the other students don't need to do that.

Clara is one of the last students to arrive, but the seats on both sides of me are already taken, so she has to sit on the other side of the big table. She nods at me and smiles, so I nod and smile back. She doesn't seem to mind the other students noticing that she's smiling at me. Maybe that means something too.

When Professor Schmidt arrives, he says he hopes we've all read at least the first part of our textbook. I nod and think about saying something out loud. But I'd better not: the other students would for sure think I'm showing off. Besides, they're all nodding too, even though I didn't see one of them in the library's reserved reading room. Either they purchased the book for themselves, or they're trying to convince the professor they did.

He says, "Okay, if you all read the textbook, you now know the history of philosophy starts with the early Greek thinkers. Now why do you suppose the book starts there? Why is it important that we learn about what those men thought when it was so long ago?" He looks around the room, but nobody is responding. I raise my hand, but only a little.

The professor spots it and says, "All right, Mister . . . ?"

"Murphy. But everybody calls me Murph."

"All right, Mister everybody-calls-me-Murph, tell us what you think. Why *do* we need to read anything about what those men were writing so long ago?"

"Uh, well, the history of philosophy book you assigned said it was less important what they said than how they thought."

"Okay. And what was so important about how they thought?"

Is he trying to test me to find out if I really read the reserved books. The answer seems obvious. I quietly say, "What was important was that they demonstrated a new way of thinking about the world around us, a way of thinking not dictated by orthodoxy."

The professor smiles and turns to the rest of the class. "Exactly right. They were not simply observing the world around then, they trying to figure out some of the basics of *why*. That is the essence of philosophy—what is and why it is. And they wanted to come up with their own answers, not the answers that were given to them by those in authority."

He goes on, explaining how from those first philosophical musings, the modern field of philosophy grew.

I glance at the other students to see if they're irritated at me for getting so much of the professor's attention, but they're all busy writing down notes. I realize I should be doing the same thing and get busy scribbling a sort of outline of what he's lecturing about, along with a few notes of my own. It's a technique I learned while listening to Father Saul's lectures, because sometimes he'd get very passionate about what he was trying to teach us and start talking very fast.

The professor continues, also talking pretty fast. He's summarizing some of the main points the early philosophical thinkers were making. The most interesting thing to me is when he gets to a concept he describes as "observation precedes reflection." He says, "Even though those early philosophers didn't have the tools to fully understand the nature of the world around them, they observed what they could and then reflected on what hidden truths might lie behind what they were seeing. The Sophists, for example, were public teachers who questioned whether we can ever arrive at true truth. They suggested that perception of truth may simply be one man's truth. As a result, they questioned from where truths, and laws, derive their authority. They even questioned such supposed basic concepts as justice."

The professor pauses, looking at each of us. All of the other students are still taking notes, but I'm finished, so I just nod to show him I understand.

He goes on to say that despite the modern era we live in, and despite all the modern sophisticated tools we have to help us better understand the world around us, such questions are just as valid today.

As the professor goes on to talk about how the Stoics emphasized the necessity of living according to nature, and how they tried to pin down the character of a wise man, I am, of course, still hung up on his previous words about justice and from where laws derive their authority. Again, I have to ask myself if I have any right to make up my own law about not reporting finding a murdered man buried in the desert.

Is my search for Father Saul's killer only a need to satisfy my own personal concept of justice?

My attention is brought back to Professor Schmidt's lecture when he says he will conclude by moving past the foundations established by the early Greek philosophers and move on to a brief discussion of philosophy in the Middle Ages. He says, "In the Middle Ages, there arose a distinction between those things that are supposedly known through theology, and that which can be known through reason. Many of the thinkers in that period, at least the ones that wrote texts that lasted, were theologists. But modern philosophy grew out of a gradual trend away from submission of thought to the authority of the church and toward definitions of reality based more on individual observations."

Although I hadn't really thought about it before, all my learning came from Father Saul who was, after all, a theologist. I don't remember much of what he taught us being based on his theological beliefs, but what Professor Schmidt is saying has got me thinking back on it. Father Saul certainly did want to protect us from what he called "the outside world." Was that because he believed the outside world was filled with evil, at least his Catholic version of evil? Or did he not want us to be exposed to any version of truth other than his own?

On the other hand, he usually forced boys to leave the orphanage when they turned eighteen. Did he believe he had instilled enough of his philosophy in them so that even as adults, they would be prepared to deal with those outside forces?

My attention is brought back when I notice the other students are standing up. I didn't even realize Professor Schmidt had concluded his lecture and is leaving the room. I hope I didn't miss too much.

Chapter Twenty-Three

I see that Clara is waiting for me by the door. I quickly close up my notebook and hurry to meet her.

She says, "I notice you were taking notes this time. Did you hear something all that interesting?"

I shrug. "I'm just trying to learn how to be a good student."

As we walk to the cafeteria, she seems less impressed by the idea that philosophy in the Middle Ages was dominated by religious philosophers like Saint Thomas Aquinas than by how little science they knew back then. She laughs and says, "Heck, you could be known as a good physician simply by bleeding the patient and having them drink a lot of hot water."

I'm beginning to think she has a tendency to be a bit cynical about things, but I decide to just keep quiet and let her talk.

She continues talking about Professor Schmidt's lecture as we walk, and when we arrive at the cafeteria, she again takes charge and chooses the same sandwich for me as the last time. I notice that she now put both of our sandwiches on one tray. I guess that means she thinks I'm now willing to share with her. I hadn't thought about that, but I am. In fact, I like it.

As soon as we sit down, she says, "I've been thinking about your murder mystery novel, Murph. Did you do what I said and look up how to tell how long a body's been dead?"

"Yes. I found a book for coroners that said there are three stages. In the first stage—"

"Good. You could have your detective read the same book. We'll decide later how long the victim has been dead. We shouldn't nail down too many of those kinds of details in advance. A lot of murder mystery novels are written backwards, with the writer having decided all the facts in advance. But my writing teacher disagreed. He said that approach takes all the creativity out of it. It keeps you from coming across interesting new ideas as you write, as you get to know the protagonist. I like his approach better, so let's just go forward and worry about the details later."

She's unwrapping her sandwich as she thinks, so I remain silent and do the same.

After she gets the first bite of sandwich in her mouth, she leans across the table closer to me and says, "Now, I bet there'd be a lot of clues related to the body he finds in the desert. He should inspect the body carefully."

I say, "Oh, okay. What should I . . . that is, he, should be looking for?"

She chuckles. "It's okay to imagine you're the detective in the story. In fact, that's what the writing professor told us to do. 'Put yourself in the story,' he said. 'Get right into it. Imagine the scene. Imagine what it would feel like and then give your protagonist those exact feelings.'" She takes another big bite of her sandwich.

As I start eating my sandwich, I think about her words. The only part of Father Saul's body I saw was part of his face and the terrible wound on the back of his head. What other clues could the rest of his body tell me? Maybe I should dig up the rest of him and examine his body.

But the more I think about doing that, the less I like the idea. After all, I'm not a real detective, and the body is that of a man I loved.

"For example, you said you wanted the victim to have died of blunt force trauma. It's important for you to decide what part of his head got hit."

"I was thinking the back of his head. That would tell us if he turned his back on the killer."

Clara nods and stares at me. "Good thinking, Murph. It could indicate he knew the killer. Maybe trusted him."

"Yes. That's what I was thinking."

"I think you're going to be good at this, Murph. You're a clear thinker. My writing professor said objective thinking about your own writing was the hardest part of writing a good story. That and having a good imagination."

"Well, I don't know about that, but I do like to think about things. Maybe too much."

She takes another hurried bite of her sandwich and shakes her head. "No such thing as thinking too much. The biggest problem in this world is people not thinking, just doing. That's what I'm learning in my psych classes. People just do whatever they've been rewarded for doing all their lives. Especially what they got rewarded for when they were young."

"Really? Is psychology that simple?"

"Actually, it's not simple at all. How you learn to act is like evolution; it happens in tiny steps, over long periods of time."

"I've never studied any psychology, so I guess I'll have to take your word for that."

"That's another mistake. Taking other people's word for things. My advice is to don't believe me. Take some psych classes for yourself."

"Actually, from meeting you, I was already thinking about doing that."

She just says, "Hmm," and continues eating.

As I watch Clara eat, I'm wondering what she's thinking about. She's an interesting person, full of advice, but at the same time telling me not to take her advice.

She stuffs the rest of her sandwich into her mouth and stands up. "Gotta go," she mumbles, her mouth still full. "'Nother class. Same time here tomorrow?"

"Okay," I say, but then I remember I might have a job now at the reservation bingo hall. "But I'm not sure. I'm trying to find a part-time job."

She hesitates. "Thought you said the military was paying you to go to school."

"Yes, but they only pay tuition. I'm looking for a part-time job to pay for living expenses."

"Speaking of living expenses, where are you living?"

"I uh . . . right now, I'm staying with a friend. Over in Mesa."

"That's a bit of a trip every day."

"I take the bus."

"Okay. I'd let you stay with me, but like I said, I'm still living with my parents." She shrugs. "I know. Embarrassing. A grown up person still living with her parents. But same as you, I can't afford to rent an apartment on my own. And I don't like living with other girls. You know how silly they can be."

I'm about to tell her the truth, that I have no idea how girls can be. But before I can figure out how to explain to her that she's the only girl I've ever known, other than the nurses at the hospital, she says, "Maybe you and I should find a cheap apartment together. Share expenses. That way we could study together."

Her words take my breath away, but before I can figure out how to react to that, she says, "But we can talk about that later. Gotta get to class. I'll eat here at this time every day. Join me if it works out with your new job."

And then she's gone. I'm left with my half eaten sandwich and my mind reeling. Did she really just ask me to move in with her? How would that work?

Oh well, I'd better not let my mind start thinking about that kind of thing. I'm so new at this living in the real world and dealing with people, I'd better not start imagining things that might never happen.

Chapter Twenty-Four

The next morning, as soon as I wake up, I remember I'm supposed to go meet with Bob at the bingo hall. I wonder what time he expects me?

I go into Cody's hideaway to ask him what time the morning bingo sessions starts, but he's not there. I guess that means he's already gone to the bingo hall. I'd better hike over there too, in case they all get going early.

I take the roundabout route, and as soon as I go inside the bingo hall, I can see there's no bingo game going on. But they do seem to be getting ready for one. The food table woman is there setting out a variety of foods, and the man who sells the bingo cards is laying out his wares.

I go up to the food table woman and ask her where I would find Bob.

She looks at me in a suspicious way, and says, "Why do you want to see him?"

"Oh, he told me to meet him here today."

She hesitates and then points toward a door in the far wall. "He's in his office."

I say, "Okay, should I just go in?"

But she's already gone back to laying out the food.

I go to the door she indicated and knock on it. When there's no answer, I open it a crack and see it leads to a narrow hallway. I go in, and the first door I come to, oddly, has a sliding panel in it. I knock and immediately, the panel slides back. A man's face confronts me. "Yeah, whada ya want?" His voice is gruff.

I say, "I'm looking for Bob. He told me to come here to talk to him today."

"Down the hall," the gruff voice says and slams shut the sliding panel.

I turn away and go on down the hallway. What was going on in that room? In the brief moment the sliding panel was open, I saw a row of ornate box-like things against a wall, and there was a man standing in front of each of them. Cody told me there were slot machines in this building. Is that what those things were? I'll have to ask Cody more about that.

I lightly tap on the next door, and a voice says, "It's open."

I go in and find Bob sitting at a cluttered desk. He looks up at me.

I say, "Excuse me, sir. You said to come by this morning. Uh, about a job? Maybe?"

He doesn't smile, but he does seem to recognize me. "Oh yeah, the Oklahoma kid who wanted to go somewhere warm."

I smile. "That's me. I like the desert. Uh, I mean, I'm already liking Arizona."

"So, how was your university class?"

For a split second, I almost tell him it was good, and that my lunch with a smart girl from the class was even better, but then I realize that would sound weird, so I just say," Fine. It's my first semester, but I'm liking it."

"Remind me. What are you studying?"

"Philosophy."

"Philosophy? I don't even know what a philosophy class would be about."

"Well, it's mainly just—"

"But I guess it won't help you work here. On the other hand, getting smarter is always good. Most of the kids on this res are about as dumb as . . . well, I guess you don't care about that, do you? You want a job, right?"

"Yes, sir."

He gets up from his desk. "Well, let's see what we can find for you. Understand we can only pay you a dollar an hour."

"That's fine sir."

He leads me out of his office into the main bingo room. He leads me to the food-table woman I had spoken to earlier.

He points at me with his thumb. "Ellen, this is . . . " He turns to me. "Remind me. What was your name again?"

"Murph."

He turns back to the woman. "Murph is from some reservation over in Oklahoma. Find something for him to do."

He turns back to me. "She'll keep you busy. You do whatever she tells you to do, okay?"

"Okay. Sure. Thank you, sir."

He walks away, and I turn back to the woman named Ellen. She's very short, but stout, and she has a hard look about her. She's sizing me up.

"So Bob offered you a job. An outsider. Haven't seen him do that before."

I smile to be friendly, but she just continues to stare at me.

"I noticed you kept on calling him sir and you're wearing them military-type pants. You been in the military?"

"Yes, ma'am."

"Vietnam?"

"Yes, ma'am."

"Wounded?"

"Yes, ma'am."

"Now I know why Bob hired you. Figures. He lost his son over there. Well, let's show you the ropes."

She leads me to a door in the side wall. She opens it and I see that it's a large closet mostly full of metal folding chairs that are hanging from some kind of rack. There are also quite a few tables with folding legs stacked up against one wall.

She says, "We leave most of the tables and chairs already set up out in the hall, but on weekends, if too many players show up, you'll have to get in here and bring more out."

"Okay."

She says, "I don't know what else Bob want's you to do. Just whatever comes up I guess. Once the players start showing up, you stand over there." She points to the side wall where I saw the group of Pima men, the watchers, standing during the bingo games yesterday.

"You'll be keeping an eye on things. Bob will usually be there too. He'll tell you what to watch out for. Are you tough?"

"Tough?"

"Yeah. Can you handle yourself in a fight?"

"I suppose I could. If necessary. Will there be fights?"

"Not likely. Most of the players are old timers. But they can get . . . uh, troublesome. Bob or one of the others can usually handle it. You'll only help if they ask for it, okay?"

"Okay. Sure."

She glances at her watch. "We've got about twenty minutes before we open the doors. You might as well just sit down and wait until then. You'll be on your feet all the time once the games starts."

She goes back to setting out the food, so I do as she suggested and sit down. But I stay close by in case she needs me to do anything.

So, she thinks Bob hired me, an outsider, because he lost his son in Vietnam. I wonder where his son was stationed. I know I never met him because I never met anyone over there that looked like a Pima Indian. Interesting that she asked me if I was tough. Is that a hint that the men that work here in the bingo hall have to be tough? Could that somehow be related to why Father Saul got killed? Probably not, but I need to keep my eyes open to everything. I need to remember why I'm here—to look for clues.

When the doors are opened and the players begin to stream in, I see that like the last time I was here, they're mostly old folks. They rush to buy their bingo cards, and once again, I see that a lot of them are buying four or even six cards. I still don't understand how these old folks can keep track of that many cards.

Once they've staked out their favorite places at the tables, a lot of the women hurry to the food table, and a lot of the men dash to the booze booth at the back of the room where they either buy beer or else tiny bottles of what I assume is hard liquor, along with different kinds of soda to mix it with.

The same group of men I saw before, the watchers, take their places along the side wall.

I go join them, but I stand a few feet away. They all look at me, and a few of them whisper something to each other. Apparently nobody told them I'd be joining them.

Bob arrives and nods to me. I guess that told the others I have the right to be here with them, because they immediately stop staring at me.

The bingo games begin when the man at the front of the room speaks into a silver microphone to announce the first game will be a "standard" game, plus a "four corners."

He starts turning the metal cage and soon a ping-pong ball falls out. He picks it up and speaks into the microphone, "Under the G, 52."

Same as the last time I was here, that triggers many of the players starting to talk, saying things like, "Got it," or "Can't hit 'em all unless you hit the first one." Others grumble. With each new number called, the sound in the room becomes a steady drone of comments about luck, good or bad.

After what seems like too short a time, B-14 is called and an elderly man with white hair stands up and shouts, "Bingo."

One of the watchers next to me goes to the old man and begins calling out numbers, all of them "under the B." The man at the microphone at the front of the room confirms each of them until it gets to "B four." At that one, he says, "Hold your cards everyone. I don't have a B four."

A general groan goes up from the crowd. Someone yells, "Damn it. I already cleared my card."

The old man who yelled bingo argues loudly: "You called B four. I heard you."

The man at the microphone says, "No, I didn't call B four. We need to move on."

But the old man won't give up. "You did too. I heard it, and I marked it."

The bingo caller says. "I'm looking right at my tray, and there is no ball with a four on it. I do have a fourteen. That must be what you heard."

"No, I know you said four, not fourteen," says the old man. "It's your mistake. You said the wrong number, so I get the money."

He won't back down, and the other players are getting upset. Someone yells, "Sit down, old man, and let us get back to the game."

But the man won't sit down. He continues to argue.

Then, Bob is next to me. He says, "Here's your chance to show us what you can do, Murph. Take care of it."

Confused, I say, "How?"

"That's up to you. If he won't stop causing trouble, you'll have to throw him out." He gives my shoulder a little push, so I go to the old man. I'm not sure what the other players would think if I do what Bob said and throw the man out. I decide to try to reason with him. I say, "Excuse me, sir. I can understand how you might have thought he said four when he actually said fourteen."

The man stares at me, and then he moves closer, his fists balled up. Does this old guy think he can take me on? I sure wouldn't want that. It would be really disruptive, and I doubt if that's what Bob wants.

I say, "Now be reasonable, sir, nobody else marked a B four did they?" Several of the other players nod in agreement. Some point to their bingo cards.

"Oh yeah! So you say." The old fellow is practically growling now. "You Indians think you can get us to come in here so you can take our money. Here's what I think. I think you can take your bingo game and shove it where the sun don't—"

Suddenly, Cody is there. He touches the man's shoulder. "Now listen, Oscar," he says softly. "You like coming here and playin', don't ya? You wouldn't wanna get banned, now would ya?" He turns to me. "I can see how this mistake could have happened, can't you, sir?"

I can see that Cody wants me to go along with what he's up to, so I say, "Sure."

Cody says, "How 'bout we say drinks are on the house tonight for good old Oscar here. He's a regular."

Cody is still nodding at me to let me know I should go along with him, so I say, "Sure, drinks on the house seems like a good compromise. Okay with you, sir?"

The old man seems to immediately soften, so Cody gently sits him down and says, "I know just what kind of drink you'd like, Oscar. How about I get it for you? Cody points at me. "And like this nice man here said, it's on the house? Hey, if we let the game go on, maybe you'll still hit a bingo, right?"

That seems to cheer the old man up, so I turn to the number caller and signal for him to go on with the game.

There is a smattering of applause from the other players, and I'm left suspecting that it might be for me. I guess they couldn't hear what Cody was saying, so they credit me with solving the situation.

As the game goes on, I go back to my place at the wall and find Bob grinning at me. He says, "Well done, Murph. I think you're going to fit in fine here."

He also seems to be giving me the credit for solving the situation, just as the players did. I think about telling him it was actually Cody that came up with the solution, but it's too late; he's already gone back into his office. I guess he just came out to see how I did on my first day on the job.

One of the other watchers, a short man with bulging upper arms that look like the arms of some of the weight lifters I met in Vietnam, edges closer to me and whispers, "Good goin', kid. But keep your eye on that old guy. We know him. He's a trouble-maker. Somethin' wrong with his brain, and he blames it on everybody but himself."

I nod to show him I understand, but I whisper, "Something wrong with his brain? Like what?"

"Some of the real old ones are like that. Can't remember what you told 'em two seconds ago. And a few of 'em are like that guy. Get pissed off about it."

I nod again to show him I understand, but it strikes me that I've never been around any older people. Except for Father Saul, of course. But his brain was top notch. We could never put anything over on him, and he hardly ever got really angry. Oh sure, he'd get irritated if we didn't do what he said, but that was mostly because he was worried about us. Anyhow, I should use this opportunity to learn more about old people. In fact, now that I'm going to be out in the "real world," I should pay attention to what the different kinds of people are. I'm beginning to think there are "types," just like there was in Vietnam, except now I'm sure I'll see a lot more variety. It's something I bet Clara, the psych major, can help me with.

The rest of the bingo session goes more smoothly, and I get to watch Cody in action. He never stops moving, hustling drinks for people, and also food sometimes. If he gets tips on each of those trips, I can see how he makes so much money. He has a way with these old people, often talking to them cheerfully about the games, and never missing a chance to congratulate anyone who hits a bingo. I can see that they all really like him.

After the last bingo game is over, I go to Ellen to ask if there's anything I can do to help her. She says no, but she says after I see Bob, I should come back to get some of the leftover food. I say, "I'm supposed to go see Bob?"

She seems surprised at my question. "Of course. Don't you want to get paid?"

"Oh, right," I say.

I turn and see that the other watchers that were with me at the wall are lined up outside the door that leads to Bob's office. I wait my turn, and when the last of them leaves, I go in.

He seems happy to see me. "I know I told you a dollar an hour, but after what you did today, I think you're due a little bonus." He hands me a wad of bills.

I say, "Thank you, and I'm again tempted to give Cody some of the credit, but then I worry that I might give away some of Cody's money-making tricks.

I start to leave, but Bob calls me back. He says, "You told me you were wounded in Vietnam. Bad?"

"Yes, petty bad. An explosion. I spent a long time in hospitals."

My words seem to make him sad. "My son got killed over there. Never did find out what happened. You didn't happen to meet him, did you?"

"No, sir. But then I wasn't there very long before I got wounded. And I was out in a pretty isolated firebase."

He nods. "All right, son, I understand. See you tomorrow morning? I assume you don't have a class on Sunday, do you?"

"No, sir. I'll be here. The same time?"

"Yep. We hold a morning session even on Sundays. Even more people show up. Can I count on you?"

"Yes, sir. I'll be here."

"I don't want to cut in on your study time, but we can use you whenever you can make it."

"Yes, sir, I'll be here whenever I can."

After Bob dismisses me, I go back to Ellen's food table where I find Cody stocking up. He greets me with a smile and says he want's to shake the hand of the man who "solved the problem."

I start to protest, but he cuts me off with, "My name's Cody, mister. What's your name?"

"Uh, everybody calls me Murph."

"Glad to have you on the team, Murph. Here, grab some food."

Ellen is putting away the packaged food, but she pushes some of the fresh food across the table toward me.

I say, "Well, I wouldn't want to take it if anybody else in the tribe can use it."

She waves off my protest. "We make sure everybody gets all they need. This food will just go to waste if somebody doesn't eat it."

Cody wraps up some of the rolls and cheese in a napkin and hands it to me. "Go ahead. Like Ellen said, it'll just go to waste."

He takes more of the food, wrapping it in napkins before stuffing it into his pockets. Then, he turns back to me. "Haven't seen you around here before. New in town?"

"Actually, I'm a student at the university. Over in Tempe."

He grins. "Ah, a starving student. Here take more food." As he shoves more food into my hands, I check to see how Ellen is taking all this in. She's busy packing up her stuff, but I'm sure she's been listening to Cody's little act.

After he forces me to take as much food as I can carry, he says, "I 'spect you'll be heading for the bus stop. Wait up. I'll walk with ya."

Outside the building, Cody slaps me on the back. "Hey, man, that worked out bettern we coulda expected. Now everybody knows you, and they'll think we just met. Even more important, they all saw that Bob likes ya, and if Bob likes ya, you're in."

"He gave me credit for what you did."

Cody looks startled. "I hope you didn't tell him I had anything to do with it."

"I wanted to, but I thought it might get you in trouble. I'm not sure you should be giving away free liquor to the customers."

"Aw, my old man is totally in charge of the booze, and he's not about to give away anything. I had to pay for it."

I stop walking to look at him. "You paid for it out of your own pocket?"

"No big deal. A few drinks. It was worth it. It got everything set up for us, just like we wanted."

I pull the bills that Bob paid me out of my pocket and hold them out to Cody. "I got paid in cash today. Here, you take it. You gave me money, and it's the least I can do for you bailing me out back there."

Cody keeps walking and waves off the money. "Naw. Keep it. I got a lotta tips today. Besides, you need money until you get your check from the Army."

I can see he's not willing to take my money, so I put it back in my pocket and keep walking. "Okay, Cody. But why are we walking to the bus stop?"

"Can't let them know you're staying right here on the res. Soon as we're outta sight, we'll cut across the desert and head back for the orphanage."

I do as he says and keep walking. I'm impressed at what a little conniver Cody is. He seems to not only know all the bingo players, but he also seems to know how the tribal power structure works. And he's right about what we now have set up. I have a job at the bingo games, and I'm on the good side of the boss, which means I could be on my way to becoming an insider. Still, I'm feeling a bit worried about how they might react if they find out I've been living out at the old orphanage. And what if they find out I was once a student of Father Saul's?

Chapter Twenty-Five

Once we're back at the orphanage, Cody suggests we take out all the food and have a feast right now. I consider heading for the university to see Clara, but it's already too late to meet her at the cafeteria at our usual time. I'm not sure she's there on weekends anyhow, so I agree to take time to eat.

I am hungry, but first I want to check on Father Saul's burying place to be sure nobody has been there.

I find the area completely undisturbed, so I head back inside the building where I find Cody sitting at the big table, already eating. "Hungry," he says, his mouth full. "All that runnin' drinks and food hustlin' makes me work up an appetite. C'mon, dig in."

As I busy myself making a couple of cheese sandwiches, Cody is jabbering about our encounter with the old white-haired man. "Old Oscar *is* quite a troublemaker, but he's not so bad once ya get to know him. He'll get mad at ya, then ten seconds later, he'll forget it ever happened."

"Yes, I got that feeling from Bob."

"You talked to Bob, eh. That's good. Best to get on his good side. There's a committee that runs things, but everybody knows Bob is the real boss."

"Well, Cody, if I'm on his good side, it's because of how you handled that situation."

Cody chuckles. "Yeah. Nobody'd think a kid could control an old fart like Oscar, but I know his secret. He's hooked on booze, but he can't afford it. He's livin' on social security and blows most of it on bingo. Sometimes, I bring him a drink or two and pay for it out of my tips. He really appreciates it, but then he forgets and accuses me of stealing his money."

"Seems like you're a real insider there at the bingo hall, like you know everybody."

Cody shrugs and says, "Yep. Been doin' it for a long time. At first they didn't like me hangin' around, but when they tried to kick me out, Ellen stepped in and said I was good for business. Said the players didn't like gettin' up and leavin' their bingo cards untended, so having somebody to run errands for 'em was actually something the tribe should have thought of. And besides, they don't have to pay me." Cody chuckles again. "Them being cheapskates is what keeps me in there. All they care about is makin' money."

"Has the tribe making so much money from bingo changed things?"

"Are you kiddin'? It's turning the whole res around. Used to be one of the poorest reservations around, but now bingo is bringing in a ton of bucks. And then there is the money those slot machines in the back room bring in. I don't know how much it is all told, but I can guarantee you that nobody is goin' hungry any-more. Ya see new TV antennas on all the trailer roofs, and new trucks and new ATVs are poppin' up all over the place."

I finish my first sandwich and start on my second while I think about that. "What you're saying is that they might kill to protect all that money coming in."

Cody points in the direction of the bingo hall. "Are you kiddin'? You saw it yourself. The bingo games and them slot machines are bringin' in more players all the time. I think it's hardly started. Gamblin' on the res is gonna get big. I can feel it."

Chapter Twenty-Six

The next morning, I walk with Cody toward the bingo hall, but when we get close, I let him go on ahead to make sure nobody sees us arriving together.

When I get there, I see that the first game is not yet underway, but people are already lined up to buy their bingo cards. Cody waves to me. He's already busy making his rounds, talking to the players, being friendly to all of them.

Ellen is busy selling food, so I guess I'm supposed to do what I did last time, take my place at the wall with the other watchers.

This time, when I join them, they hardly seem to notice. Except for Bob; he smiles at me and give me a little greeting wave.

That gets the attention of the watcher I think of as "Mr. Muscles." He glances at me, not smiling. He must be a weight lifter, like the men in my unit in Vietnam that spent amazing amounts of time lifting up heavy stuff or else doing pull-ups on the steel bar they'd placed between two tall piles of sandbags.

Once the first game gets underway, the watchers take turns going to check the cards of each winner. Bob doesn't ask me to do that, so I don't have much to do other than watch the players. The games are repetitive, but watching the players is kind of interesting. As soon as each new game gets underway, the players all put their heads down, closely looking at their cards and putting beans on any number that's called. And then, once somebody calls out a bingo, there is always the same kind of murmuring. It makes for a kind of timed group sound that I'm starting to get used to.

Many of the players complain about losing, but they don't really seem all that unhappy about it. Whether they're winning or not, these old folks seem to be enjoying themselves.

I get the feeling that for many of them, this is the highlight of their day. Maybe it's not so bad that the tribe is making money off of them.

Between games, I count the number of players. It's almost a hundred. With only one winner per game, it means the tribe must be making quite a bit of money from these games. And except for me, the "employees" are all members of the tribe. I assume the tribe owns the building, so they don't have to pay any rent. That again leads to the thought that the money from these bingo games could be becoming so much a part of their existence, that some of them might be willing to kill anyone who threatened it.

The session is almost over when a woman causes a ruckus. When one of the watchers tells her she doesn't really have a winning bingo she stands up and starts yelling about how "you Indians" are cheating us and "we're not gonna stand for it anymore." She's obviously drunk, and she seems to be trying to get others to join her protest. Most of the other players are just sitting quietly, but a few are grumbling about her always disrupting things so the game can't go on. A nearby woman stands up and yells at her to shut up and sit down so the game can go on. The two of them get nose to nose, looking as if they might actually get into a physical fight. Quickly, the guy I think of as Mr. Muscles goes to intervene. Is that his main job? To step in when there's trouble?

I glance at Bob, and he waves for me to go get involved. I guess he wants me to try to calm the situation like a I did with the old man the last time. Have I become the resolver?

By the time I get there, Mr. Muscles is holding back the drunk women, and Cody is trying to calm the situation down by offering her free drinks. But it's not working, She's yells, "You dirty redskins take our money, and then you don't pay us even when we win."

It's obvious she's drunk, so I'm surprised she doesn't seem to be much interested in Cody's offer of free drinks. I go to her side and try to talk to her reasonably, telling her that maybe the number just called might have sounded a lot like the number she was hoping for.

But she's not paying much attention to me. She seems more interested in going after the woman who told her to sit down and be quiet.

I again try to reason with her by again reminding her that a winner is paid after every game.

She finally seems to hear me and turns to face me. She says, "Oh yeah, who are you? I ain't seen you in here before."

"No, ma'am. I just started working here."

"Just started working here? Does that mean you're not a member of this stupid tribe? Are you even an Indian?"

"I'm just a college student, ma'am. But that's not important. What is important is that you're holding up the game. The number caller says he didn't call the number you thought he did. Listen, how about if you—"

But I don't get the chance to continue trying to calm her down because a man jumps up and gets right in my face. He yells at me, "You calling her a liar, kid?"

He's an older man, but he's a big fellow. Despite his age, he's acting very threatening.

I look at Muscles for help, but he's busy holding apart the two troublesome women who are still trying to go after each other.

I keep my focus back on the man who's threatening me. He's getting red in the face, as if he's barely able to hold himself back from attacking me. I sure don't want to get hit in the face in front of all these people. They've all gone silent, watching and waiting to see what's going to happen. I remember getting hit in the face once. It was in Vietnam. It happened soon after I got posted to the firebase in the jungle. A guy just walked up to me and hit me. I didn't go down, but it sent me reeling backwards. I didn't have any experience at that kind of serious fighting. The only fights we kids got into at the orphanage were mostly just pushing and wrestling. As a result, when that guy in Vietnam hit me, I didn't know how to respond. I didn't want to get into a fight and make enemies on my first day at the firebase, so I just backed off, and that was the end of it.

Afterwards, a couple of the other guys took pity on me and told me not to worry about it. They said it was just that guy's way, showing every newcomer that he's the top dog.

One of them advised me that if it ever happened again, just watch the guy's eyes so I'd know in advance when the blow is coming. The other guy disagreed: he said no, watch the hands, always watch their hands.

From then on, I took both types of advice: in the few other fights I got into over there, I found that never taking my eyes off of the other guy's eyes *and* his hands worked pretty well. I was always able to either duck the blow or else divert it to the degree that I never again got hit very hard. I was able to keep any fights from escalating, and that gave me the chance to talk my way out of it.

As a result, I'm not afraid of this old fellow. But I sure wouldn't want to hurt him.

I try explaining that I didn't mean to insult the woman.

But that doesn't calm him down. He's still ready for a fight.

When it comes, I'm ready for it. He winds up and takes a swing at me, but by keeping my eyes on his hands, I see the blow coming, and I'm able to easily avoid it. But the old fellow swings so hard, he falls forward, and I have to catch him. His attempt to hit me was so comical, some of the other players laugh. That makes the old guy so mad, he winds up to try again to hit me.

But this time, Mr. Muscles is there. He grabs the guy by the back of his collar and starts pushing him toward the exit. Apparently, he's the one who decides when it's time to throw out a troublemaker. The poor old guy, clearly overpowered by Mr. Muscles, can't keep himself from being pushed right out of the building. He complains all the way that he should have been able to stay and finish the bingo game, but it's no use; Mr. Muscles pushes him out of the building, and then stands guard at the door to make sure he doesn't get back in.

When that's over, the troublesome woman turns her attention back on me. "You aren't one of these damn redskins, are you? So why are you helping them cheat us white people?"

I say, "Listen, ma'am, nobody is trying to cheat you. Look at your bingo card. You only need one more number for a bingo, I-20. Why don't you sit down and let young Cody here go get you a fresh drink. On the house. Maybe one of the next numbers called will be the number you need. You never know."

She stares at me for a long moment, then finally she sits down. I stay by her side, waiting for Cody to bring the free drink.

The number caller says he's going to resume. He calls out, "I-20."

The woman shrieks out "Bingo," and grabs my arm. "I won, I won. Now don't you go anywhere young man. You're my lucky charm."

I smile and pat her hand. I point toward the far wall. "I'll be right over there, ma'am, wishing you good luck on every game from now on."

One of the other watchers comes to pay her off, and I go back to my place against the wall.

The other Pima men at the wall briefly stare at me, but then a new game starts, and they go back to watching.

Bob smiles at me, nodding his approval. It means I've now had two seeming successes out of two tries at being the resolver. Pretty lucky. Maybe the word will get around and other members of the tribe will now accept me. I hope so because it might mean I can learn more about how things work here. Most important, I might be able to talk to a few of them and find out what they knew about the orphanage, and if anybody had it in for Father Saul.

As I go back to watching the bingo game, I'm wondering if the number caller intentionally called the number that troublesome woman needed. Would he do that just to avoid more trouble? Nobody but him sees what ping-pong ball numbers fall out of his spinning cage, so he actually could call out any number he wants. And as soon as a game is over, he quickly dumps the balls back into the cage, so no one can check to see if every number he called really was dropped.

I guess I'll never know about that one, but from now on, I'm going to watch more closely how the games are run. I don't think they're cheating anybody, but I still think I'd like to know if they ever manipulate the games.

I wonder how many of the players are like that woman? Could a lot of them be harboring prejudice against Indians? I wonder how common that kind of racism is here in Arizona. Funny I never thought about that before. But why would I? I grew up with Indian kids, and the only non-Indian I ever knew was Father Saul. That one guy in Vietnam named me Geronimo, and I guess that was meant to be an insult. But he made up an insulting nickname for everybody.

After the next game is over, Bob comes to get me. He leads me to his office and invites me to sit down in front of his desk. Am I in trouble? Did that woman's words remind him that I'm not a member of his tribe, so he's going to have to get rid of me?

But no, the first words out of his mouth are, "You did a good job out there, son. Did you learn to fight like that in Vietnam?"

I smile and say, "No sir. In Vietnam, I learned how to avoid fights."

He lets out a slight chuckle. "Good plan. We also try to avoid any trouble during the games. I'm glad you understand that. But tell me more about what you did over there. You said you were in the jungle, so you couldn't have met my son. He was up north. Plenty hot up there, according to his letters. The enemy kept on trying to overrun the base he was in. I guess they must have finally succeeded. The Army didn't tell me much. Only that he was dead and that his body would be shipped home soon. They said he could be buried in the big military cemetery out north of Phoenix if I wanted. I liked that idea, so I said yes, and got him the best casket I could afford. But there was no funeral out there. Only me and the employees of the cemetery. I stood out there under a tent with his casket until one of the workers asked me if I wanted to say any words. I couldn't think of anything to say, so I just shook my head, and they took him away."

He stares down at his hands that are folded together as if in prayer, but so tight they are shaking. "They said I could go to his grave after the grave digging machine was done burying him, but I didn't want to think about him being in the ground, so I didn't go."

After he falls silent, I try to think of something to say, but I can't come up with anything that might make him feel any better, so it's probably better to just stay quiet and let him deal with his grief on his own. Finally, I say, "Maybe it would be better if I left."

He looks up at me and holds up one hand. "No, no, stay. Sorry to go quiet on you. It's just that the only memory I have of him was the day he left. I couldn't think of anything to say to him that day either. I just shook his hand and told him to be careful over there. He laughed at that and said I should have thought of that before I made him register for the draft. That upset me. The counsel had all agreed that even though the government didn't have very good records on children that were born at home here on the reservation, we should send all of our young men out to get registered for the draft. It seemed like our patriotic duty. Now, they're all coming back to us in body bags, so why did we do that?"

He again stares down at his desk, but quickly looks up and says, "Did many in your unit get killed?"

"Yes, sir. Actually, all of the men in my patrol group were killed, except for me."

He seems surprised. "All of them? How did you survive?"

"I just about didn't, sir. I was wounded so bad I think the enemy thought I was dead. Or about dead."

He nods and stares at me for several moments before saying, "Well, I'm glad you made it back. And got into college too. I always hoped my son would go to college. He would have been the first one in our family to go. I suppose it's the same for your family too."

"I don't know about that, sir. I was an orphan and never found out who my parents were."

"Oh, that's right. You told me that, didn't you. Sorry. It was an orphanage over in Oklahoma, wasn't it. We have a lot of that here too. Kids get left alone when their parents run off. Or die. Used to be an orphanage here. Out in the desert. Run by a Catholic priest."

"Used to be?"

"Yeah. An old priest took in any of our kids that got abandoned. He was out there for as long as I can remember. His orphanage wasn't sanctioned by the tribe or anything. It was way out in the desert, but it was actually on reservation property. I hear the building is still out there somewhere, but the priest left. I don't know why. The tribal counsel was not all that unhappy when he disappeared because he kept on making trouble about the bingo. He called it illegal gambling."

I try to decide how to respond. I don't want to lie to a man who's being so nice to me, but until I can figure out who killed Father Saul, I'd better just stay quiet about what I know. Still, even though Bob doesn't seem to know anything about Father Saul's disappearance, maybe he has some ideas about it. I say, "Maybe he got run off."

Bob looks at me sharply. "You mean because of the bingo? Naw. The lawyers took care of that. All cleared up now. I guess maybe the old priest just got tired of doing what he was doing. Or maybe he was ill. He was an old guy. All I know about is somebody said he was gone and the orphanage was shut down. To tell you the truth, I wouldn't mind if the Catholics sent somebody to get it going again. Even though some on the tribal council didn't like him running his orphanage on reservation property, I thought he was providing a real service for us. Like I said, kids get abandoned here all the time, and it's a real burden on their extended families to take them in. I liked the old priest. He was an interesting guy. I even slipped him a little money from time to time."

I have a lot more questions, but I decide to hold off seeming too interested. If he ever finds out that I actually grew up in an orphanage here, I don't want him to be any more angry at me than he probably already will be.

I just say, "Yes. I was lucky to find an orphanage to take me in."

Bob says, "Well, I'd better get back to work. I'll pay you now so you can go do your studying."

He opens one of his desk drawers and counts out a few dollar bills. He stops and seems to think about it for a moment, then he adds a few more bills to the pile. "Plus a bonus for doing such a good job." He hands the bills to me.

I take them, but I think about telling him I don't need the bonus, that I was just doing what I thought my job was. I'm beginning to suspect he's paying me extra to make sure I don't have any money problems that might interfere with my studies at the university. And maybe, in some strange way, by my being a college student, I'm taking the place of his lost son. I just say, "Thank you, sir." He doesn't say anything else and seems lost in his thoughts, so I quietly leave the office.

The bingo games are still going on, but I have the feeling by paying me in advance, Bob was telling me I can leave. However, if I just leave, what will the other watchers think? That I'm Bob's pet project? In Army basic training, the guys that got the most harassment from the others were the ones that seemed to be the sergeant's favorite. I don't want to become known as that one, so I go back to my place against the wall. The other watchers look at me briefly, as if wondering why Bob took me into his office. I'm glad I decided to resume my place along the wall. I hope they aren't getting suspicious of me. As far as I know, I'm the first non-member of the tribe to work the bingo games, and that means they probably wonder why I was hired. If I get an opportunity to tell them I was in Vietnam, just as Bob's son was, I should do that.

Luckily, there are no other problem incidents before the afternoon bingo session ends, and the players all seem happy as they file out the exit door.

The other watchers line up at Bob's door to get paid, but since I've already been paid, I figure it's time for me to leave.

But before I can make it to the exit door, I'm intercepted by Cody who reminds me that I can now go to Ellen's food table to get us some of her leftover food.

There aren't as many leftovers this time, but it's more than we will need. I take a little, but Cody loads up, and then we head for the exit.

Chapter Twenty-Seven

As we start our secret roundabout route back to the orphanage, Cody says, "You handled that big guy good, Murph. It was really funny how he tried to take a swing at ya. He almost fell on his ass. You gotta teach me how to fight. It can be part of our lessons."

"It wasn't a big deal, Cody. And besides, fighting isn't ever a good thing. There are other ways to resolve disputes."

"At least tell me your secret, Murph. You had no trouble at all beating that guy. And he was pretty big."

"I didn't beat him, Cody. All I did was make sure he didn't hit me."

"Okay, then tell me how you did that. There must be a trick. I been hit plenty of times."

"Well, I don't want you getting hit, so I will give you one piece of advice. Watch your opponent closely. Especially watch his hands."

"That's it? All you have to do is watch their hands?"

"Well, you also have to duck."

"Oh, right. And then when they're off balance, you get ta hit 'em first, right?"

"No, you just want to keep them from hitting you. Then you talk your way out of it."

"Just talk? Isn't that kinda chicken?"

I wonder if I should even be talking to Cody about something like this. He's a smart kid, but when you're just starting into your teenage years, you're going to be mostly concerned about looking good. I say, "Listen, Cody, I was just answering your question about how I handled that big guy back there at the bingo hall. You said you wanted me to teach you things. What I can teach you is that fighting never solves anything. If you beat somebody in a fight, you'll just make an enemy."

Cody is silent for several seconds, then he says, "Ah hell, they don't like me anyhow. And they're bigger than me. And they stick together."

He's frowning and looking at the ground as we walk. I can tell he doesn't want advice about how to avoid a fight; he was hoping I could tell him how to beat the boys who've been attacking him. I wonder who they are, so I say, "So, some bigger boys have been attacking you. Why?"

"Aw, they think they rule this place. Like I said before, they see me as an outsider. And they don't like it that my dad gets to run the booze business at the bingo hall and how I get to make tips running drinks."

"So, who are they? Are their fathers important members of the tribe?"

"Yeah. And they think that makes them big shots." He turns to look at me. "Not only that, they call my old man a drunk. I can't let them get away with that, can I?"

"Didn't you tell me your father does get drunk?"

"Yeah. He does, and I hate it. But I can't let others say it, can I?"

"I guess it's up to you, Cody. But are you sure you want to fight your father's battles?"

"Ah hell, I don't wanna talk about that anymore. I saw you go into Bob's office. What did he want to talk about?"

"He mostly just wanted to talk about Vietnam."

"Yeah, too bad about his son getting killed over there. You didn't happen to know him, did you?"

"That's what he asked me, too, Cody. But no, I only knew the guys in the unit I was assigned to."

Cody slows his walking and looks at me. "You know, Murph. I don't get that war. Why did we invade somebody else's country in the first place?"

I'm not sure how I should answer him. Thankfully, nobody else has asked me that question, and I wouldn't know how to answer them if they did. I say, "I don't know any more about that than you do, Cody. It's part of the Cold War I guess."

Cody is still looking at me. "Well, you said you were going to teach me stuff. What about that? I know we got involved in a bunch of wars in other places. Europe and all that, but those were world wars. That's what they taught us in school. Vietnam isn't a world war. It's only us there. Why did we invade a little country like that?"

"To tell you the truth, Cody, it wasn't something I ever thought about. I knew our country was at war in Vietnam, and when I got drafted, that's were they sent me."

He's still staring at me. "Is that how the other soldiers felt?"

"I expect so. Actually, nobody talked about it. I didn't even know there were protests about it until I got back here. When I was hitchhiking, an old guy picked me up and told me about that. And then, when I got to the ASU campus, I saw there were protests going on there."

"Really? Are a lot of students protesting?"

"Not all that many, really. But that old man who gave me a ride said protests were going on all over the country."

"Yeah, my old man has a TV, and they were showing protests on the news. I didn't pay that much attention to it, but I guess if they're showing it on the news, it must be a big deal."

I don't know what else to say to Cody about that, so we just walk on in silence. Not being able to answer any of Cody's questions is making me feel a lot less like a teacher. In terms of what goes on in the world, I guess I've always been out of it. At the orphanage, we didn't even have electricity, let alone a TV. And not even a radio, except for the little transistor radio one of the older boys got ahold of somewhere. But he only listened to rock and roll, holding it up to his ear. If there was ever any news on his little radio, I guess he must have just changed the station because I never heard any. After seeing the protesters at the university, Clara did talk about the war a little. She said her parents were in favor of it. She said they thought we had to stop the Communists in Vietnam before they took over the world. I wonder if that's how most Americans see it?

When we finally get to the orphanage, the first thing I do is what I always do, go check to see if anybody has disturbed Father Saul's grave site. I check the ground all around it, and I can't find any footprints or any other indication anybody has been there. And thankfully, it doesn't look like Blackie has been back. As usual, I use a branch off of a shrub to erase my own footprints.

Back at the dorm building, Cody is waiting for me outside. "Well, has anybody been there?"

"Not a sign of anybody. No footprints anyhow. I'm wondering how long we can wait before we call the police."

"No, Murph. Please don't do that. That'd ruin everything. I'll get punished for sure. Maybe even get sent away again."

"Well, sooner or later, we'll have to do it."

"Just wait a little longer. Now that you've got an in at the bingo games, I'm sure you'll figure out who killed him."

"Maybe, maybe not. But I will wait a bit and try to find out more before we call in the police."

"Good. Did you find out anything more today about who might have wanted to kill him?"

"No. I was thinking sure his death could have had something to do with him being so against the tribe getting into gambling, but after talking to Bob, I'm not so sure."

"Oh? Why?"

"Bob actually liked Father Saul being out here. He said the orphanage was proving a great service for the tribe."

"Yeah, maybe, but I know some of the others didn't like him being out here. Not one bit. Because of his being against gambling."

"Yes, I get that. By the way, speaking of gambling, I think I saw the slot machines you were talking about. Are they in a room near Bob's office?"

"Yeah. That's them. Nobody knows how much money they make, but the word is it's a lot. They got the lawyers to get the okay for the bingo games, but I bet they didn't tell the lawyers about those slot machines. Anyhow, come inside. Let's eat. I got the food all laid out."

Inside, it's clear that Cody's made a big deal out of setting the table, and I think he's doing to for my benefit. Interesting. Nobody has ever treated me like that before.

As we eat, Cody again wants to talk about the Vietnam war. I don't have much more to say about it, but I do mention that students at the university are protesting against it, saying it's an illegal war.

"Illegal? What does that mean?"

"I'm not really sure what they mean. All wars start because the leaders say the country has to go to war, so I guess that's what makes it legal."

Cody is wolfing down his food, but he continues to talk, his mouth full. "What about you? How did you end up over there?"

"I got drafted, and that's where they sent me."

"But did you have to go? Couldn't you have said no."

I start eating while I think how to answer him. I guess I might as well tell him he truth. "It's not a matter of saying yes or no, Cody. If you say no, they'll put you in jail. But I never thought about that. I got drafted, and I went where they told me to go."

"But how did they find you to draft you? Did they know you were living out here in this orphanage?"

"That's an interesting issue, Cody. Actually, they had no way of knowing I was in the orphanage. But Father Saul made me go in to the draft board and register, even though he wasn't sure exactly how old I was. When I told them I didn't know for sure how old I was and that I didn't have an actual address so they had no way to contact me, they drafted me and sent me off for basic training right away."

"Wow, you must have been the youngest soldier there."

"No, some of the other soldiers there had volunteered to go into the Army as soon as they turned eighteen. One guy told me he was really only seventeen, but he had lied and said he was eighteen, and they believed him. He said he'd seen the war going on over there in Vietnam on TV and he didn't want to miss out."

Cody has stopped eating and is staring at me. "Really? I hear the older boys in the tribe talking about it, and they mostly talk about how to get out of it."

"Well, I guess they've been hearing about how dangerous it is over there."

"Is it really all that dangerous? For everybody?"

"Well, actually, it's not dangerous for all the soldiers. It takes a lot of soldiers behind the lines to make a war. Somebody has to provide the food and ammunition and service the airplanes. Things like that."

"So, couldn't you have done that?"

"It takes special training, and the only special training I got was physical training and how to handle a rifle."

"So they were training you to be a soldier. To fight."

"I guess that's what they need most, so that's what they trained me for."

"Geez, Murph. If you woulda got killed, I never would have got to meet you. Like Bob's son. I heard he didn't want to go, but his father made him."

I let that sink in. No wonder Bob is so broken up about his son's death. He must blame himself. Jimmy told me they'd all heard I'd been killed. If Father Saul also heard that I wonder if he felt guilty for making me go.

"That got you quiet, Murph. What are you thinking about?"

"I didn't know that about Bob. But with so many being killed, there must be a lot of parents thinking like that now."

"But they keep on saying on TV that we're winning that war. They say we're bombing the hell out of them."

"From the number of planes I saw going over every day, that's probably true. But the word in my unit was that the enemy has started digging tunnels to hide from the bombing. The dirt over there is mostly damp and soft, so it wouldn't be hard for them to dig tunnels and hide. On patrol, we found some tunnels, but there was nobody in them. They must have heard us coming and left. We blew the tunnels up, but I don't think it would have been very hard to re-dig them."

Cody says, "This is great, Murph. I like it when you tell me stuff." But he suddenly stands up and says, "I guess I'd better head back to the bingo hall to get ready for the next session. You going?"

"No, Bob said I should spend the rest of the day studying, so that's what I'll do. I think he's treating me a bit like his lost son. He said he wanted his son to go to college."

"Is that right? I don't think any of the kids from the tribe have gone to college. June is the only one I know about. Mostly the boys just hang around, or else they go into town. They go to the bars, and I hear a lot of 'em get into fights in town. The people in town don't like us. That's what I hear anyhow." He stuffs a little more food into his mouth, and then he hurries toward the door. But then he turns back. "So, what ya gonna study?"

"I'll head back to the university library this afternoon. But right now, I think I'll go for a brief run out in the desert. I'm getting out of shape."

"A run? In those Army boots?"

I chuckle at his question. "I can't tell you how many miles I've run in these boots, Cody. In Basic, we ran and ran and then ran some more in boots. Actually, these boots work pretty well here for running. A lot better than they worked in the Vietnam swamps."

He grabs one more handful of food and says, "Swamps? I'd like to hear more about that later, okay?"

"Okay."

And then he's gone, heading off to the bingo hall.

I go outside and start a slow jog toward the distant mountains. It's still hot, but I don't plan to be gone for long. I need to get to the university library to get caught up on the required reading. And it sure would be great if I just happened run into Clara there.

As soon as I start jogging, I realize how out of shape I am. Not only are my legs hurting, but I'm getting a little bit out of breath. It's a hard reminder of how long I spent in those hospitals, lying down.

It'll take a lot of this kind of slow jogging to get strong again.

I sit down to rest. The desert is quiet, except for the call of a roadrunner. Another bird answers in the distance.

Every time I come out here, I realize how much I missed the desert when I was in Vietnam. Whenever I was on guard duty at night over there, I didn't recognize any of the bird calls. And I was always trying to figure out if the bird calls I was hearing where real bird calls or the enemy signaling to each other. Now, here in the desert that I know so well, with all the familiar sounds and smells, it feels remarkably safe. But is it? After all, somebody killed Father Saul right here in this desert.

But no, this desert is safe. It must have been somebody Father Saul knew. But who? Now that Bob has told me it wasn't the tribe, who could it have been. I guess it could have been some members of the tribe that didn't tell Bob what they were up to. But what could have been their motive?

Now that I know Bob actually liked the orphanage being out here on reservation land, none of it makes any sense. I must be missing something. But what?

Chapter Twenty-Eight

I'd better head for the university to get more of the required reading done. And then I'll go to the cafeteria and hope Clara is there, even though I'm not sure she even comes to the university on weekends.

I jog to the bus stop, and when the bus arrives, a lot of folks are getting off. They all hurry toward the bingo hall, some of them almost at a run. Obviously, Sunday is a big bingo day.

I get on the bus and see that it's entirely empty. That's fine with me. I need to think about what I saw today at the bingo session. It seems that most people like the chance of winning some money almost as much as winning it. Except for a few trouble-makers, everyone seems to enjoy the game, even if they don't win. I think Cody could be right about gambling getting big on the reservation. Father Saul told us about Las Vegas, a town in Nevada, where the whole economy is based on gambling. The problem is, Nevada is the only state that allows gambling. I wonder if Indian reservations could find a way to get in on that kind of gambling. Not likely, but they did get their bingo games legalized by saying state gambling rules don't apply to Indian reservations.

After I get off the bus at the university, I think for a moment about going by the big fountain to see if the anti-war protesters are there, but I quickly discard that idea and head straight for the library.

When I get there, I go to the reserved books section, and I'm happy to see that no one else from my class is there. But I wonder why. Don't the other students think it's important to have read the required books? Or do they come here at night? That doesn't seem likely. Maybe Clara isn't the only one who bought the book. Do they want their own copy so they can get ahead of students like me that can't afford them?

I guess I shouldn't think like that. That's not the reason Clara ordered the book; she just wanted to have it for herself. But maybe the other students are just not bothering to read the assigned reading. Maybe they figure they can just listen in lecture and get all they need.

Who knows? What do I know about being a university student?

I check the textbook out from the reserved desk and pick up reading where I left off, with the Skeptics. It says the Skeptic position was that we only know how things *seem* to us. They saw the only legitimate philosophical problem to be a search for truth, to distinguish between what appears to be true and what is really true. They said if we are to account for the real world, we can only do it in terms of our personal experiences. Life, they said, then becomes a challenge to determine if what we *perceive* is truth, or only the appearance of truth. They suggested that the experiences we perceive through our sense organs may only be a "sign" of actuality, not the "real" reality. They asked, Is the only reality what we can touch?

That makes me stop and think about special knowledge. Like that of scientists. To a scientist, aren't atoms and molecules real, even though they cannot be touched? I guess that means the perception of reality depends on the knowledge of the individual who is doing the perceiving. And what if the scientist explains to an average person that the object he is observing is actually made up of invisible tiny objects? Would that change that person's concept of reality? What if that person doesn't believe the scientist?

In general, it seems like the more an individual learns about the true nature of things, the more that person's definitions of reality will change. Assuming, that is, that the person believes what he is being taught. There may be some individuals who want to hold onto their beliefs at all costs. I turn back to the textbook. It says that is exactly what happened in the early days, when much so-called knowledge was in the hands of religious scholars. They said they were writing facts, but they were actually trying to get people to believe in their version of reality.

That reminds me of something Father Saul taught us. He said Socrates was accused of corrupting the youth of Athens by telling them "the truth." He was sentenced to death, and was forced to kill himself by drinking a cup of poisoned hemlock. I guess that's an extreme example of needing to know, and teach, the truth.

I put down the book again. Did Father Saul have to die for some reason like that? I can't imagine what that could be, but I do know he was determined to teach us "the truth." Is it possible that, as with Socrates, someone so objected to his version of truth, they killed him to silence him?

Chapter Twenty-Nine

"There you are."

It's Clara, standing right next to me, her hands on her hips. She says, "You didn't show up for our lunch meeting. Are you mad at me or something?"

I reach out to touch her arm. "No, of course not, Clara. I had to work. My part time job, remember?"

"Oh, all right then. But next time you can't make our lunch meeting, let me know, okay?"

"Sure. Yes, I will." But as soon as I say it, I don't know how I could do that.

"Now," she says, pointing at the bookshelves, "tell more more about how long it takes for a body to decompose."

"Okay. In the early stage, most of it is going on inside the body. Maggots and other bugs go to work eating up the person's internal organs."

"Ugh. Do I really need all the details?"

"Oh, sorry. But you asked."

"Just kidding. Go on."

"Okay. During the first few days, there's what they call skin slippage. And hair loss. After that, the skin begins to get leathery."

"Leathery?"

"That was the term in the book. Maybe it's how the skin feels."

"Good. So, our detective would need to feel the victim's skin. That would show that he's smart, and he knows about dead bodies."

"Oh, right. Anyhow, the final phase is skeletonization. I guess that term explains itself."

"Okay. Good work, Murph. I'd say we'd better have our victim not be dead all that long. Otherwise, the clues might all be gone and the killer will have gotten away clean."

"Right. Uh, I was thinking maybe a few months."

"A few months? Why not a few days."

"I'm not sure why I came up with that. Maybe I wanted to make it harder for the detective to solve."

"Good point. We need the reader to know how smart our detective is. Now, we need to start thinking about clues and suspects. But for now, maybe we should go to the cafeteria. It seems to be our traditional talking place. Are you hungry?"

"Not really. But I guess I could go for a piece of that good apple pie made by the secret little lady in the back room."

She smiles at my remembering her joke, and after I turn the book in, she takes my hand as we walk.

This hand holding is something entirely new for me. It's another of my "first-time" experiences, and as usual, I don't know what to make of it. Is this something friends do, or does it mean more than that? How I wish I still had Father Saul here to ask him those kinds of questions.

But then, I have to laugh at myself. Me, just back from war, asking an unmarried Catholic priest advice on how to be with a girl?

Still, I'm sure he'd have some advice. Would it be to proceed with caution? Or would he say to go for it? You could never tell with Father Saul; sometimes, if you asked him for advice, he'd come up with the most surprising answers. I sure do miss him.

"Thinking again?"

"Uh, sorry, Clara. Yes, I was thinking."

"Thinking about me, I hope."

"Actually, Clara, I was. I was thinking—"

"No, don't tell me. Let me imagine they were good thoughts, better thoughts than you could possibly really think about me."

"Of course they were good thoughts. How could anybody ever think anything but good thoughts about you?"

She laughs and squeezes my hand. "Boy, do I ever have the wool pulled over your eyes."

I squeeze her hand back and say, "Pull wool over my eyes. I haven't heard that one before."

We've arrived at the Union Building, and she shakes her head, as if in frustration. But she's still smiling, and she's still holding my hand. "Of course you haven't heard that saying. You're the original left-behind-the-door boy. I keep forgetting you were raised under a rock. Anyhow, let's go in. Allow me to open the door for you, sir."

She opens the Union Building door for me and bows as I go in.

She's in quite a playful mood today. It's a side of her I haven't seen before, but I think I like it.

We get in the food line, and I only pick up a piece of pie. Clara does the same, but then she tells me she's a little bit hungry, so she tells me to go on while she heads back to get a sandwich.

I pay for my piece of pie and take it to our usual little table.

She soon joins me, and I see that she got one of our usual packaged cheese sandwiches, but that's all.

I say, "No apple pie?"

"I'm trying to cut down." She pats her stomach and laughs.

I assume it was a joke relating to how skinny both of us are, so I say, "Yeah, we both need to cut down."

She grins at that and says, "Besides, I was hoping you'd give me a bite of yours."

"Sure, but I'll go get you a piece if you want."

I start to get up, but she reaches out to touch my hand. "Why, that's very gallant of you, Mister Murph, but can't I just share with you? You don't have any cooties, do you?" She's grinning at me, so I know it was some kind of joke. Or is she laughing at me?

"I don't know what a cootie is, Clara, but I don't think I have any." I push the plate of pie toward her. "Here. Sure we can share."

"Why thank you, Mister Murph." She uses my fork to take a small bit of pie. "My, that is downright good, Mister Murph. How downright kind of y'all."

She's using some kind of fakey accent. Southern maybe? Some of the guys in Vietnam had a Southern accent that was sort of like that.

But now, she's no longer smiling as she says, "Sorry, Murph. I don't know why I'm in such a weird mood today. I'll knock it off."

I reach out to touch the back of her wrist. "No, don't knock it off. I like you in a happy mood."

"Naw, I shouldn't play around with you. With what you've been through, I think you have a need to take things seriously. I understand that it's a hard world, so you probably don't need some silly girl around."

This time I take hold of her wrist. "That's not true, Clara, I want you to be any way you want to be. I mean, I . . . I like you the way you are."

She frowns and pulls her hand away. "No, you're a serious person. I know that. You've been to war, and after all, you are a philosophy major, the only philosophy major I've ever met. That should have told me something."

I have to smile at that comment, remembering how it was mostly an accident that I ended up registering to be a philosophy major. But before I can explain that to her, she's on her feet, getting ready to leave. I hope I haven't done something to drive her away. I reach out toward her. "Do you have to leave already? I've already put my time in at my job this morning, so I can stay as long as you want."

She grabs my hand in both of hers and squeezes it in a way that I hope is trying to reassure me.

"No," she says, "it's my mother. She insists on buying me stuff. Today, she's taking me to buy some new school clothes. That's what she calls them, 'school clothes.' What they really are is clothes that reflect the type of person she wants me to be. She hates it that I wear jeans. She wants me to wear girlie dresses." She shrugs. "But I shouldn't complain. I don't have any money of my own, so if she didn't buy my clothes, I guess I'd have to go naked. You probably wouldn't want that, would you?"

She's looking at me with raised eyebrows.

To go along with her joke, I say, "Oh, no, I sure wouldn't want to see that."

She gives my hand one more squeeze, and says, "I gotta go. I'm late already. Same time, same place tomorrow?"

I say, "Sure. See you then."

She hurries off, and after she's gone, I try to imagine what she might be like with her mother. For some reason, I feel like she might be a somewhat different person at home. But then, maybe she's always a different person when she's with me.

I wonder why I had that thought. She said she thinks I'm a serious person. Am I too serious? Maybe. She was in an especially playful mood today. I wonder what drew that out of her today? Maybe it's only because it's a weekend and she isn't under the pressure of taking her heavy load of classes. So why is she here on a weekend? It seemed like she must have come to the library's reserved book section looking for me. She told me she'd ordered the philosophy textbook, but maybe she had assigned reading for some another class. No, she didn't indicate that. She must have come to campus today specifically looking for me. I wonder where she usually spends her weekends. With friends? At parties? She's never mentioned friends, but I expect she could be a very popular girl, if she wanted to be. So why is she spending time with a weird person like me?

She's right, I probably am too serious. Was it almost dying in Vietnam that did that to me? Because of that, and Father Saul's murder, death has become a concept that is often on my mind.

Actually, I guess I was pretty serious before I got drafted. I did have fun with the other boys at the orphanage sometimes, but I have to admit that I did like being alone. If anybody wanted to find me, they knew where I'd be: out by myself exploring the desert, and thinking.

Father Saul would sometimes catch me lost in thought. He sometimes called me "the thinker." I got the idea he meant that as a compliment, but maybe he thought I spent too much time alone, just thinking.

Not that he thought being alone and thinking was bad, but he thought a big part of his job as our teacher was preparing us to go out into the world, and that would mean getting along with other people.

Well, maybe I need to think more about all that later. Right now, I guess I'd better head back to the orphanage. It's been a long day.

On my way to the bus stop, I start to worry about leading Clara astray with the story that I'm writing a murder mystery novel. I wonder if I should try to put a stop to that, or at least divert it. And why did I get that going in the first place? Could it really help me solve Father Saul's murder, if did I go along with it just so I could keep on meeting her for lunch? There are moments when I feel like I should just go ahead and tell her it's not a story, it's real.

But I know I can't do that. She'd probably tell me to call the police. She probably wouldn't be as sure as I am that the police wouldn't do much about it. And I'd also have to explain how that would mess things up for Cody. And mess things up for me with the tribe, especially now that I've got the part-time job at the bingo hall. Doing that job, I can find out more about what goes on at the reservation, in addition to making some much-needed money. I feel uncomfortable lying to her, but maybe it's not like a real lie, just a way to skirt around some troublesome facts by letting her go on believing what she wanted to believe in the first place. If I ever have to tell her the truth, I hope she'll understand.

And what about not telling Bob the truth about where I'm living? He's been so nice to me, it just doesn't feel right to deceive him. I think I've mostly been a truthful person in my life; how did I get myself into a situation where I have to hide the truth from people I like?

Chapter Thirty

The next morning, when I wake up, it feels like I'm alone in the dorm. Sure enough, when I go to check on Cody, he's gone. Where could he have gone so early in the morning? I again worry that he might be out there trying to solve Father Saul's murder on his own. If he goes around asking too many questions, the killer might get nervous and come dig up the body. Or even worse, do something to shut Cody up.

I guess I'll just have to trust that Cody will be careful. He's a smart kid.

Right now, I should grab a bit of the leftover food and head for the university. I'm not sure what time it is, but from the position of the morning sun in the eastern sky, I think I have plenty of time to get some reading done at the library before my philosophy class.

I hike to the bus stop in front of the reservation main entrance, and when the bus arrives, I'm surprised to see so many people already on it. I've never seen so many on this bus. Most of them seem young enough to be college students. Are they all going the university? If so, why are they all going there this early in the morning, and all at once?

As we go along, more and more young people get on the bus until it's really crowded. I can hear that they're talking excitedly, but I can't quite figure out what they're so excited about. Something about how great *this* is going to be.

So they're not just going to class. This bus is heading for Tempe, but maybe they're not going to the campus. Maybe there's some kind of early-morning festival or something like that going on in downtown Tempe.

As the bus pulls up at the campus bus stop, I stand up, and I'm surprised when all of the others stand up too. Why is everybody getting off here? They can't all be going to a class. And why are they so excited?

They all seem to know where they're going, so I follow them. We pass by the student union building, and then they head down the long wide walkway that's lined with tall palm trees.

It isn't long before I hear the murmur of a large excited crowd in the distance. The people I'm following are heading straight for that sound, and we soon arrive at the fountain in front of the old building where I previously saw the anti-war protesters. A group of those same type of protesters are again up on the edge of the fountain with their war-protest signs, and a few more guys are wading around in the fountain water, also carrying anti-war signs and chanting "NO MORE WAR! NO MORE WAR!" The big difference is, the last time I was here, there were only a few onlookers; now there are hundreds, with lots more still arriving. How did they all find out something was going to happen here today? Was it published somewhere? And exactly *what is* going to happen here today?

The growing crowd soon picks up on the chant of the anti-war protesting boys: "NO MORE WAR! NO MORE WAR!" Everyone in the crowd seems very excited. Are they excited about ending war, or are they just excited about being part of such a large ant-war demonstration?

I stay well back, close enough to hear, but not so close I might be noticed. The same guy with the bullhorn that berated me the last time is again shouting through his bullhorn about what an illegal war the Vietnam War is and how thousands of innocent Vietnamese people are being killed over there just for defending their homeland.

Is that true? I suppose some of those we thought of as the enemy did believe they were defending their homeland, but weren't they mostly carrying out the wishes of the Communists? That's what we were told. We were told that taking over Vietnam was part of the Russian and Chinese Communist's plan to take over the whole world.

Now, thinking back on it, it kind of surprises me that I didn't think more about that.

If Father Saul saw me as a thinker, when I ended up in the Vietnam War, why didn't I think much about what the war was all about, and my role in it? I've been telling myself that it was because I was too busy staying alive, but that's no excuse. I guess once I was in it, and my duties became my day-to-day life, I just didn't want to think too much about it.

The crowd is still growing, but I know I'd better head for my class. I don't want to be late, but as I walk, I can't stop thinking about what that guy with the bullhorn was saying, and about the whole crowd chanting against the war. I'm pretty sure I was the only person in the crowd that had actually been in the war they were chanting about. I wonder what they would have thought about me if they knew that.

I know I need to get that out of my mind and start thinking about my philosophy class. Or should I? Aren't we supposed to be thinking about large concepts like war and peace? Isn't how people feel about their homeland the domain of philosophy? Maybe with this unrest going on today on campus, the professor will be lecturing about that.

Or will there even be a class today? Maybe all the students are at the anti-war rally.

I get to the classroom early, so I'm not surprised that I'm the first one there. I sit in my usual place, and I'm hoping Clara gets there in time to sit next to me.

By the time the professor arrives, there are only two other students besides me. Professor Schmidt seems surprised to see so few of us in attendance, but he doesn't comment on it. He just takes his place at the end of the table, opens his notes, and begins lecturing.

He says that in our last class meeting, he described the importance of the early Greek philosophers, but now he wants to move into the significance of the Middle Age philosophy. He says that in the Middle Ages there was dissonance among philosophers about acquiring knowledge through reason as opposed to "supernatural revelation." "

But," he says, "we should not restrict our study of philosophy to unaided reason. Philosophy should attempt to investigate all aspects of human knowledge, including what can be determined through scientific study *and* moral science. A good part of the formal study of philosophy in the Middle ages was conducted by theologians like Saint Thomas Aquinas."

That again reminds me that essentially all of my learning came from a theologian, a Catholic priest. As Professor Schmidt continues to talk about the authority of Aristotle and the church during that period, I start to pick up a sharp chemically-smelling odor. I don't recognize, it, but one of the other students says, "Tear gas." He said it right out loud, and he's staring at the open window at the end of the room.

The odor isn't all that strong, but as the professor tries to continue with his lecture, he keeps on coughing. He seems to be having trouble getting the words out. I wonder if he has some kind breathing problem that's being especially affected by the tear gas. He stops talking and puts a handkerchief to his face. He points to the open window, so I immediately jump up and go close it.

Without thanking me, he tries to continue his lecture. But it's no use. He's coughing repeatedly now, and he's holding the handkerchief close over his nose and mouth.

Now that the anti-war demonstrations are affecting him so directly, maybe it's time to bring up the topic of war. I raise my hand, and without waiting for him to call on me, I say, "With all that's going on, sir, maybe we should be talking about war. I mean about how, or why, humans are always getting themselves into wars."

At first, I'm not sure he's going to answer me. He seems to be really bothered by the tear gas fumes. But then, he says, "Well, it certainly does seem to be impinging on us right now, doesn't it? What do you think, Mr. Murphy? Is war a necessary aspect of all human civilizations?"

Uh oh, I should have realized he'd turn it back on me. "Well, sir, I was in the war, the Vietnam war, so maybe I'm not the best person to answer that. But my old teacher taught us that people have been engaging in wars since . . since the time of the Greek philosophers, and probably long before that."

The professor nods, but because he's still got a handker-chief over his face, I'm not sure if he likes me asking him such questions.

He says, "Well, Mr. Murphy, it seems you do have a unique position from which to view the subject. I think we'd like to hear more about your experience at some time." He pauses to cough into his handkerchief, and then says, "As to your reference to the fact that war has been with us for a very long time, yes, we have literature from the era of the ancient philosophers that has been handed down to us. Stories about the Trojan wars, for example. But whether getting involved in wars is a necessary condition of humans, maybe we need to leave that to the psychologists. But I would say that the grand narratives of a society, the universal acceptance of such concepts of patriotism and heroism in a soci-ety, do have a strong predictive element." He again pauses to cough several times into his handkerchief, then says, "But for now, with the obvious influence the local affect of the issue is having on me, I suggest we continue this discussion next time."

With that, he gathers his notes and hurries out the door, still hiding his face behind his handkerchief.

I go to the window to see what's going on out there, and the other students do the same. The same student that had mentioned, "Tear gas," now says, "Cops. Damn, they called in the cops." He runs out of the room, and the others quickly follow him. I assume they're heading toward the demonstration to see what's going on.

I stay at the window, Uniformed police are streaming down the sidewalks between the buildings, all of them heading for the site of the demonstration.

Maybe I should also go see what's going on. I suspect the students that just ran out of this room are going to go join the anti-war demonstration.

I'm a student too, but as an Army vet, I'm not sure it would be appropriate for me to even be in the area of the demonstrations.

But why not? I guess the question is, am I ready to think like a real student? I believe I am. Or more accurately, I'm willing to be. If so, why shouldn't I be involved in student activities? I'm also a philosophy major, so shouldn't I at least go observe what's going on? I should do what an interested student should do, try to figure out the meaning of what's going on. I hurry out of the room.

Before I even get close to the demonstration area, I meet students running toward me. They seem panicked. I stop. What could be going on over there that is causing them to run? I decide to continue on, cautiously.

The closer I get to the demonstration site, the stronger the smell of the tear gas. It's not strong enough to give me too much trouble breathing, but it is making my eyes water. The students in class seemed to think it was the campus authorities that called in the police. Are they so against such demonstration on campus that they would call the police? Is there some rule at this university against students holding on-campus demonstrations? Or is it only because it's a demonstration against the war?

When I get to the plaza in front of the Old Main building, I see right away why so many student were running away: a line of uniformed police in gas masks is confronting a line of young men, most of whom have wet handkerchiefs over their faces. The young men are obviously willing to challenge the police. They're not only standing up to them, they're yelling at them. I can't hear all of what they're yelling, but I hear enough to tell me they're demanding to know on what authority the police are breaking up the demonstration.

A haze of tear gas hangs in the air, but the police are not firing any more of it right now. I'm not liking the way the tear gas is making my eyes sting and water, but I'm too fascinated by what's going on to run away.

For a few minutes, the situation seems to be at a standstill. But then, the police, all together, begin to move forward, pushing the young men back. Was there some kind of command I didn't hear?

At first, the young men stand their ground, but then the police began to hit them with clubs, a type of long thin black baton.

Hitting students on their own campus? That can't be right. I step forward and yell, "Stop that! Those young men aren't doing anything wrong."

The policemen either don't hear me, or they're ignoring me. I yell again, "Stop that!"

That causes one of the policemen to turn and look at me. He taps another policemen on the shoulder, and nods toward me. Together, they start walking toward me.

Uh oh, now I've done it. Never in my life have I ever had any dealings with police. But what they are doing just doesn't seem right. If those young men are students at this campus, just as I am, don't they have a right to make their opinions about the war known?

The two policemen close in on me, holding their batons in a threatening way.

A jumble of questions run through my mind. Are they going to hit me? Should I try to stop them from doing that? Is it illegal to stop a policeman from hitting you? I sure wouldn't want to end up in jail.

As they close in on me, I hold up my hands. "I don't want to fight you. I just wanted to know why you were hitting those students."

For some reason, that stops them. Maybe they can sense I'm not like the other students that have been confronting them. I should try to keep that image of myself going. I say, "I may not agree with what those students are saying, but it's their campus, isn't it? Why should they be stopped from saying what they think?"

The face of the bigger of the two policemen is getting red. He must be getting more and more angry at me. He holds up his baton and steps closer to me. "Oh yeah, what's makes you the expert?"

I shrug and say, "I'm no expert, officer, but it doesn't seem like they were hurting anybody. They were just yelling."

"Yeah, and I'm telling you it was an illegal assembly. Now get your ass out of here before you get yourself hurt."

I point to myself. "You're going to hurt me? For just talking to you?" I keep my eyes on that baton he's holding. Would he really hit me with that thing?

Sure enough, he raises his baton higher. "Okay, smart ass. You've been warned. Now I'm forced to take action against you."

I can see the other policeman doesn't seem quite as eager to get involved against me, so I nod toward him and say, "Your partner seems more willing to talk about it, so why can't we just talk? I think those students have the right to express their opinions. It's their campus. Isn't that partly why they come here to this university? To talk? In fact, in the class I'm taking, the professor says we should—"

Luckily, I was keeping my eyes on his baton, because whatever I said didn't seem to work. He swings his baton down toward the top of my head. Of course, I duck, but it does manage to hit my shoulder. It hurts, a little. I take a step back and hold up both of my hands. "Hold on, sir. I'm not challenging you. It's only that I just got back from Vietnam, so maybe I don't know the rules yet."

That stops him. "You were in Vietnam?"

"Yes, sir. I'm here taking classes on veterans benefits."

My words have obviously confused him. He lowers his baton. "Well, why didn't you say so? If you're military, why are you sticking up for these asshole anti-war protesters?"

"Well, sir, whether I agree with them or not, I think they have a right to say what they believe. That's what we were fighting for, wasn't it? The right to say what you believe?"

He shakes his head, clearly still angry. "Well, they don't have the right to say we shouldn't be trying to stop the Goddam Communists before they destroy the world. And if you don't agree with that, then you're just as stupid as they are." He turns and walks away.

The other policeman stares at me for a few seconds before he also turns away.

I watch them go back to join the line that's attacking the young men, and now the policeman that confronted me seems to be hitting out at the students even more aggressively. Obviously, my well-reasoned argument didn't work with him.

I'm ready to go try to stop them hitting the students, but the students, after getting hit a few times, break ranks and run away.

That seems to satisfy the police. Some of the policemen chase after them, but most of them pull back. They're gathering back at the fountain. One officer, probably their superior, is up on the concrete lip of the fountain talking to them. I'm too far away to hear what he's saying, but I wouldn't be surprised if he's congratulating them on a job well done. If so, I expect we'll be seeing police on this campus again.

As I walk away, I'm still thinking about that policeman's attitude. He was sure he was in the right. Is that how everybody thinks? One you're convinced you're on the right side of something, are you then unwilling to change your mind, no matter what anybody says? That seems like a good topic for discussion in my philosophy class. It's obvious something important is going on here, and it seems like an appropriate topic for a philosophy class. Professor Schmidt said he'd be willing to talk about it in our next class meeting. I'll be sure to hold him to that. I'll ask him if the study of philosophy ought to have significance in the real-world, not just how it was interpreted by some old Greeks. He may not like me saying that, but how can he disapprove of me wondering how things going on in the world relate to what we're studying? I'm sure if Father Saul was still alive, he'd encourage me to speak up about something so important.

As I walk to the student union cafeteria, I'm hoping Clara will be there. It's starting to feel like my meeting her in the cafeteria has become the most important time of the day for me. What does that say about me? What am I really feeling toward her? For the thousandth time, I wish Father Saul was here to advise me.

My thoughts are interrupted when more students run past me. It's as if the whole campus is in an uproar.

I think the university administration made a big mistake bringing in the police. They must have thought they could use the police to stamp out such demonstrations, but they might well have done just the opposite.

I watch the students run. They look so frightened. Is it because they are afraid of the police, or are they just scared and confused that something has so disrupted their normal life?

I again wonder what those students would think if they knew I had been part of the war they're protesting against? Would they tell me I was wrong to go, that I was wrong to participate in killing people in a far-away country? Well, was I?

Now that was an odd thought. I don't think I've ever thought about the war and my role in it in quite that way before. Did it take a student anti-war demonstration and an aggressive police response to start me thinking about the meaning of the war?

I have the sudden thought that Father Saul would have wanted me to have such thoughts. He would have asked me how could I have spent all that time in Vietnam without hardly ever thinking about the bigger meaning of what we were doing there? I'm sure he would have been very disappointed in me. He always told us to think for ourselves.

Is that what war does to us? Does it get young men involved in something they say is very important, and then get them so caught up in staying alive they're willing to kill other human beings without stopping to think about why they're doing it?

As I approach the student union building, I'm actually feeling sort of grateful to that policeman; it's like him hitting me with that baton woke me up, forced me to think about the bigger meaning of the war.

All right, Father Saul, I'm awake now. I'm ready to start thinking about what the hell is really going on out here in the *real* world.

Chapter Thirty-One

When I get to the cafeteria, I'm disappointed to see that Clara is not waiting for me at our usual table. That table is occupied. In fact, almost all the tables are occupied. This must be where a lot of the students at the demonstration ended up when they ran away from the tear gas.

I wander through the crowded tables, hoping to find Clara, but she's not here. Maybe she doesn't want to have lunch with me anymore. No, that can't be. We only recently met, but she's the one who suggested we meet here everyday.

Maybe she went to the demonstration. Maybe she got hurt by the police. She's a straightforward person. Maybe she confronted the police and got arrested. Did they arrest people, or were they only here to break up the demonstration, to hit people? Maybe she got hit and is out there hurt somewhere. I should go look for her.

I head for the exit, but then, thankfully, I see her coming down the stairs. She's hurrying and seems out of breath. I wave to her, and luckily she sees me despite the crowd.

She joins me and puts her hand against my chest. She's leaning forward and panting. "Sorry I'm late, Murph. I was hiding in the psych building. I hoped those cops wouldn't come in there."

"They chased you?"

"Well, not just me. A bunch of us ran when they started in hitting with their clubs. I yelled to the others to go to the psych building 'cause it's a place I know. I ran up the stairs to the top floor, but none of the others followed me." She's breathless, and she's gripping my arm as she talks.

I put my arm around her shoulders and lead her to one of the few empty tables. I get her seated, and then I say, "Should I go get us some sandwiches?"

"No. I couldn't eat now." She grabs my arm to pull me back down. Still out of breath, she says, "I ran up the stairs without stopping. Went into the rat lab. Luckily, nobody was there. I heard shouting in the hallway, so I just stayed hidden there, crouched down in the darkness between the rat-testing cubicles. When it finally quieted down, I figured you'd be waiting here, so I took a chance and went out. I ran all the way here."

"Are you sure you don't want me to get us something to eat? Maybe it would relax you."

"No. I'm probably too het up to eat. Let's just sit here for a few minutes until the crowd dies down. I expect they're all here to talk about what happened, but they'll leave soon 'cause I think a lot of them aren't students. Can you believe those damn cops? Beatin' the shit out of students? Just 'cause they were demonstrating against the war?" She stops talking and stares at me. "I didn't see you there. But maybe the crowd was too big."

"I went to class."

"You went to class?"

I can tell she's disappointed in me. I say, "I could tell there was going to be some kind of demonstration, but I figured it would still be going on after class was over. As it turned out, I made it to the demonstration in plenty of time because Professor Schmidt ended the class early. The tear gas was bothering him."

She lets out a sarcastic chuckle. "I expect it was bothering everybody on campus. Can you believe those cops tear gassed us? What right did they have to come onto our campus and do that?"

"I was wondering the same thing. Do you think the administration requested them to come?"

"Christ, I wouldn't put it past 'em. They've been restricting what the student newspaper can say about the war, and I'm sure they didn't want the demonstration to happen on what they think of as 'their' campus. I knew it was going to happen here sooner or later." She pauses, and I can tell she's still angry, but she does seem to be calming down a bit.

She looks up at me. "You told me you haven't ever watched TV. But if you did, you'd know this kind of anti-war protesting has been going on all over the world. When that Buddhist monk burned himself to death on a street in Saigon to protest the war, that really got the protests going."

"A Buddhist monk burned himself to death?"

"You didn't even know about that? Didn't the soldiers in Vietnam talk about things like that?"

"No, this is the first I've heard about it."

"Well then, I'd better educate you. I've been following it pretty close. After the anti-Vietnam War student protests started in England and Australia, it didn't take long to spread to this country. At first it was mostly at the universities back east, but then it became a real anti-war movement and began to spread all over the country. A lot of students began starting on-campus demonstrations. Guys of draft age are burning their draft cards, sayin' they won't go."

Her words are telling I've been completely out of it. How could all this have been going on, and I never heard a word about it?

She stops talking and stares at me. "Well, don't you have anything to say? What about what they did? Cops beating up students on their own campus? Or are you on the cops' side?"

"No, Clara, I'm definitely not on the side of those police. In fact, one of them went after me with his baton. Tried to hit my head."

"Really? What did you do?"

"I ducked."

"Then what?"

"I talked to him."

"Talked to him? Are you kidding? What made you think you could talk to those assholes?"

"I'm not sure, Clara. It's just that what they were doing didn't seem right, so I thought I should say so."

She lets out a sarcastic chuckle. "I bet that went over well."

"I guess it wasn't a smart a thing to do. That's when he swung at me with his baton. He said I must be on the side of the Communists."

"Why didn't you tell him you'd been in Vietnam fighting the Communists?"

"I did tell him I'd been there. That was after he attacked me."

"Good for you. What did he do after that?"

"He backed off, but I wouldn't say it made him think about the error of his ways. He went right back to hitting the demonstrators."

"So, now that you've seen it, which side are you on?"

I scratch behind my ear while I stall. I'm not sure I should tell her that I'm really not sure there is actually a side to be on. But I should tell her the truth. "Listen, Clara, we have to talk about this. It seems to me everybody is just playing their part, the protesters, the police, the university administration. Think about my position. I'm here now, trying to be a college student, but it wasn't all that long ago when I was with a bunch of other young guys like me out in a jungle fighting other young Vietnamese guys who were probably also just playing their part. For sure, I didn't feel like I was fighting against Communism; I was just trying to stay alive, and I'm pretty sure that's all the other guys in my unit were thinking about. I suspect that's what the so called enemy guys were also thinking. Were we wrong to try to kill an enemy that we weren't even sure needed to be our enemy? Probably, but like I said, we were all just playing our parts."

"Wow, Murph, that question sure got you thinking. So, have you decided? Is the war right or wrong?"

"I'm still trying to think it through, Clara. I don't want to think the guys in my patrol group, my friends, died for nothing. Should I now believe they were fighting for something that was wrong?"

She leans forward. "Yes! It seems to me you have to be on one side or the other."

Her statement doesn't seem right to me. "Listen, Clara. We're learning in our philosophy class that there is no black and white about things. Isn't that right?"

"No, it's not right. The war is wrong. The university administration is wrong. Those police hitting students are dead wrong. You have to take a side."

"I'm sorry, Clara, I guess to me it just seems more complicated than that."

She shakes her head. She seems angry. At me?

She says, "Saying it's complicated is just a way to avoid taking a stand. I think we have to react. Otherwise the university administration and the cops will just keep on pulling this kind of crap."

"I do agree with that part, Clara. Students, anybody actually, should be allowed to express their opinions. But the war itself . . . well, that's the part that seems the most complicated. It's a big question."

She's frowning. I can tell she's not going for it.

She says, "It doesn't seem all that complicated to me. I was already pretty much convinced that the war over there was wrong, but what happened here today really decided it for me. You saw what those cops did. They even went after you, a wounded war veteran. I'd think that would have made up your mind too, if nothing else did. Isn't it obvious? Vietnam is a pointless war. An illegal war, just as those protesters were saying. The university administration knows it. The cops know it. Even the government knows it. It's simple psychology 101. They all know they're in the wrong, so they have to act aggressively to prove to themselves they're on the right side. The university administration knew this first demonstration might only be the start of it, so they had to try to stamp it out quick."

She's getting angry again, it's leaving me not knowing what to say to her. All I can do is repeat that I see it as more complicated, but I don't want to keep on staying that. It'll just make her feel like I'm against her.

But I'm not, so I'd better say something to let her know that. "Listen, Clara, I'm not disagreeing with you. What happened here today kind of woke me up, so I can see what you're saying is true. But everybody is getting so polarized, it makes me feel kind of stuck in the middle."

She starts to object, but I keep going. "Like I said, Clara, I can see you're right. The government has committed tremendous resources to the war, so they can't back down now. But I was over there. I was in it, and I don't want to think those guys in my unit were wrong to be there. They just thought they were doing their duty."

"So, is that how you felt?"

"How I felt? I don't know how to answer that, Clara. What did I know? I was young. I got drafted, so I went where they told me to go and did what they told me to do."

"Yeah, well, like I heard somebody else say, they need young men like you to fight their wars. So what if they gave a war and nobody showed up? It's young men like you that make it all possible." She looks right into my eyes. "Come on, Murph, what do you really think? Do you really believe sending young men like you to die in some stupid little far off country is really necessary? The government sure is trying to convince us it's necessary. They want us to believe the Communists have some big plan to take over the world, starting with Asia. Do you really believe that?"

She's trying to convince me of something, and she really wants me to agree with her. I should say something before this turns into an argument between us. "Listen, Clara, I agree with a lot of what you're saying. I just need more time to think about it."

"Okay, then why not just say it? This war is wrong."

I lean closer to her and say, "Listen, Clara, I can see why those students are protesting. Vietnam isn't like stopping Hitler. But I'm not ready to say there was no real reason for me to go fight over there. I mean, how much do we really know about the real reasons for the war? There may be reasons we don't know about. Things going on behind the scenes that they can't tell us."

She waves off that idea. "Aw, I don't believe that bull for a minute. The whole stop the Commies before they land on our beaches is just a ploy to get young men like you to go get themselves killed. If they think it's so damn important, why don't they go?"

I can tell her anger is building up again. I'd better say something to show her I really am listening to the points she's making. "I can see you're still angry at those policemen for attacking the students, Clara. And I agree with you that they shouldn't have done that. But give me some time to digest it all, okay? I've been kind of out of touch with everything that's been going on. I didn't even know there *was* an anti-war movement."

That seems to calm her down a bit. She says, "Aw, you're right, Murph. I don't want it to cause trouble between us. I 'spose you had your own good reasons for going over there. But the one thing you've got to come to grips with is that this stupid war isn't really worth you almost dying for."

Before I can respond, she says, "Oh never mind. I can see we just disagree about this. How about your murder mystery novel? How is that coming along?"

"I didn't say we disagreed, Clara. I only said it was complicated. I just need to think about it more."

"Okay, fine. You think about it more. In the meantime, have you been to the library to do more research for your novel?"

"No. I've just been reading the philosophy textbook."

"I figured as much. Are you really writing a murder mystery novel?"

I'm not sure how to answer her. I hate not being able to tell her the truth. Her life seems so isolated from anything going on outside of this campus. Actually, if I'm going to be a real student, I should be like that too. I should give up trying to figure out who killed Father Saul and move on with my life here on this campus. I'm becoming pretty sure my future life will be here, studying philosophy at this university. That means I should just turn the murder mystery over to the police. But first, I have to go tell Cody. He won't be happy about it, but it's what needs to happen.

Clara is staring into my eyes. "You went silent. You aren't writing a novel about some body being found out in the desert, are you? Did you really find a body?"

After our difficult talk about the war, I don't want to get into an even more troublesome topic. She'd tell me to call the local police immediately. I say, "You're pretty smart, Clara. No, I'm not writing a novel about a murder. I never said I was. You just inferred that from the library research I was doing."

"Okay, then tell me why you were doing that kind of research."

"Actually, I am trying to solve a mystery. Remember how I told you about the great old teacher I had at the orphanage?"

"Yes. Was he murdered?"

"Well, he's disappeared. Very suddenly. And nobody knows where he went."

"So, you think he might have been murdered? Why? Did he have enemies?"

"Well, yes. He got into trouble with the reservation people when he reported them for illegal gambling. There's a lot of money involved. You said yourself most murders are committed over money."

"And you think they might have killed him for that? And buried him out there in the desert?"

"Well, it's possible. I can't think of any other reason why he would just disappear so suddenly. And nobody saw him go. How could that be unless he's still out there somewhere."

'It does sound like a real mystery. And the cops don't have any ideas?"

"I haven't gone to them. Not yet anyhow. I did get in touch with the archdiocese, and they were surprised to hear he was gone."

"Well, I can't blame you for not going to the cops. You saw today what they're like."

"Yes, I hope I can figure it out myself before I contact them."

"Oh, Murph, everything with you is complicated. But I get it. Okay, I'll try to help you search for him, if you want me too. But right now, I've got to get to class. I'm already late."

She starts to stand up, but I touch her wrist and say, "Listen, Clara, our talking got us into some troublesome areas today, but we actually may not be that far off from each other. Regarding the war I mean. Give me some time to think about what you said. Let's meet up here tomorrow at the usual time so we can talk some more, okay?"

She smiles at me, which I take as a good sign.

"Okay," she says. "Besides, we can't actually go two days in a row without eating some of their wonderful cheese sandwiches, can we?"

"No indeed. They'd be wondering where we are."

She smiles at my joke and seems about to hurry off, but then she turns back and leans down to kiss me, right on my lips.

It takes me by surprise, and at the moment our lips touch, I lean back.

She seems surprised and says, "No?"

I let out a self-conscious chuckle and lean forward to try to kiss her more firmly this time. But I'm too late, she's already hurrying away. I wish I could have explained why I leaned back, that it was only that she caught me by surprise. But maybe she didn't really want to kiss me. Maybe it was just some kind of test. Would she do that? Did she test me, and then pretend to be in a hurry to avoid actually kissing me in a serious way? Well, what do I know about such things. I really do want to spend more time with her, but clearly, I've got a lot to learn.

Chapter Thirty-Two

I stay seated at the little table, watching the students. The place is thinning out a bit, but there are still a lot of young people gathered at tables excitedly talking about the demonstration and what the police did. From what I can hear, there seems to be general anger at the police, mostly for them daring to come onto the campus in the first place, but also anger at them for using their batons to drive students away from the demonstration site. I can't blame them for being angry about that. Breaking up a peaceful demonstration with such aggressive tactics was completely unnecessary. And I suspect it will only create more anti-war demonstrations, and the next ones might not be so peaceful.

I head for the bus stop, and I get there while the bus is still in the process of loading. I hurry to get in the back of the line, and when I get on, I'm lucky to actually get a window seat.

As we pull away, I see that the university parking lot is just about entirely full of police buses. Geez, did they really need that many cops just to break up a peaceful demonstration? I guess it proves what Clara was saying, that they're personally involved, angry at the student demonstrators. They must think the students aren't being patriotic, so they deserve to be taught a lesson.

Some of the police buses are identified as being from Phoenix. So they not only used local police, they brought in outside police. Why would they do that? Do they hate anti-war demonstrations that much? It makes me think of what Clara said about them knowing they're in the wrong so they have to respond with force to prove they're in the right. It also makes me remember that a lot of the demonstrators also came in on the same bus I was on. That probably means it was not only students at the demonstration. Those other people thought today's demonstration was important enough to take time out from their lives to get on a bus and go to a college campus to join in.

Clara said this was the first demonstration on this campus, and that was why the university administration and the police tried so hard to stop it. She's probably right about that, but it seems to me that could have the opposite effect. When the word gets out about what happened here today, the next demonstration will probably be even bigger.

Well, welcome to the real reality, Murph. The other day, when you saw those guys at the fountain with their bullhorn, you thought they must just be some students that didn't want to get drafted. But now you learn it's not just a few guys with a bullhorn, it's actually a worldwide anti-war movement. I need to think about that.

And Clara said some draft-age students were burning their draft cards. When I got drafted, it never even occurred to me that anybody might refuse to go. When Father Saul told me I had to go register for the draft, I just went. I guess I just thought they were in charge, so I should do as I was told. It was the same when I got to Vietnam: it didn't take me long to learn that to get along, just go along. So that's what I did.

But I keep coming back to the same question: why didn't I think more about what the war itself meant? Maybe it goes all the way back to what I learned from Father Saul. He was a caring person, but he ran the orphanage with an iron hand. He said to learn to be an adult in the adult world, you had to learn discipline. But did his rules about discipline turn me into a person that wouldn't question authority? Maybe. The one thing I know for sure is that none of the boys at the orphanage ever thought about questioning Father Saul's rules. I guess that was because we knew how much he cared for us.

I keep wondering how much of what we learn when we're young makes us how we are as adults. I'll have to ask Clara what she's learning in her psychology classes about that.

And what about the other people? Why do they support the war? Was it something they learned as children? Mr. Foucher gave me a ride in his old truck and helped me just because he knew I had been a soldier.

Mr. Gibson at the post office was really nice to me for the same reason. And Bob at the bingo hall gave me a job when he found out I'd been a soldier in Vietnam. I wonder what they'd think if they knew I was now having doubts about what we were doing over there.

At the firebase, at lunch mess, I once overhear two guys talking about somebody they knew back home who had refused to be drafted. They said the guy had been sent to a military prison, and they both agreed that he got what he deserved. I didn't think about it much at the time, but now, it's got me wondering. If there really is a worldwide anti-war movement, and a lot of young men are refusing to go, are they all ending up in prison? It again reminds me of what Clara said: what if they gave a war and nobody showed up? Obviously that's not happening— the United States was involved in Korea, and now in Vietnam, and they keep on getting plenty of young men to go fight their wars.

Chapter Thirty-Three

All the way back to the reservation, I try to think through all that happened this morning. First, the tear gas fumes forced professor Schmidt to cancel the class. And then, I went to see what was going on and saw the police attacking the protesters. First off, why would so many people show up to protest the war in Vietnam? And why would the university administration try to put a stop to it by bringing in the police? Father Saul always told us to make our decisions based on facts and reason, not on emotion. But now everybody, on both sides, seems to have an emotional response to the Vietnam War, even if it has nothing to do with them. That policeman was obviously angry and upset with the student protesters. Why? He said we had to stop the Communists before they "destroy the world." Does he really believe that? And is that what a lot of people believe?

Father Saul taught us that the Cold War was about thwarting Communism. But do people really think our fighting in the jungles of that far-off little country has anything to do with the rise of Communism?

Of course, if anybody heard me say that, they'd think I was agreeing with the protesters. Or at least agreeing with Clara. But I'm not; I'm only trying to think it through. Why are so many people upset about this war when they apparently agreed with previous wars, even Korea?

Clara was upset with me because I said I hadn't made up my mind yet about the war. Because of what happened to her at the demonstration, she's decided that the war is wrong, She feels strongly about it. Does my failure to agree with her mean she won't want to spend time with me anymore?

No, I can't believe that. Clara may have been upset about what the police were doing to the students, but she's a rational person. When she calms down, she'll want to think through it logically, just like I do.

She'll be there tomorrow at the cafeteria at our usual time, and we'll talk it through then.

That reminds me: I should tell Bob I can't make it to the morning sessions anymore. I don't want to miss anymore of my lunch meetings with Clara. Right now, that's the most important thing.

When the bus lets me off near the entrance to the reservation, I go straight to the bingo hall to find Bob. Ellen is busy setting up the food table, so I know they're getting ready for the next bingo session. I ask her if Bob is in, and she tells me no, he had to go to Phoenix for some kind of meeting.

I think about asking her to give my message to Bob when he gets back, but then I decide it's better that I tell him myself. I don't want him to think I'm letting him down; I'll just tell him I need to spend more time at the university library.

"Hey! That's him. That's the queer."

I turn to see who's yelling. It's a Pima man I don't know. He's pointing at me. And he's with Cody's father.

"That's him? The one you told me about? The queer from the old orphanage?" says Cody's father. He sounds drunk, and he's yelling really loud. What could he be talking about? Did Cody tell him something about me?

The other man runs off, but Cody's father is staggering toward me, his fists raised.

This could be big trouble. I sure don't want to get into a confrontation with Cody's father. I say, "Excuse me, sir, do I know you?"

He comes to a stop right in front of me, swaying back and forth. He seems so drunk, he might fall over, and I could be blamed for it even though I haven't touched him.

"It's all your fault!" he yells. "You're the reason I can't keep track of that dammed kid. Have you been keeping him locked up out there, you damned queer?"

"I don't know where Cody is, sir. He comes and goes. But maybe you don't understand who I am. Bob hired me to help out at the bingo sessions."

He jabs the front of my chest with his finger, hard, and says, "We were gonna get a posse tagether ta go out there and teach ya a lesson." He grabs the front of my shirt in his fist. "But now that I gottcha, by God, I'll take care of ya myself."

He keeps ahold of my shirt with one hand as he takes a roundhouse swing at me with his other fist.

I quickly duck down so it only glances off of my forehead. Then, I grab the wrist of his punching hand and twist it hard to force him to his knees. He yelps, and starts screaming as if I'd really hurt him.

I shouldn't have done that. It's just going to make him more angry. I let loose of his wrist, and tell him I'm sorry, but he's sputtering mad as he tries to scramble to his feet. He stumbles toward me and goes down again. Now he's really angry. He starts yelling, even louder: "Help! Help! Somebody come help me! I caught the queer, and he's attacking me."

Three Pima men come running out of the back room. One of them is the man that was with Cody's father, but I don't know the other two.

Cody's father scrambles to his feet and starts backing away from me, still yelling, "Getta hold of him. And watch out. He'll hit ya. He knocked me down."

I try to explain that I did no such thing, but the three men do as he said and pin my arms behind me.

Cody's father says, "Let's take the queer out back and teach him a lesson."

I say, "Now wait a minute. I have no idea what this man is talking about. You all know me. I work here, same as you."

The men look at each other, apparently unsure of what to do.

I look at each of them. They don't work the bingo sessions, so they must not know me. What a time for Bob to be out of town.

Cody's father is still yelling, "He's the one, I'm tellin' ya. He's the one Carl saw in the tub out there with my kid. Hit him! Kick the shit out of him."

The man he's calling Carl seems unsure. He says, "I don't know, Jake. Maybe this is something the police should handle."

"Aw, Christ," says Cody's father. "The cops will just give him a slap on the wrist and let him go to do it again. It's just like when they arrested that old queer priest. They let him go. Don't ya remember?"

"Yeah," says Carl, "but this time we got evidence. I seen 'em. And you know how the cops in this town hate queers. I say we take him to the cops."

I realize what's going on. The man they're calling Carl, must have seen Cody and me living together out at the orphanage

"Wait a minute, sir," I say. "I don't know what you think you saw, but I—."

"Save it for the cops," says Cody's father. He turns to Carl. "All right, if you want the cops to handle it, go ahead and call 'em. But I say first we teach him a lil lesson about how we handle queers here."

Luckily, Carl won't go along with that suggestion, and I soon find myself in the back seat of a police car with my hands handcuffed behind myself. As we go along, I lean forward and try to talk to the officers in the front seat. "Excuse me, officers, I'm afraid this is just an innocent mistake. I can explain it if you'll only let me."

"Save it for the judge," says the driver. "From what they told us, you're lucky those guys didn't beat the shit out of you. If I'd been the one to catch you at doing something like that . . . Well, you'd be smart to just sit back and keep your damn mouth shut."

I do as he said and sit back, although it's not easy with my hands behind my back. I've never been in a situation like this, so I'm not sure what I should do. I probably would be better off to quit trying to explain the situation to anybody until I get in front of a judge, assuming that really is what's going to happen.

But going before a judge is not what happens. They throw me into a jail cell, and they're not very gentle about it.

I sit on the narrow cot, trying to think what might happen next. How will Cody or Clara find out where I am? I wonder how long they can keep me here since I didn't commit any crime.

I try to think through what happened. They seem to be accusing me of being a homosexual because I've been living out at the old orphanage with Cody. Not only that, previously somebody at the reservation accused Father Saul of the same thing. That could explain why he ended up dead and buried out in the desert. Could Cody's father have been the one who killed him? He seems like a man who prefers to solve things with violence.

Chapter Thirty-Four

No one comes to talk to me in my jail cell, and although there is no light in my cell, and only a bit of light from the hallway seeps in under the steel door, I can tell time is passing by the changing sunlight that shines through the little barred window way up high near the ceiling.

After what I think is several hours, someone opens a small trap door in my jail cell door and pushes through a food tray. The food is unrecognizable and almost inedible, but I try to eat a little bit of it.

It gradually gets dark outside my little window, so I lie down on the very hard cot. The only sound is an occasional angry-sounding outburst from somebody nearby, probably another person in another cell just like the one I'm in.

The night passes in near total darkness, and I'm starting to wonder how long they're going to keep me in here. I remember somebody in Vietnam saying the way to treat draft dodgers was to lock them up in prison and throw away the key. In other words, lock them up and forget about them. Is that what they've done to me because of what kind of person they think I am?

After many long hours, someone again shoves through a tray of food, but he does it in a way that makes the food fall on the floor. I'm sure he did that on purpose. I can't imagine what's been on the floor of this cell, so I know I can't eat that food now.

Another long hungry night passes, and after many hours, someone again shoves a tray of food though the trap door. He again tries to make the food fall onto the floor, but I manage to catch some of it. I try to eat it, but it doesn't taste very good. Are they putting something in it to it to make it taste so bad? I know I can't let myself get weak from hunger, so I force a little of it down.

Another mind-numbingly boring day and night passes, leaving me with nothing to do except worry about what Cody and Clara might be thinking happened to me. I can't imagine what they might think. What if they think I've left for good? After all, from their point of view, I did only recently appear out of nowhere.

No, more likely, they'll think something bad has happened. Maybe they'll think the killer got to me.

And what if the killer knows I'm in jail and uses the opportunity to go dig up Father Saul? With nothing to do but think, your mind turns to doubts and fears. Is that a normal thing for a mind to do? I'll have to ask Clara about that. Assuming I ever get to see her again.

The next morning, I wake when the sun comes up outside my little window. I'm feeling very hungry, but that's not what's important; what's important is that I'm not getting a chance to explain to anybody that I haven't done anything wrong.

The main thing I keep thinking about is what Clara will think when I don't show up for our lunch meetings in the cafeteria. Will she think I'm mad at her because of our hard conversation about the anti-war protesters? And what about my class? What will Clara think when I don't show up for our class? And what about the professor? Will he think I've dropped out of the class? Will he flunk me?

But Clara knows how much I've been enjoying the class, so when I don't show up, she should realize something has happened to me. At least I hope so. But even if she realizes that, where would she go to look for me? She doesn't even know where I've been living.

I'm feeling really down when I hear the guard again starting to open the little trap door in my cell door. This time, I'm so fed up with it all that I don't even care if he dumps my food on the floor.

But this time he's not delivering food. Instead, he tells me to put my hands through the trap door. When I do, he puts handcuffs on my wrists.

Soon, a uniformed guard unlocks the door and leads me down the echoing hallway. I ask where we're going, but he won't answer. It would only seem right for them to at least tell me where I'm being taken, but I decide I'd better do what that other policeman told me and keep my mouth shut. In a way, it's like being back in the Army again: just keep your mouth shut, and do what you're told, and you'll be better off.

The guard leads me out of the cells area and into an elevator. We go up, and when we get out of the elevator, he leads me down another hallway and into a large deserted room that has a lot of padded seats in rows and a high counter in the front made of polished wood. This must be a court room. Maybe I'm finally going to get to go before a judge. The guard leads me to a chair that's behind a table near the front of the room. He takes the handcuffs off of me, but he stays close behind.

Soon, I hear voices. I turn and see Cody's father and one of the men who turned me over to the police come in through a door in the back of the courtroom. They stare at me, still obviously angry.

Next, a man comes in through a door at the front of the room and sits behind the high wooden counter. He's wearing a dark robe. He must be the judge.

He looks at some papers, and then he looks right at me. "I have the charge sheet here," he says, "but I don't have your name. Tell me your name."

"My name is Murphy, sir. But everybody just calls me Murph."

The judge stares at me for a few moments and then says, "Mr. Muphy, do you understand the charges against you?"

"No, sir. Actually, I'm not even sure what you mean by charges. Does somebody think I did something against the law?"

"Surely you know why you're here, Mr. Murphy. You have been accused of committing unnatural acts, acts that are clearly specified as unlawful in the Arizona statutes. Do you deny those charges."

So is this because they found out I was living out at the orphanage with Cody? I'd better think about my answers carefully. Apparently, they think I broke some kind of weird Arizona law. "Well, sir, I'm not sure what charges you are referring to. Apparently that man saw I was living out at the old orphanage with my young friend Cody. He must have thought it was wrong for me to do that."

"Don't let this queer fool you judge. We saw what he was doing with my son."

I turn and see that it's Cody's father that spoke. He's standing up and pointing at me. He seems really angry.

The judge points at him and says, "So you saw this man commit unnatural acts with the young boy?"

Cody's father starts wringing his hat in his hands. He seems nervous. "Well, I didn't see it. Not personally, I mean. But Carl here saw it, and I—"

The judge interrupts him. "If you have only hearsay to add to these proceedings, sir, I suggest you sit down and keep your mouth shut."

"Well, it was my son we're talking about here, judge. So I figure I have a say in this."

The judge says, "You do not have a say in this proceeding. Didn't I just tell you to sit down and keep quiet?"

Now it seems like it's the judge who is angry.

Cody's father quickly sits down.

"Now, sir," says the judge, pointing at Carl, tell me what you actually saw. Not what you think you saw, what you actually saw."

"Well," says Carl standing up, but looking down at the floor, "I was out hunting doves, you see. I usually don't go out that way. The best dove hunting is up in the foothills, but that day I thought I'd check the weedy areas over that way for a change, so I—"

"Get to the point, sir. What did you see? Exactly."

"Well, they were naked. Both of 'em. In a tub."

"And?"

"And they seemed to be having a heck of a good time. Laughing and splashing water on each other."

"Both of them? Splashing water?"

"Well, thinking back on it, I guess it was mostly the boy, Cody."

"So you're saying the boy was having a good time in the water. And that's what you saw?"

"Well, I—"

Now I understand what's going on here. That man named Carl must have gone by the day Cody and I took a bath in the old wooden tub. Is that against the law in Arizona?

The judge again turns his stern eyes on me. "And what do you have to say about it, Mr. Murphy?"

I try to make myself as calm as I can, and then I say, "All I can say, sir, is the truth. After hitchhiking here from California, I went to the orphanage to see Father Saul, but the place was deserted. Nobody was there except for a young fellow who said his name was Cody. After a few days, I needed a bath, so I got out the old wooden tub. Cody said he needed a bath too, so he joined me. The well water was very cold, and Cody thought it was fun to splash around. But as soon as I was clean, I got out and—"

The judge says, "So you claim all you were doing was taking a bath. Is it your normal custom to take baths with young boys while you both are naked?"

"Yes, sir, it is. When I was in the orphanage out there, every Saturday evening, Father Saul made us boys fill up the old tub from the well and take a good bath. He put as many into the tub as would fit."

The judge again stares at me. I wish he'd stop doing that. It makes me feel like he's trying to see inside my head.

"You were at the orphanage? The one that used to be out there in the desert. The one run by that old Catholic priest?"

"Yes, sir. I grew up there. Since I was a baby, and now I've been staying out there again. I don't have any money, so I didn't know where else to go after I got out of the Army hospital."

"So you claim that's why you thought it was all right to take a naked bath with a young boy."

"Yes, sir. It was what we always did. Father Saul insisted on us boys being clean, so every Saturday night, we got out the wooden tub and we all—"

"I have something to offer to these proceedings, your honor."

I turn to see who spoke. It's Bob. He's standing just inside the courtroom door. Boy, am I glad to see him. Maybe he'll tell the judge I wouldn't do anything wrong.

Bob says, "You know me, your honor, and you know I represent the tribe. At the time in question, this young man was just back from Vietnam where he was seriously wounded. Like he said, he went out there to his old orphanage because he had nowhere else to go. But since then, he's become a valuable employee of the reservation. He's earning money, and he's now also a student over at ASU. I don't know what Carl here thinks he saw, but I don't believe Murph is capable of doing what he's being accused of. I've gotten to know him pretty well, and I know him as an honest and honorable young man who served his country and came back to our community to find a place in it. Is this how we want to treat a wounded veteran, your honor? I think we should immediately drop these ridiculous charges and let this young man go back to living his life. And like I said, being a responsible member of our community."

The judge says, "Noted." He points at Carl. "All right, sir, do you still want to prefer charges against this young veteran who was wounded serving his country in Vietnam?"

"Uh, I guess not, you honor. If Bob here says he's a stand-up kid, that's good enough for me."

I raise my hand, and the judge looks at me. I say, "I'm sorry I didn't inform the tribe that I was staying out there at the orphanage, but I've been waiting for my discharge check to come from the Army, and I—"

The judge interrupts me. "You don't need to say any more, Mr. Murphy. We understand."

He turns to look at Cody's father and Carl. "And I'd advise you men to be sure you have your facts straight before you bring serious charges against someone. Not all that long ago, you dragged that old priest in here. That time too, you were making plenty of wild accusations, but you had absolutely no evidence. And now you come up with the same old accusations again against a young man who was wounded in service to his country. I dismissed your ridiculous charges against that old priest back then, and I'm going to do the same this time. This case is dismissed. Release him. Now!" With that, the judge abruptly stands up and exits the courtroom.

The guard looks at me and says, "Well, the judge says you can go, so I'd suggest you take off." He turns and walks away.

Cody's father and Carl quickly leave the courtroom without a word, leaving only me and Bob in the room.

Bob is frowning and shaking his head. "You'd think they could at least apologize, but no, off they go with their tails between their legs. I think I'm going to have to do something about those two."

"You don't need to do anything on my account, sir. They thought they saw something they didn't. No harm done."

Bob shakes his head. "I'm sorry, Murph, but I'm afraid there has been harm done. I'm not sure Carl will do anything else, but Jake is one mean son of a bitch, and he won't let it drop. I've tried more than once to get him kicked out of the bingo games for getting drunk while he's supposed to be working, but he's got friends on the council. And now, you've made him look bad. He won't take that lying down. He'll spread his nasty rumors about you, and he'll make sure you don't get to work at the bingo games anymore."

"I don't mind, sir. I can probably find other work, maybe over at—"

Bob raises his hand to stop me. "Don't worry, son, I think I have a better job for you, one that's more suited to your capabilities. Come on, I'll give you a ride back to the reservation and tell you my idea."

Chapter Thirty-Five

On the way back to the reservation in Bob's big car, he's strangely quiet. I consider asking him what he's thinking about, but I decide to leave him alone. He'll talk to me when he's ready.

I keep thinking about what I learned in that courtroom. The judge said they previously accused Father Saul of accosting Pima children and had him arrested. But the judge threw out their accusations. Did they kill him because of that?

Finally, Bob says, "All right, son, I've decided. After what happened back there, Jake and his friends will make sure you can't work at the bingo sessions anymore. And now that they know you and Jake's son have been living out at Father Saul's old orphanage, they'll try to kick you off reservation property. They might even try to have that old place torn down. Like I told you before, the old priest was something of a troublemaker, but we really miss having him out there. He provided a valuable service to the tribe, taking good care of our youngest boys that had nowhere else to go. I understand why you couldn't tell me you were staying out there, but I heard about it. I'm wondering if you've been trying to fix the old place up."

"Yes, sir, I have. As best I can. With Cody's help, of course."

"Well then, what about if we turn that into a job? A real job, with the support of the tribe. I think I can convince the council that we should get the orphanage and school going again."

"Oh, I think that's a really good idea, sir. Being brought up out there in that orphanage was a great experience for me, and I know it was for the other boys too."

"Well, are you interested in the job? We wouldn't want it to interfere with your college classes, though. I think we can work around that."

"Uh, are you offering me a handyman job out there?"

"More than that, son. If we can find a good teacher to run the school, we'd put the orphanage under the auspices of the tribe. That means we'd need a representative from the tribe to oversee it."

"Me? You'd want me to . . . uh, what is it you'd want me to do, exactly?"

"Like I said, oversee the place. We could send some of our young men out there fix the place up. And keep it in good repair once it's up and running. You'd be their boss. We could pay you a regular salary so you wouldn't have to get any other job that might interfere with your studies. In fact, you could even study out there. While you're getting paid. And live there for free, of course."

"Uh, I appreciate you saying that, sir, but I've never been a boss."

"I've seen you in action, Murph. You've got a good head on your shoulders, and you know how to handle people. Those boys, the one's that aren't yet old enough to get drafted, haven't been doing a damn thing except gettin' themselves in trouble. When they're not out chasing girls or getting drunk, they're begging their parents for money. It's about time they learned about responsibility. We'll pay them some. They'd like that, at least."

I think about the ramifications of what he's saying. If I am going to stay in college and try to get a degree, I will need to earn some money. I like the idea of continuing to stay at the orphanage, and like he said, it would be helpful to be earning some money while I do my studying. I say, "All right, sir. I'll do my best."

He smiles and says, "Good. Now, tell me a bit about the place. What does it need?"

"Well, sir, it would probably need a lot. It was all we boys could do to keep the place from falling down. And it was everything Father Saul could do to keep us fed."

"No problem with the food, son. Ellen knows all the food wholesalers. And with the new money bingo is bringing in, we could fix up the old place to make it very comfortable. Build you an apartment, and one for the teacher. What about heating and cooling? What kind of shape are they in?"

"Uh, there was none, sir."

"None? No cooling in the summer months? Not even a swamp cooler?"

"We had no electricity, sir."

"What? I didn't know that. Well, we'll get an electric line strung out there right away. I'm sure some in the tribe will complain that we could just bring in a trailer and make it closer to headquarters, but I like the idea of keeping the young boys out there and away from the influence of those trouble-making older boys I was telling you about. Sort of like sending them off to summer camp, but still having them close by if they need help."

"I like that idea too, sir. Being out there, we learned about nature. About the weather and the seasons. I learned to love the desert. Still do."

"Exactly what I was thinking, Murph. If only my son was here now. I think he'd like this idea."

With that, Bob stops talking and seems to move into a more contemplative mood. As we drive along, I suspect he's thinking about his dead son, so I decide not to interrupt his thoughts. It gives me a chance to think seriously about what he's proposing. Am I ready to take on that kind of responsibility? I think I am. And Father Saul provided me with a good model of how to handle young boys.

As Bob pulls into his reserved parking place next to the bingo hall, he says. "Why don't you just go on back out to the orphanage and wait, Murph. Before I bring this to the council, I want to approach the key members to explain why I think we need it. Once it's voted on, I'll send young Cody out there to tell you what the council said. But don't worry, I think I can convince them we really do need it."

After we get out of the car, he shakes my hand and pats me on the back. Then, he hurries away into the bingo building.

I start to head for the secret route back out to the orphanage, but then I remember I don't have to hide anymore.

I head straight across the desert toward it, thinking about the major change my life is about to undergo. I can hardly wait to tell Clara. I wonder what she'll think of everything that's happened.

Chapter Thirty-Six

When I get to the orphanage, Cody is nowhere around. I assume he's at the bingo hall. But just in case, I check inside his little makeshift hideaway, and there he is. What is he doing in bed this time of day? He's got his back to me, and his legs are pulled up to his chest, as if he's trying to roll himself into a ball. Something's wrong with him.

I go to him and touch his shoulder. "Sorry to wake you, Cody. I'm back."

He rolls over to face me, and I'm at first shocked, and then angry, to see how beat-up his face is. Like before, his face is again all red and puffy and one of his eyes is partly swollen shut.

I try to make my voice as calm as I can and say, "Did your father go after you again?"

Cody just sits up on the edge of his cot and does an exaggerated shrug. "He caught me off guard. Not as bad as it looks."

"Well, it looks pretty bad. I guess I'm going to have to go to town and get you some ice again."

"Already got some." He reaches back onto his cot and pulls out a dripping bag. "Ellen made me an ice bag. Boy, was she pissed at him. Said she was gonna call the cops on him. I tried to talk her out of it, but I think she's gonna do it."

"Maybe it's time somebody did something."

"Aw, hell with him. But what about you? They said the cops took ya away. My old man said they were gonna lock you up in jail and throw away the key. That's when he started socking me. It was all I could do to get away and run back out here. So, did they really throw you in jail?"

"Yes, they did. Your father and a man named Carl accused me of . . . well, something not even worth talking about. But the judge dismissed the charge. The important news is that Bob came to my aid. He wants to restart the orphanage. He says the tribe will pay to fix this place up, and I can be the manager."

Cody seems so excited he can hardly contain himself. "Great! That's really great, Murph. Then you can be the real teacher, and I'll be your student."

"Bob says they'll hire a real teacher, but I'll be a kind of supervisor over the place. He says they'll bring in an electric line, and put in heating and cooling."

"Wow, Murph. That's really great. I'll be able to live here and go to school here too. I've always wished I coulda been in this orphanage like you were. It'll be fun."

"I agree, Cody. I think we could turn this into something really good. And I hoped you'd want to help. But you know what else it means."

He looks puzzled. "What?"

"It means we'll have to tell the police about Father Saul."

Cody is frowning and shaking his head. "No, no, Murph. That'd ruin everything. Can't we do what you said before? Dig him up and move him to a place he'd like better?"

"I wish we could, Cody. But the police will need to find out who killed him."

Cody keeps on shaking his head. "The cops won't do that. They won't do nuthin'. They won't care about some old dead body out on the res."

"That may be, but I'm afraid we have no choice, Cody. Everything here is going to change. There'll be a lot of people out here. Workers."

He doesn't seem convinced, but I say, "Come on. Let's go see if anybody has disturbed his grave site. We can talk more about it out there."

I lead the way to Father Saul's grave site with Cody slowly following. I'm happy to see that he's at least trying to keep the ice bag on his swollen face.

As we go over the top of the hill, I see somebody is at the grave site. We both start running, and before we even get there, I see who it is: it's Jimmy, and he's hurriedly digging up Father Saul's body.

I yell at him, and he turns to see me. I half expect him to try to run away, but he doesn't. Instead, he throws down the shovel and runs to me. As he throws his arms about my neck, I can see he's been weeping. He tries to talk, but then he starts crying so hard he can barely mumble the words, "I'm sorry, Junior. I'm so sorry. I couldn't stop him. I tried, but I couldn't stop him."

I hold him at arm's length and look into his eyes. "Couldn't stop who, Jimmy."

"It was Brent. When we got back from trying to catch some fish that day, Father Saul was waiting for us. Somehow he'd found out we'd lied about getting registered for the draft, and he was pretty pissed off about it. He said we had to go right then and get registered or he was going to report us as draft dodgers. I'm so sorry, Junior, but I couldn't stop Brent. You know how crazy he can get. He blew his top. Said the draft board couldn't know about us, so there was no way he was gonna get drafted like Junior did and get killed over there in Vietnam. Father Saul said that even if the draft board didn't know about us, it was our patriotic duty to our country to register for the draft. He said he was going to go to the draft office himself and give them our names. As soon as he turned away, Brent picked up a rock and hit him on the back of his head. Hit him hard. It happened so fast, I couldn't do anything about it, Junior. I'm really, really sorry."

I say, "But you didn't report it, did you, Jimmy? You and Brent just buried him here, didn't you?"

Jimmy looks down at the ground and says, "Brent did it. It wasn't me. I wanted to call the cops. I said we could say it was an accident. But Brent said they'd never believe that a priest with a bashed in head was an accident. And even if they did, we'd get sent off to Vietnam to get killed. He said we should just bury him quick and take off for Canada. He said he'd heard about other guys getting out of being drafted by going to Canada. Brent ran to the tool shed and got a shovel. He dug a hole and put Father Saul in it. Brent was really pissed off at me for not helping, but I didn't know what to do."

"You could have stopped him, Jimmy. Or you could have at least tried. You just left Father Saul out here in the desert. And when I saw you on the street down in Mesa, you told me some made-up story about him just being already gone when the two of you got back from fishing."

"I know, Junior. I know. I felt really bad about lying to you, but by then, I thought it was all over and done with. Brent took off for Canada, and nobody seemed to care that Father Saul was gone. Like I said, the orphanage was pretty much shut down by then anyhow. And I thought you were dead too. Killed in Vietnam. It was like everything was falling apart, and I couldn't do anything about it. For a long time, all I could do was lie on some guy's borrowed couch and cry. I couldn't even get up to try to find a job. I lost a bunch of weight and . . . "

He's trying to make me feel sorry for him, but he's the one that let Father Saul get killed and then didn't do anything about it. "So, you let Brent kill the man who took care of us, the man who raised us and taught us so much. And then you just walked away and felt sorry for yourself."

Jimmy sinks to his knees and starts crying again. He's moaning over and over about how sorry he is.

I again grab his shoulders to make him face me. "Stop that and answer me, Jimmy. Why did you come out here today to dig him up?"

He finally manages to stop crying. "All along, I thought about coming out here to dig him up and move him to a place he'd like better. Like that hill where he used to take us out at night to teach us about the stars and the planets. You remember that place, don't you, Junior? I knew he'd like it better out there. But when you told me you were staying out here, I knew I'd better not do it when you were around." I've been coming out here sometimes, but either you were here or this young man was." He points at Cody who's been standing back watching it all. "And then, for the past few days, you weren't here, so I decided now was my chance to do it. I wanted to dig him up and move him, and then I'd go off to Canada, like Brent did."

Cody steps forward and says, "I think he's right. Murph. Nobody's missed the priest at all. And all the cops will do is lock this guy up for not reporting it. You said yourself we should move Father Saul to a place he'd like better to be buried."

I point at Jimmy and say, "But what about Jimmy here, Cody? You're saying we should just let him go?"

"Like he said, it wasn't his fault. He couldn't stop the other guy from hitting Father Saul with a rock. I think we should just let him go off to Canada, if that's what he wants to do. If we bring the police in here, it'll just mess up everything. And what about what Bob wants you to do? With the orphanage. Calling the cops will mess that whole thing up."

I shake my head. "Father Saul taught us that the world doesn't work if there's no honesty, no justice."

"So, you're idea of justice is to let this guy get locked up. And then maybe get him sent off to Vietnam to get killed."

"Not everyone who gets drafted gets killed, Cody."

"Well, you just about did. And so far, just about everyone from the tribe who gets sent over there comes back in a bag."

Suddenly, Jimmy is on his feet and running, fast.

I know with my bad legs, I can't catch him, so I tell Cody to go after him.

Cody shakes his head. "I don't want to, Murph. Let him run off to Canada. Who cares? I think we should do what we talked about before, move the priest's body to that hill Jimmy talked about. Otherwise, the police will burn him up."

"Burn him up? What are you talking about, Cody?"

"I've been asking around. Just being curious, like every-body knows I'm curious about stuff. They said if no relatives come to claim dead bodies, they put 'em in an incinerator and burn 'em up."

I watch Jimmy disappear into the distance and think about what Cody is saying. I suspect he's right. After all, the police can't keep dead bodies lying around, and they probably don't want the expense of burying them. The question is, what would Father Saul want?

Cody picks up the shovel and holds it out to me. "Well?"

I need to make a decision. Father Saul probably wouldn't want Jimmy to go to prison. And I'm sure he really would rather be buried out here in the desert he loved instead of being burned up in some police incinerator.

Cody is still trying to get me to take the shovel.

I take the shovel from him and start digging.

Cody says he'll run get another shovel from the tool shed, but I say, "No. I don't want you having anything to do with this. It may be what Father Saul would want me to do, but moving a dead body without reporting it is probably some kind of crime."

Cody insists he wants to help, so I tell him go get the wheelbarrow.

By the time he gets back with the wheelbarrow, I've gotten Father Saul's body mostly dug up. Cody brings the wheelbarrow closer, but then he hangs back.

I say, "Isn't it about time for you to go to the next bingo session, Cody?"

He shakes his head. "No, I want to stay here with you."

"Cody, listen to me. You have to go. We should keep everything as normal as possible. Besides, if anybody ever questions you, I don't want you to know where I rebury him."

He's not happy about it, but Cody finally heads out across the desert toward the bingo hall.

Part of Father Saul's body is stiff, but other parts seem in danger of falling apart. I grit my teeth and try not to think about what I'm doing, and eventually, I get him into the wheelbarrow.

Now, where should I take him? I can't take him to that hill Jimmy mentioned. I don't want him to know where Father Saul is buried.

But then, while I'm filling in the hole that's been dug up, I remember just the place. One day when I was out exploring the desert by myself, I came upon Father Saul. He was kneeling on the top of a hill that's not all that far from here. He was looking up at the heavens, praying. I think he would like that to be his final resting place.

I start taking his body to that hill, being careful not to let the wheelbarrow tip over whenever I go through soft sand. It's not easy going, but I finally get there, and then I take plenty of time to dig a really deep hole. It takes a long time to get it deep enough, but I don't want Blackie or any wild animal to dig him up. I think the hole is deep enough, but just in case, I stand up and say out loud, "Blackie, if you're out there watching, don't dig here. This is sacred ground."

Once I've carefully placed Father Saul's body in the grave and filled it in, I place a flat stone there to mark it. Then, I use a broken off part of a bush to erase any sign that the desert has been disturbed.

As soon as I've finished that final task, what I've done finally hits me. I sit down in the dirt to stare at the flat stone.

Then, I start crying, and I can't stop. I don't want to stop. I'm crying as hard as Jimmy was, but my crying is not because of regret, but because of remembering. It hits me now that Father Saul really was like a father to me. Jimmy might have been right: Father Saul very well could have been my real father.

I'm not going to even try to stop crying. This is the first time I've cried since I was very, very young. Actually, this is the first time I've felt anything strongly since Vietnam just about wiped all the emotion out of me. For now, I just want to sit here in the sun and cry and remember.

Finally, I calm down enough to lie back and let the hot sun dry my face. I've got to remember how it felt to feel something this strongly. From now on, I've got to stop suppressing my emotions. That will be especially important if I'm going to provide a good model for young boys at the new orphanage.

I sit up and again stare at the flat stone. I hope I've done the right thing. I guess I don't mind that Jimmy and Brent will be up there in far-away Canada, hiding from the draft board. Maybe that means I'm feeling different about the war now too. Cody said a lot of the boys from the tribe who got drafted and sent off to fight in Vietnam never made it back alive.

And I saw how broken up Bob was that his son died over there. Is whatever this war is about really worth all this death and suffering?

With that final thought, I get up and slowly start pushing the wheelbarrow back. I stop once in a while to go back and use the same broken off branch of a bush to erase the wheelbarrow track I'm leaving.

When I get closer to the orphanage, I think about Bob wanting to restart it. I'm sure Father Saul would be happy to know that what he started will survive, even if he can't be here to see it. I'm even fairly sure he'd be happy to know I'm going to be part of it.

By the time I get the wheelbarrow put away and sit down to rest, I'm feeling completely overwhelmed by everything that's happened today. It seems hard to believe that only this morning I was locked in a jail cell.

I look back toward the hill that is now Father Saul's final resting place. Burying him there seems like a fitting ending to my journey that started with me being released from that Army hospital in California and two truckers giving me a ride here where I met Cody, and ended with me getting registered as a university student and meeting Clara. What a journey it has been.

As I look out across the beautiful desert, I wonder what Father Saul would think about everything that has happened to me since that day he sent me off to the draft board office. I sure wish he was here now so I could tell him about it all and find out what he thinks. I'd especially like to know what he thinks about the war. What would he think about so many young men dying. Would he still think it's our patriotic duty to go fight in it?

And what about Clara's growing feelings against the war? Will she think I've disappeared because of the hard talk we had about the war? She might even think I've given up on her. I sure wouldn't want her to think that. I should go there right now and try to find her and tell her everything.

But how much can I actually tell her? I'll have to tell her I've been in jail, of course, but I can't tell her about moving Father Saul's body. Just as I didn't want Cody to have to lie if anybody ever asked him about it, I wouldn't want her to know so she won't have to lie about it either.

If she asks about Father Saul's mysterious disappearance, I'll just tell her I've given up playing detective in order to focus on my studies.

But she probably won't ask about that. She'll probably still be focused on the war and the campus demonstration. So, what am I going to say when she wants to talk more about that? I'm still not sure what my position is, but I know she won't accept that as an answer.

One thing I really am sure about is that I'm looking forward to seeing her again. It's too late for our usual meeting at the cafeteria, but I should go to the university and try to find her. Maybe I can catch her walking between classes.

I get up and head for the usual bus stop.

But then I change my mind and decide to go down to the Mesa post office. Maybe my check from the Army has arrived by now. After that, I can catch a bus there in Mesa to get to the university.

Chapter Thirty-Seven

When I get to the post office, Mr. Gibson seems very happy to see me. He claps me on the back and says, "Glad to see you, Murph. You got an envelope from the U. S. Army yesterday afternoon. Official business it says. But I didn't know how to get in touch with you."

"Oh, good. That'll be my discharge check."

"Well, come on in. I'll get it out of your box for you."

He unlocks the door, and as he leads me inside the post office, he says, "I've been thinking about you, son. You're the first wounded Vietnam vet I've met. I told the guys at the American Legion about you." He leads me behind the counter and then behind the PO boxes. He seems to know which one is mine without even looking it up because he grabs the envelope out of a box and hands it to me. He says, "There you go, son. Now you can pop it into your bank account and start using the money right away."

"Oh, right. Uh, actually, sir, I don't have a bank, so I guess I'll have to go to some bank to cash it."

He stares at me, and for a moment, I worry that he might start asking me questions about where I'm living and how I've been surviving without money.

But he doesn't. Instead, he just says, "Well, son, I'm not sure a bank will cash it if they don't know you. Why don't you open it? Let's see how much it is."

I tear open the envelope and hand the check to him.

He looks at it and says, "Well, that's not so much. We can probably cash it for you here." For a few moments, he continues to stare at the check, and then he shakes his head. "A man serves his country and gets himself wounded, and this is all he gets? It's a shame. A cryin' shame if you ask me." But then he shrugs. "Well, at least they gave you something, right? Here, let's get you your cash so you can be on your way."

"Thank you, sir. This money will really help me. I'm taking classes over at ASU in Tempe now."

That brightens him up. "Really? A college student now? And at ASU. That's where I went. I think you'll like my old alma mater. Hey, I hope the Army is paying for it. That's the least they can do."

"Yes, sir, they are."

"Well, that's something at least. Let me get you your money so you can be on your way. Heading for the campus now, are you?"

"Yes, sir."

"Well, good. Very good. Just give me minute to open the safe."

After only a few minutes, he's back, and he's stuffed the money into the same Army envelope. He hands it to me, and I don't bother to count it. I wouldn't want him to think I don't trust him after all he's done for me. I just stuff the money into the pocket of my Army pants, thank him again, and hurry out of the building. Out on the sidewalk, the growing heat of the day is already noticeable. It's going to be another hot one.

The last time I was in Mesa, I spotted a bus stop just down the street. I hurry in that direction, thinking about the big wad of money I now have in my pocket. For the first time in my life, I could actually walk into any one of the stores I'm passing and buy something.

But that's not what I want to do. I should buy one change of clothes and save the rest of the money for later. Or maybe I should buy something for Cody. Or something for Clara. I should ask them if they need anything.

Chapter Thirty-Eight

As soon as the bus drops me off at campus, I start looking for Clara. But there are so many students flowing by, I realize there's not much chance of running into her.

But then I have another idea. I'll go to the library get caught up on some of the reading I've missed. If by some chance Clara is looking for me, that's where she'd probably go,

At the reserved book section, I check out the same history of philosophy textbook and reread the section about the period of Aristotle and the church dominating learning. The book says as the sciences gain more credibility, the old authoritarian ways of looking at things gradually gave way to meaning based on scientific observation.

The book says the middle ages of philosophy were between the fall of old Rome in 476 and the fall of Constantinople in 1453. It says that although the way philosophers looked at things was slow to change, new ways of thinking were pioneered by Francis Bacon and Rene Descartes, and that would later lead philosophy into what the book's author says is the era of modern philosophy. It says the period had been foreshadowed by Aristotle's interest in knowledge for its own sake.

Knowledge for its own sake. That's an interesting concept. Don't we acquire knowledge in order to better understand the world around us? The book clarifies that concept by comparing it to prior periods in which thinkers were supposed to acquire knowledge to better understand "correct" ethical conduct or to better understand the rules of religion.

That concept also makes me think about the lessons Father Saul taught us. Oddly, he hardly ever mentioned the Catholic religion, or any other religion for that matter. He did talk a lot about ethical conduct, but he talked about it in terms of our responsibility to our fellow man, not to God.

Interesting that everything I read in this book on the early history of philosophy makes me think about lessons Father Saul taught us.

I fight down the emotion that memory elicits and put down the book. I try to think through how much of my thinking, and maybe the choices I've been making in life, come from the lessons he taught me. Is that how it is with everybody? It almost feels like the learning we acquire when we are very young is like the main trunk of the tree and all of the branches that sprout later grow out of that early learning. Did all my "branches," everything I've done since I left the orphanage, grow out of my early learning tree? Not only what I learned from Father Saul, but also what I learned growing up in an isolated environment, in a desert, along with boys who were orphans just like me? That would also mean that what I've done since I left that Army hospital in California was somehow "caused" by what I learned at Father Saul's orphanage school? I think I'd like to talk to psychology-major Clara about that. Assuming that is, if I can ever get her to sit still long enough to have a serious talk with her.

I stare at the book on the table in front of me. Is this what my life is going to be like from now on, thinking about things I read in books? How will that change me?

"There you are! Where the hell have you been?"

It's Clara. I was so deep into my own thoughts, I didn't even see her come in.

The woman behind the counter tells her to shush, so Clara takes the book away from me and drops it onto the counter. Then, she grabs my arm and pulls me all the way out of the library. Outside, she gets up very close to my face and says, "Well? What do you have to say for yourself?"

I say, "I'm sorry, Clara. But I couldn't help it."

She still won't let go of my arm. Is she afraid I'm going to get away again?

"You couldn't help it? What's that supposed to mean?"

"Well, it's kind of a long story."

Standing outside the library, in the hot sun, with other students flowing around us, Clara won't let go of my arm. She's not smiling.

She says, "You miss class, and then, for days, you don't show up at the cafeteria like you promised, and all you can say is it's a long story? I'm going to say it again. Where the hell have you been all this time?"

I pat her hand. "That's the longest part of the story, Clara. I was in jail."

I feel increased pressure on my arm as she says, "In jail? What are you talking about?"

"Now don't get worried, Clara. It was all a mistake."

With that, she seems to recover at bit, but she still looks upset. I should have broken it to her more gently.

"In jail? A mistake? What kind of mistake?"

"Come on, Clara. Let's go to the cafeteria. I can explain it to you there."

She lets me lead her toward the student union building, but she continues to hold onto my arm. Before we even get into the shade of the building, she stops us and says, "I hope you know I've been worried frantic sick about you, Mister Murph. I kept thinking about that weird murder mystery you've been trying to solve, and that got me to thinking your disappearance might have something to do with that."

I quickly say, "No, not at all. In fact, I've given up on that. I got put in jail for a few days because somebody accused me of something ridiculous, and the judge couldn't see me until this morning. He knew the charges were crazy and let me go right away. But let's not talk any more about that. I have something more important to tell you. Something good. Actually, a couple of good things. First off, I got a job and—"

"You got thrown in jail, and then you got a job? A full time job? How are you going to study if you have a full-time job?"

"No, it's only a part time job. And it's one I can study at."

"Oh. You need money. I guess everybody needs money. I'm so naive. Of course you need money. Not everybody can live at home like I can. I'm such a child. You must think I'm a naive child, letting my parents pay for everything while you went off to war and just about got yourself killed, and now you come back and have to get a job while I just sit around and do nothing like some kind of fancy damn princess, like I'm a—"

I get ahold of both of her arms so she has to look me in the eyes. "No, Clara. I don't think any of those things about you. Everything is fine. In fact, better than fine. I finally received my discharge money from the Army, and now it looks like I'm going to get a job where I can study and make a salary at the same time."

She stares at me. Then, she looks down at the ground. "I did it again, didn't I? Got all nervous and started talking a mile a minute. You must think I'm an absolute idiot."

I pull her to me and hug her tight to let her know that her nervous talking didn't bother me a bit. In fact, it only showed me she really did care about me, that she was worried about me.

She whispers, "So you don't hate me?"

I pull back and look into her eyes. "Hate you? Clara, don't you know how much I love you? How much I want to be with you every time I'm away from you?"

She folds herself back into my arms again and is quiet for a moment. Then she whispers, "When you went away, I thought you were mad at me. And I couldn't blame you. I know I got too upset about the cops beating kids, and then the way I talked to you about the war and . . . and everything. But I was so mad. Those damn cops even tried to hurt you, you who could have been killed over there in that damn war, and then I wouldn't have even ever got to meet you. Oh. I'm doing it again. I get all nervous and can't stop talking. I've told myself a million times I wasn't going to do that anymore, and then I go and do it again. I'm sorry. "

"Listen to me, Clara. You don't have anything to be sorry about. I like you being honest with me about how you feel about . . . about everything. From now on, I'd like us to do that. There are a lot of things about my life that I haven't shared with you. I'd like to do that from now on."

She stares into my eyes. "It's a deal. From now on, we'll always be honest with each other. No matter what."

"Right," I say, "it's a deal. No matter what, we'll tell each other the truth. Always."

We finally release from our hug, and I realize classes must have let out because even more students are flowing around us. They're all smiling at us. I suppose that's not surprising seeing as how we're standing right in the middle of the hot sidewalk, in the sun, hugging.

Clara doesn't seem to notice them. She seems happy now, and she pulls me toward the entrance to the student union building. But then she stops and looks at me. "Didn't you say you'd got your money from the Army? So, why haven't you bought yourself some new clothes? You've had that shirt and those Army pants and those boots on ever since I met you."

"I just received the money today. Actually, I kind of hoped you'd help me buy some clothes. I've never had to buy my own clothes."

That makes her laugh. "You're a grown up person, and you've never bought clothes? How does that work?"

"Well, you know. The orphanage. And then the Army."

She grins at me. "Well then, we'd better go buy you some right now. I'm surprised those clothes you're wearing aren't standing up by themselves."

I smile. "They probably would if I ever took them off. But of course, I can't."

She gets my joke and is still grinning at me. "Okay," she says, "where should we go?"

I do my usual shrug, and say, "How would I know?"

That makes her laugh again. "Oh right. I guess I'm going to have to get used to the idea of being with a person who's never done anything before. It's a weird idea. How about we go to the mall?"

"What's that?"

She does her odd grin again. "Right. Of course you wouldn't know what a mall is. Every person in this country knows what a mall is, but of course you don't. A mall is a big place with a lot of different kinds of stores in it. They have everything, from shoes to hardware, from cookware to clothes."

"Sounds like an interesting place."

She chuckles. "Yeah, but maybe you won't think it's all that interesting once you get there. Hey, here's a trick I learned. I'm skinny, so I can buy clothes cheaper in a teen store. And you're skinny too, so shall we go there?"

"Sounds good to me."

Chapter Thirty-Nine

At the mall, I see that she's right, there are a whole lot of different kinds of stores. An amazing number of stores. How can they all be here in one place? Can they all make money?

She leads me inside the mall, and then to her favorite clothes store. I'm again amazed, this time at all the clothes for sale. A lot of them are identical. Who would want that?

She finds a pair of white tennis shoes in my size and picks out a couple of shirts and two pairs of pants.

She insists I go into a dressing room and put on one of the shirts and one of the pairs of pants. When I come out, she smiles and says that now I look "just like every other student." I'm not sure that's quite what I want, but it's all right with me if she makes all the clothes decisions. After all, what do I know about clothes?

The only thing I'm not so sure about is the dark sweater she picks out for me. It has a hood on it. I say, "It's a hundred degrees out there, Clara. Are you sure I need a sweater?"

"Oh yeah. You'll need it for our long walks in the desert at night. You know, when winter comes."

I suppose I could use a sweater, and I do like the idea of long walks in the desert with her. There are so many things about the desert I can show her.

On our way back to campus, she says, "All right now, Murph, what's this new job you managed to get? A job that lets you study and make money at the same time?"

I know explaining where I've been living and how Bob, the reservation boss, wants to rebuild the old orphanage and make me the manager is going to take some time, so I ask her if she still has time to go back to the cafeteria to talk.

She says, "You bet. I'll make time. I want to hear it all."

Back at the cafeteria, we get our traditional sandwiches and apple pie and sit at our usual table. Then, I start explaining it all, starting with how I hitchhiked here from California and went out to the old orphanage in the middle of the night.

She says, "I bet they were happy to see you."

"No, the place was deserted. The only person there was a young boy from the tribe. I found out later that the old priest that ran the orphanage had shut the place down. He'd managed to get all the boys adopted out."

"Why?"

"I'm not sure about that. Maybe he thought he was getting too old. Or maybe he just ran out of money. Anyhow, he was gone. I'll tell you more about that later. The important thing is that I met Bob, a boss from the tribe. He says he wants to fix up the orphanage and get it running again. He said they'll bring in a teacher, but he wants me to manage the place. Like I said, it'll be a job that'll make me some money, and give me a free place to live while I study."

"A place to live? Does that mean an apartment?"

"Well, yes, that's what he said."

"An apartment where I could come and visit you?"

"Uh, sure. Why not?"

With that, she picks up her books and says she'd better hurry and get to her next class.

She only takes a few steps away from the table, before she turns back to give me a quick kiss.

This time, I'm ready for it, and I don't pull away.

That makes her smile, and she squeezes my hand before she hurries off.

I'm left sitting there, thinking about what that kiss meant. Up to now, I've been afraid to even hope our relationship could be more than just friendship. But now, with her kissing me, and her talking about coming out to visit me at the orphanage, I think I'd like to start making plans that include her. Once I start making some money, I might even buy myself an old car so we could do some traveling together.

For example, we could drive up to the Grand Canyon. Father Saul told us about it. He said he'd been there, and it was wonderful. He said it made him think about nature and the age of our earth. He told us if we ever got the chance, we shouldn't miss the opportunity to see it for ourselves.

And we could go other places. Clara said she'd visited some of the other reservations in Arizona as part of a class she took. Once I get a car, we could go visit those reservations. I might even be able to find out more about who my mother might have been, and whether Father Saul could possibly have been my real father.

I look around the big cafeteria. It's full of students, eating and talking. And with the way I'm now dressed, I suppose I do look just like them. Actually, today I think maybe I really am one of them. As quickly as it happened, I think this is exactly where I belong. And with my new job at the orphanage, and with Clara wanting to be with me, it feels like I'm leaving one life behind and starting an entirely new one. It's hard to tell where this new life will take me, but I'm ready to take it on. Most importantly, I think Father Saul would approve and be proud of me.

www.ingramcontent.com/pod-product-compliance
Lightning Source LLC
Chambersburg PA
CBHW072204170626
46813CB00003B/783